VIOLETTE'S EMBRACE

VIOLETTE'S EMBRACE

A NOVEL BY MICHELE ZACKHEIM

Riverhead Books · New York · 1996

Care has been taken to trace ownership of the works of others and obtain permission, if necessary, for quoting excerpts from them. If any errors have occurred, they will be corrected in subsequent printings, provided notification is sent to the publisher.

RIVERHEAD BOOKS
a division of G. P. Putnam's Sons
Publishers Since 1838
200 Madison Avenue
New York, NY 10016

A list of permissions and acknowledgments of sources can be found on pages 211–213.

Library of Congress Cataloging-in-Publication Data

Zackheim, Michele.
Violette's embrace / by Michele Zackheim.
p.   cm.
ISBN 1-57322-036-1 (acid-free)
1. Biographers—France—Fiction.   2. Leduc, Violette, 1907–1972—Fiction.
3. Women authors, French—20th century—Fiction.   4. Americans—
Travel—France—Fiction.   5. Biography—Authorship—Fiction.   I. Title.
PS3576.A274V56   1996   96-11063 CIP
813'.54—dc20

Printed in the United States of America
10 9 8 7 6 5 4 3 2 1

This book is printed on acid-free paper. ∞

Book design by Iris Weinstein

Reader, my reader, I was writing outside, sitting on the same stone, a year ago. My square-lined writing paper has not changed: the grapevines run in the same lines below the plunging hills. The third row is still covered with a haze of heat. My hills are bathed in their halo of gentleness. Did I go away, have I come back?

THIS BOOK IS DEDICATED
TO THE RETURN OF VIOLETTE LEDUC.

VIOLETTE'S EMBRACE

I flew to Paris to find a dead writer. On the airplane, in the bag on my lap, I carried a lilac-colored copy of *La Bâtarde*. It was tattered and underlined, with red paper wrappings from chopsticks marking the pages. Many years ago, I had found this used copy in an old bookstore on Broadway in New York. The writer, Violette Leduc, wrote on an edge that reminded me of myself. I bought it for a dollar and devoured it forever.

Around Paris we flew, around, and twice around again. It was a pale-gray dead-day of winter. Paris seemed bare. Brown, tan, drab hushed squares of earth surrounded the city. All that was visible was the very tip of the Eiffel Tower and the nightclub on top of the ugly skyscraper in Montparnasse. The pink, glowing aura that usually surrounded the city from above was missing. The plane landed on the tarmac before I even knew we were near the ground.

❧

Violette Leduc was a perplexing woman. She was demanding, discourteous, and intensely neurotic. She was obsessive and possessive. She didn't understand the word "no"—and paradoxically, didn't understand the word "yes." She groveled at the feet of Jean Genet, she worshipped at the altar of Simone de Beauvoir. I would probably not have liked her.

Yet the language she uses to describe her life is splendid, it is passionate, it is powerful, it is brave.

She was glaring with the truth—stark, nude, abandoned. I adore her pen, but am embarrassed by her eccentricity.

Still—Violette Leduc is my accomplice.

Her sighs slip through her language.

She places letters, then words, rising and falling like waves in the sea. The *t*'s are a moment's pause—the *c* and *s* carry her toward the shore. Sometimes a *z* confuses the water—carving an undertow. But gracefully they land on the beach.

She moved her Blanzy-Poure pen forward to the next tide of language, she created—she was fearless. She wrote.

I shall write, I shall open my arms, I shall hug the fruit trees and give them to my sheet of paper.

❧

I was fifty years old and a visual artist. Yet as the years went by, my work had become more and more literary—until I realized that I had almost written myself off the canvas.

One autumn evening I was sitting with my husband in a bar complaining about not writing.

"Why don't you do something about it?" he dared me warily. It happened just like that. The idea of writing a book settled on the dark wood bar between our two glasses of red wine and looked me straight in the eye. I suppose I was waiting for the right moment to conjure the courage to make the leap. Now my husband had presented the challenge. And I decided to cast my lot with Violette.

So, my fingers covered with ink, I began to move along this white paper with the blue squares in the large orange notebook—having only an intuition about what I was going to find.

· I ·

My *mother never gave me her hand,* is the first sentence of the first volume of Violette Leduc's autobiography, *L'Asphyxie,* or *In the Prison of Her Skin.* Violette's mother barely gave her anything beyond her delivery into the world. Her childhood was lived in disquiet, upheaval, devoid of love. Yet Violette had the most remarkable thirst for living. In her heart she stored her real self. And in her books she explored who this was. I invited myself to try to put together all the pieces.

Thérèse Andrée Violette Leduc was born on the seventh of April, 1907, at five in the morning, in the north of France, near the Flemish border.

Her mother, Berthe Leduc, although most definitely French, shared the Flemish proclivity for hard work. But she could not resist her heart and succumbed to the son of her wealthy employers—André Debaralle, a sickly, pensive man who sloped toward melancholy. When Debaralle heard his mistress was pregnant, he begged her to leave their town of Valenciennes, so as not to embarrass his family. She convinced herself that if she followed his wishes, he would be grateful and marry her.

Berthe Leduc left her home and traveled the sixty kilometers west to Arras for her *accouchement*. Three weeks later, with her newborn daughter, Violette, and her mother, Fidéline, Berthe Leduc returned to Valenciennes. The three women settled into a new, small house near the outskirts of town, and Berthe found work as a saleswoman.

André Debaralle refused to marry her or to help her financially. He ignored her. Berthe was obsessed. She haunted him as he hid behind curtained windows. He crossed the street when he saw her. She harassed him even more. His rejection inflamed an already raging heart. It took years to ease her fury.

On the outside, Violette and Berthe's relationship was perfectly ordinary. Violette was fed and clothed, and better educated than most other children of her class. But she was cared for as if she were a block of wood.

Children who are fed, but starved of love, cannot survive. If it had not been for her grandmother Fidéline, Violette would have died. Fidéline nurtured her environment. This was not the traditional environment of the mother, the *entourage maternant*—but fortunately for Violette, it was what I call an *entourage grand-mère*.

In school, Violette was mischievous and had constant, but innocent, misadventures. But her mother felt they were somehow malicious. She was more fearful of how society would perceive her daughter than she was of her daughter's safety. Berthe Leduc was so powerful that Violette and Fidéline were both terrified of and greatly devoted to her. Violette loved her mother perilously.

❧

The Avenue Rodin is in a petit bourgeois part of Paris. It was fifteen minutes past noon on a Saturday and I had been warned that if I didn't arrive by noon, the concierge, Mme. Silva, would have left for her afternoon off.

There she was, her back disappearing around the corner. She had pretended not to see me. I had no option but to sit on the step and wait for her to return to let me into my blindly rented flat. I sat for one hour, two hours, and finally Mme. Silva's daughter arrived and took compassion on me. Hauling bags of books, a computer, and a satchel of clothes, we walked through a long corridor, and down a dark, gloomy hall to Studiette Numéro 2. The many keys were inserted into the many locks and the door opened.

In front of us was a visceral tunnel. Everything was pink. The walls were pink. The rug was pink. The tiles were pink. The curtains, the towels, the sheets, the cups, the saucers, the handles of the flatware, the hangers, the toilet paper, the paper towels, the handles of every appliance including the scrub brushes—all was pink. And the room was five feet wide by eighteen feet long. The sofa opened into a bed I had to step on to get from one side of the room to the other. I could use the toilet while washing and could cook and stir on the stove while taking a shower. There was one small window, looking out upon a courtyard with floors and floors of flats climbing like vines around it. The sunlight was an accident, a coincidence that occurred only because of the reflection from so many windows.

I sat on the pink sofa, my feet touching the opposite pink wall. For the moment there was no choice. My budget was limited. I was tired, paralyzed with fatigue, lonely, and disappointed.

When my moorings are severed I become uncomfortably afloat. But since I travel alone a lot, I have learned some tricks. The first is to rent an apartment, not a hotel room. This way I can go to the market and buy window cleaner, soap, a towel, my own sheets. By making the apartment into my home, I try to ease the disturbance, the experience of despair and loneliness that lodges itself against the back of my throat—it doesn't move, it sticks. I call this my "existential cusp" and totter upon its edge when I am off on one of my walkabouts.

Here in my pink apartment, it didn't take long to put away my things—the books on the pink shelf, the computer on the tiny pink Formica table. Pictures of my family . . . talismans from my friends . . . Hindu prayer beads . . . icons of the Virgin Mary . . . mandalas . . . a tiny bronze butterfly made by a sculptor friend . . . a theater poster from a play about Virginia Woolf . . . the hand of Fatima . . . a silver image of Lilith . . . a photograph of Violette . . . sweet-smelling sandalwood . . . all reminders carried from the desert, from that sea of air and wind, from my home.

Fleeing the room, and my inner chatter, I set out to explore the neighborhood. The Avenue Henri-Martin is wide and tree-lined and runs past the Place Tattegrain to the Bois de Boulogne. I walked as far as the green edge that meets the gray concrete, then paused to get my bearings.

In my desert home, I am accustomed to the sun being my compass. In Paris, in the winter, the sun rarely appears and I have to depend on left-side/right-side directional landmarks.

I am the center of the compass. I memorize the points of my compass—the yellow daffodils in the blue-framed shop on my right—the dark green sign on a white background that reads "Tabac" on my left—the bookstore, Les Livres de Pologne, on the corner—the colorful posters all around me advertising concerts.

After walking for a while I relaxed and tried to convince myself that the tiny room was adequate. I stopped and bought a baguette, cheese, a small salami, and a bottle of wine for tomorrow's lunch. If nothing else, I knew I could make myself happy by tearing off a large piece of bread, spreading it with Camembert, topping it with a chunk of salami, pouring a glass of red wine, and reading an English mystery.

⁂

French is a difficult language for many people—for me it is almost impossible. I am able to read it, indeed enjoy translating, and understand when someone is speaking. But when I am faced with participating in a conversation, my right ear turns toward the speaker, my tongue becomes numb, and my mouth gets up and leaves me, waiting impatiently by the door. I muddle through my request, my situation, my manners. My mouth knows I will make mistakes, serious mistakes, stupid mistakes, and is already twisting with embarrassment.

So there I sat in a restaurant, miserable, tired, and now having to face ordering my dinner—no English spoken in this part of town. Still, the white tablecloth and single red carnation comforted me. The menu seemed simple. My choices were few and this was a relief. I thought the waiter sensed my discomfort, for he was patient and didn't crack a grimace as I ordered *en français*.

My dinner arrived, and I realized that in my nervousness I had ordered a lamb steak, not the beef.

After dinner, I walked up the Rue Mignard, feeling my loneliness beside me. I question myself on these journeys: Why am I doing this? Unquenchable curiosity? Probably—but it takes its toll. It requires at least a year to invoke enough nerve to try it again. Yet I do it repeatedly. More easily than I had expected, I found my way back to the right building, recognized the long corridor, and finally my room. Sleep came easily and I was grateful.

The next day, Sunday, I slept until late morning and woke rested but still numb.

I read.

André Gide spent the day with me—consoling me. "Such boredom, such lugubrious fatigue strikes me as soon as I am in a new town that I can think of nothing else but the desire to get away again . . ." he wrote. "I sleep every afternoon to be able to at least dream a little. Or else I read."

So I slept and read and dreamed and read until the evening arrived and the darkness beckoned me onto the street. This time I wasn't going to take a chance. I walked to the Bois. Following a lovely smell, I came upon a man selling crêpes from an old wooden wagon on the sidewalk. I ordered one with butter and sugar, another with *confiture*, and sat down on a bench to eat my supper. Cold, but far more comfortable than a restaurant.

The next morning, after a coffee and *petit pain* in a nearby café, I left my neighborhood to investigate libraries. I needed a library with everything written by and about Mme. Leduc and other French writers of the first half of the twentieth century. Before leaving America, I had arranged to obtain credentials from a local college. As I marched along the boulevards I felt secure with my professional papers safely placed in my satchel.

Leduc said that when she first arrived in Paris, she *set off on a voyage of discovery along the Boulevards. . . . Paris had enslaved the four corners of earth.* As I followed her footsteps, I saw a glimmer of me, fluttering in the corners of soon-to-be-written sentences.

I arrived at the American Library on the Rue du Général-Camou, in the shadow of the Eiffel Tower. The library was a placid building, inviting in its American familiarity. It cost three hundred dollars to join and its holdings were scanty. I realized the library was just a snug front for my fears, a stepping-stone to where I had always wished to study. To me, the Bibliothèque Nationale was where intimate, hidden perceptions might be stacked amongst the books.

I left the Rue du Général-Camou and walked along the Seine, then crossed to the Place de la Concorde with its obelisk and fountain and closely packed herd of galloping traffic. I was pleased that I had actually pursued this project to Paris, but I was also scared. I followed the Seine, with the Tuileries on my left, and finally turned and headed for the Rue de Richelieu. Along the Rue de Richelieu, all these men once lived: Stendhal, Thomas Paine, Balzac, Tallemant, Molière, Diderot—all drawn to the library too. They may also have been enticed to the Rue Chabanais backing the library. In the 1880s, and until 1946, number 12, Rue Chabanais housed one of Paris's most notorious brothels. It is said that the Prince of Wales, along with many of France's most famous men, would retire there after a hard day's work at the Bibliothèque.

The Bibliothèque Nationale is the repository for more than eleven million volumes. Its reading room has embroidered itself into my imagination for many years. Tourists are never allowed to enter the main reading room—they are allowed only to peer into it through a window. It is magnificent, with one hundred forty-nine miles of shelves holding very old books, and a domed ceiling with a mysterious, diffused light. On the old oak tables, small, green-shaded lamps cast a warm radiance across the readers and their books. After much battling with language, and fussing with bureaucratic formalities, I was given number 921094E and found my seat among the four hundred chairs. My search for Violette Leduc began in earnest.

The first day of research flew. I looked for work by all her writer friends and started to gather my own bibliography. When I grew tired and looked up from my books, I saw an allegorical dark curtain being lowered over the room. Night had come. The green-shaded lamps were glowing warmly—but I turned cold dreading the return to my room. I got up and went to the next room, where the computers are kept. I worked a little while longer. I went back to my table and wrote a letter. I looked at my budget. I knew I had to move from the Avenue Rodin.

The next morning I walked the Latin Quarter until I found a place I could afford. It was called the Hôtel Senlis, after the flower painter Séraphine de Senlis. The atmosphere was pleasant, with a large vase of tulips on the front desk; the hotel was used mainly by academics lecturing at the Sorbonne. My room was on the fifth floor. It had a rough-hewn beamed ceiling with two perfectly scaled windows overlooking the street. It was adequate. I returned to the Avenue Rodin and in one hour cleaned the room and packed. I think Mme. Silva was feeling guilty about having disappeared on Saturday, because now she kindly helped me. We communicated well enough for me to understand that she thought I had made the right decision. She told me to wait at the curb while she fetched a taxi. I waited, and finally a taxi, driven by an amazingly beautiful woman, appeared with Mme. Silva perched on the backseat. She proudly introduced me to her friend the taxi driver and handed me into the car as if I were royalty.

The Hôtel Senlis is on the Rue Malebranche, in the Fifth Arrondissement. The small, narrow street is named after Nicolas Malebranche, a seventeenth-century philosopher, famous for the remark, "The imagination is the eccentric of the family." This is fitting for both Violette Leduc and me. We were both considered peculiar and perplexing by our families.

That evening I sat at my spacious nonpink desk and made telephone calls on my nonpink phone. Many people had given me names of people who might have known Mme. Leduc or who might know people who had known her. In America, I had compiled a long list, but there was one person I particularly wanted to meet. Everyone I had spoken to mentioned Lili Jacobs as an old friend of Mme. Leduc's who had kept a journal about literary life in Paris after the Second World War. She had also saved all of Mme. Leduc's letters to her and her husband, Alain. Over the years Lili had researched and copied many other letters written to friends by Violette Leduc, and these were also included in her archives. I had gathered from speaking to a friend at the University of Nebraska that Lili Jacobs had been planning to write a book about Mme. Leduc but had never gotten around to it. Other writers had thirsted after this material, but Jacobs had been unwilling to share.

I was afraid to phone her. What if she rejected me? What if I didn't sound "professional" enough? I decided to try two other people first. Neither seemed to be at home—and the French messages on the machines were far too daunting to deal with.

I walked around my room. I read the newspaper. I washed my face. I poured myself a cognac. I dialed the third number and a woman answered. In French I asked to speak to Lili Jacobs.

"This is she," she answered in English.

I told her my name and fumbled through my reason for calling. I said I was writing a biography of her friend Violette Leduc, because I wanted to introduce her to a new generation of readers.

"I know she is still published in France," I said, "But did you know that the English-language editions of her books are out of print?"

"Yes," Lili Jacobs said. "A pity."

She agreed to meet me that very night at ten at the Café de Flore. I was astonished.

By nine, I was wandering along the Boulevard Saint-Germain, relishing my success. My footsteps rang sweetly. After strolling along the boulevard for thirty minutes, I reached the café. It was filled with tourists looking for literary flavor, using their imaginations to summon the atmosphere of the thirties, forties, and fifties.

Especially during cold and unheated winters, the Flore was home to many writers. Simone de Beauvoir, for one, wrote here every day during the war. It was warm—it was her living room. From 1945, twice a month at four in the afternoon, Mme. Leduc came to visit Mme. de Beauvoir. Mme. Leduc was terrified of being late and missing Mme. de Beauvoir, so she always arrived early and waited at the first table on the left behind the door.

I arrived early, as I always do. There, on my left, was a woman sitting with a cup of coffee in front of her. She was lighting a cigarette.

She looked to be about seventy years old, and like most Parisian women was beautifully dressed. Her elegance magnified my baggy black clothes. Her hair was deep auburn, artificially colored and superbly accomplished. She seemed fluttering, ready to fly. She caught me watching her and smiled.

Part of me is insatiably curious. Shyness gets in its way, but desire often propels me through it. *I still haven't overcome my desire to juggle with words so that people will notice me,* Leduc once wrote.

The woman at my table caught my eye again and I could do nothing but smile back. Is that Lili Jacobs, I wondered. The café was very busy—the din was impenetrable—the smoke was coagulated. My anxiety was strung on a necklace around my neck— each bead I nervously slid along the string was named by my interior thesaurus: ambiguity, ambition, appetite. I fingered the last bead, then the clasp, and finally walked over to her table.

Smiling, she reached up and shook my hand. "It is so nice to meet you," she began.

"Madame Jacobs, it is so nice to meet you too."

"Please sit—and you can call me Lili."

Her voice was soft, melodic, lovely. I had to turn my left ear to hear her. Her demeanor was a bouquet. She smiled and I was captivated.

I marveled at her composure. I was very nervous. My head felt full of air, my throat was constricted.

"Thank you for meeting with me," I said awkwardly. "I know you were a close friend of Madame Leduc's. I have many, many questions to ask. I should have written you from America but I was afraid of being refused."

Lili laughed. "You were correct in being nervous. Many people have approached me and I have always refused."

"But why?" I asked.

And she laughed again.

"Most of the people researching Violette have been more interested in theory than in the beauty of her writing. I am really not interested in theory. So I thought maybe one day I would write about my friend myself. Time went by and I didn't get to the project. And then, last month, I received a letter from a friend at the University of Nebraska telling me about your project."

I was bewildered. Lili laughed.

"The academic world is very small, especially with many people writing about one person. Everyone knows what everyone else is doing. My friend, Eva, in Nebraska, told me about you. Just this morning I came across her letter. And then you rang me. You startled me into making a decision.

"I realize I must do something with all this information. It really is not fair to Violette to keep this material to myself."

"So, you will let me interview you for my book?"

Lili smiled and said, "*Oui*. Yes, you can ask questions, of course. But I would like simply to tell you the story. Let us see how we work together tonight, and then we can come to a decision about how to proceed. Do you have a tape recorder?"

I fumbled in my bag and brought out a mini-cassette. "I just happen to have one here." Lili and I laughed together.

"Let me speak—and as one memory invites another, you will get all the information. But of course, please interrupt if you have questions. Shall we begin?"

"Yes," I said, as I searched for the right buttons to push.

Lili ordered two coffees.

And then she started.

· II ·

"Violette's mother, Berthe, had a hard blue glare that cut like ice," Lili said. "Those cruel eyes taught Violette she was ugly— that she had the ugliest big nose in the world—that she was stupid. Luckily she had her grandmother Fidéline's soft lap as her refuge. Still, there was her mother's brutality. It invaded Violette's self and settled in for life."

In recalling her childhood, Violette had said of herself and her mother, *We were spectators at a tournament of lightning flashes. The ecstasy in the guttering had become a debauch. Her labors were unend-*

ing. The downpour became unending. The light was holding on by less than a thread. . . . And at that point grief took hold of me. It was a sap raging through me like the water in the gutter overhead. . . . I forgot my mother, I forgot myself as I wept with all my strength for both of us. I was swollen with it.

"Do you know what's she done, this idiot child? . . . Lost the umbrella I gave her. Don't you think that she deserves slaughtering?"

Violette understood defeat. Her mother called her an idiot, a little idiot. And on and on this went as Violette was awkwardly molded—forcing her later to cry out in her writings, *Oh please, I'm nobody.*

"I met Violette's mother." Lili shivered, a Frenchwoman's display of disgust. "She was a cold woman, narrow in a provincial way. She put on airs and I didn't like her. After what I saw, I am convinced that Violette was fortunate not to spend her life locked away in a mental institution. Her grandmother saved her."

Lili lit another cigarette, while I tested the tape. I wanted to be sure that it was picking up her gentle voice amidst the din of the café. I pressed Rewind, then Play. Lili was clear enough but my own tense voice was lost.

"Why don't you move closer," Lili said. "It will be better." We shifted our chairs and I placed the tape recorder between us on the table, leaning it against the sugar bowl. I smiled and nodded. Then we began again.

"It is hard to understand how Madame Leduc's grandmother could be so humane and her mother such a monster," I said. "This kind of behavior is usually passed from generation to generation."

"I know very little about Fidéline's history," Lili answered. "But I do know that she lived on a farm into her middle age and that she passed on to Violette her love of nature. When Violette was a little girl, they often went together to the countryside to pick greens and herbs. Fidéline taught her the names of flowers the way some children are taught the names of distant cousins. Nature was Violette's religion. Her daffodil stanzas and geranium litanies sat on her windowsills. *Naturam expellas furca, tamen usque recurret*— you may drive nature out with a pitchfork, still she will ever return."

Listening to Lili, I thought, is like hearing a flower bloom. I could see why she and Mme. Leduc had been friends—they shared a style of language that was sprinkled with poetic images.

However, Mme. Leduc's poetic language could also describe horror. Besides enduring her mother and her shame of being an illegitimate child and her homeliness, Violette suffered another kind of terror. *It is no good looking at men as though they're paintings,* Mme. Leduc's mother told her. Men were the enemies—threatening—dark shadows sliding past their windows—midnight clouds obstructing their view of the stars—bulbous noses, slits for eyes, gaping blow-holed gullets.

In 1913, Violette Leduc was raped by a man in the village—she was easy prey. M. Pineau was huge, obese, with thighs like an elephant. She wrote about the incident in *In the Prison of Her Skin.*

I had no time to stop him. He had unbuttoned my dress right down to the waist. I begged him to stop. I threatened to call my grandmother. He squeezed my neck between his prelate's hands. I sensed that he might squeeze it even tighter. When he sensed my defeat, he took his hands away.

Poor Violette, I thought. She too experienced violation of the human flesh, of the human spirit. She too was baptized in the waste-waters of a man.

"When Violette was nine years old, Fidéline died," Lili said, while taking out an ebony comb from her hair, catching some loose strands of hair, and replacing it again. "After she had listened for weeks to her grandmother's coughing and spitting, the sounds ceased. Violette lay in her bed waiting to hear the familiar sounds of life. But all she heard were murmurs. Assuming they were going on a holiday, Violette got up and dressed, and took along a marble to play with. She ran out her door shouting, 'I'm ready. Wait for me.'"

My mother opened the door. There was no answering sign from the figure stretched out on the bed. She was dressed in her pleated poplin blouse, her long grey plait coiled round her head.

"Go back to bed. Your grandmother isn't here any more."

The story made us sad, and we paused to listen to the noise in the café. "Years later," Lili resumed, "Violette wrote, *Fidéline has not grown dim, you cannot dim a forest of stars.*

"So you see," Lili said, looking straight at me, "from the moment of her grandmother's death, Violette had no shelter.

"Berthe was more impatient than ever before. She decided to find work in Paris and sent Violette to her sister Laure's farm in Douai. Later that same year, Violette's father died. He died before she had the opportunity to meet him. Now there was no hope for reconciliation, only abandonment and the nightmares."

Most everything I had read about Violette Leduc had a hardness, a judgment stapled to it. I was pleased to hear Lili's narrative, for her compassion supported my intuition. I had always felt Leduc had hidden tender facets, which one had to glean through her writing.

The café was suddenly quiet. I knew this was the lull before the midnight crowds.

"Madame Leduc's books," I said, "are filled with line after line—page after page—apologizing for her insatiable need for attention. Sometimes I have to force myself to read these pages—they create such dread that I want to skip ahead, I want to close my eyes, avoid her groping."

"She was starved," Lili said, "she was constantly hungry for attention. Her hunger was unremitting. Normally, skipping one or two meals sharpens your appetite for your next meal. But her hunger gnawed away at her and could not be appeased with her next meal or her next encounter. Violette always knew in advance that whatever attention was showered upon her would not be enough—her hunger would never diminish."

Lili leaned forward with her elbows on the table, one hand holding the other. "I met Violette in 1945, when I was twenty-five years old. I lived next door to her on the Rue Paul-Bert, which is in a working-class area of Paris. Near the Bastille.

"We were both poor, although my poverty was by choice. My family was quite wealthy. You have to remember that Europe had just been through a war. France was numb. I was numb. Pieces of myself were scattered all about France. These pieces had departed with dear friends and family who had died in the violence or were destroyed by sorrow. I moved to the Rue Paul-Bert to escape my family's mourning, to try to forget the past five years.

"This street is near the Rue de la Roquette, where Cyrano de Bergerac lived, died, and was buried. Noses are strange," Lili mused. She seemed to be relaxed and enjoying herself while telling me the story. "They are different from hands, feet, ears, even large bellies! They are a signal of who you are and where you come from. Cyrano's gigantic nose was immortalized. So was Violette's."

I laughed with the image in my head of his nose—three blocks long and six stories high. I imagined the nostrils as entrances to the Métro. Yet I knew that Leduc's nose was very important to her. It was her hated trademark. It was truly large and out of proportion to her long, thin face. *My ugliness will set me apart until I die,* she wrote with resignation.

"A few years before we met, she had a traumatic experience." Lili shook her head. "She was walking on the Place de la Concorde with her friend Hermine. They could hear a group of people coming up behind them. The only woman in that group turned, looked straight at Violette, and said, 'If I had a face like that I'd kill myself.'"

Once Violette admitted to Simone de Beauvoir that she had attempted to have her nose made smaller. Before de Beauvoir could stop herself she blurted out that the attempt had obviously been unsuccessful!

"Violette's looks were confusing to me," Lili said. "Sometimes you could ignore her face because she had the figure of a fashion model. She was five feet, seven inches tall and weighed only one hundred six pounds. She called herself a *skinny pendulum.* She loved clothes and often dressed in mannequin samples of great fashion designers—she could appear quite grand. Sometimes she would knock at my door and ask me how she looked. I always felt a great relief when I could honestly say to her, 'Violette, you look beautiful.' Once she told me that she thought one's personality could be changed by wearing expensive clothes."

Violette would compare herself to Jean-Paul Sartre—she felt they were equally ugly. *I love Sartre's face. They say he's ugly. He can't be ugly: his intelligence irradiates all his features. Hidden ugliness is the most repugnant.*

One day when I was seven, I remember, the doorbell rang. Standing on the front porch was a little girl who lived on my block.

"Hello," she said with an arrogant tone of voice. "Can I feel your head?"

"Why do you want to feel my head?" I asked, fearing the worst.

"I want to feel your Jewish horns."

I felt ripped in two. One part of me wanted to show her that she was wrong, the other was speechless and horrified. She stood there waiting. I let her feel.

If Mme. Leduc had been beautiful I would not have been attracted to her. Her descriptions of the physical self are hand-drawn maps leading me to my own landscape, familiar. When I was a teenager, I peroxided my hair and it became a bright and brittle orange—not the right color blond for my white, blue-collar neighborhood. I ironed it under a towel on the ironing board, so it could be straight like all the other girls in school had.

I had a pubescent moustache. My arms and legs, moving in America, were covered with the dark down of Semitic peoples. But my nose was what truly betrayed me. I was convinced it was a flag proclaiming my Jewishness, my oddity.

I remember when my family acquired a television set. For the first time, I could see how the rest of America looked, how the rest of America lived, how the rest of America thought. And I could plainly see the difference. By the age of thirteen my alienation was complete.

It seemed to me that Lili was growing bored, so when the waiter approached I assumed she would ask for the check. But she ordered a cognac, and so did I.

I sank back into my chair with relief.

She lit another cigarette.

I thought out loud, "I know it's going to be difficult to write this biography. Absolute truth is impossible, intuition is not good enough. Gathering and writing this material reminds me of raising my children. Their lives could be shaped on the turn of a dime. If I said the wrong thing at the wrong time to them, it could forever interfere with their development. A chance remark could be devastating. Well, it's the same with Madame Leduc's life. If I write the wrong impression, I can, unfortunately, alter the reader's perception."

Lili nodded. "I agree with what you are saying. If only you will try to remember this when you are writing about Violette." She looked directly at me and smiled. "I think you will."

"The failure to relate to others has resulted in that privileged form

of communication—a work of art," Lili quoted. "That is what Violette wrote in *Trésors à Prendre.* Do you know the book?"

"Yes," I replied, "but it has never been translated into English.
Is this something you might do? Your friend from Nebraska told
me you're a translator."

"Before the war," Lili said, "I attended school in London. I
loved the English language and had a special affection for its literature. When the war broke out, I returned to France—but by then,
I had already decided to become a translator. It was a comfortable
decision."

We both looked up. There was a line outside the Flore, and the
red light was blinking on my recorder. It was time to say good
night. Lili signaled for the check, but I won the battle to pay.

"My dear, you flatter me with your generosity."

"Lili," I replied, in a rational American style, "we have to be
clear here. I'm asking for a lot of your time. You must permit me,
in return, to treat you. I understand it isn't always welcome, but
please allow me to do this."

She raised her shoulders in acquiescence.

We left the café together, making plans to meet the next
evening at Les Deux Magots. She hailed a taxi, and just before she
stepped in, she turned to me and we shook hands.

"I will see you *demain soir*," she said, and was gone.

· III ·

In 1960, when I was nineteen and living in California, I was in
love with Camus, beguiled by Sartre, and thinking myself en-
lightened by Simone de Beauvoir. I decided to drive across America to settle in New York City's bohemian world—and I needed to
make two important stops along the way. The first was Virginia
City, Nevada—my hometown for the first two years of my life—
and the other was Nelson Algren's home in Chicago.

I arrived in Virginia City to find the sidewalks were still made
of wood. They were raised off the ground and ran like a long, continuous porch up one side and down the other of C Street. As I
walked, on my left I saw a woman sitting inside the post office at an

old-fashioned telephone board. I passed her window, tall, many-paned, and open to let in the September air.

Suddenly she called out to a man approaching me.

"Well, Lucius, meet our old teacher's daughter." The man stopped beside me, took off his hat (not a pint short of ten gallons), and bowed.

How in the world did this woman know who I was? This was the first time I had been here since my family moved away almost seventeen years before.

"Pleased to meet you, Miss," the man said. "My name is Lucius Beebe and I knew your dad years ago."

My incredulous face must not have surprised him, for he reared back on his cowboy boot heels and bellowed to the woman, "Well, Ida, you are one amazing gal."

Mr. Beebe laughed loudly—indeed his every move was noisy. Lucius Beebe was well-known in Nevada, where he revived *The Territorial Enterprise,* the newspaper made famous by Mark Twain.

"My father always spoke highly of you, " I ventured. "It's nice to meet you after all these years. But who is that lady, and how does she know who I am?"

"Well, my dear, let me introduce you to Ida, our town's only telephone operator."

It was strange to find myself standing in a nineteenth-century town, dressed in the black, 1960s style of bohemia, with a red beret, talking to a man I had read about in history books

Ida must have known we were going to greet her, but she sat still, in the same position, and didn't turn her head.

"Pleased to meet you, I'm sure," she said. The two of them broke out laughing and we chatted for a few minutes.

After we left Ida, Mr. Beebe and I walked down the street and he told me her story.

"Ida is blind," he said, "and every day for the past forty years she has come to work in this very same place. She knows a person's footsteps, even recognizes the sound patterns of a family. She hears them the same as a sighted person can see different patterns of fingerprints. The town won't install a modern telephone system as long as Ida is still working. People put up with the inconveniences, including not being able to call out after eight in the evening, just to accommodate her. When she retires in two years, we'll make the transition."

Mr. Beebe, now Lucius to me, invited me to have dinner with him. So later that evening I met him at Piper's Opera House, a red-flocked, crystal-chandelier-lit eatery. It was magnificent. The aisles between the tables were wide, and like the traditional western gentleman he had become, Lucius offered me his arm and we paraded to our table. My nineteen-year-old romantic imagination transformed us into Fred Astaire and Ginger Rogers on a grand white stairway—or Moira Shearer dancing to her death on the tracks of an oncoming train—or Nana in Zola's *Les Rougon-Macquart* making her grand entrance onstage.

We sat at the white-clothed table with candlelight and glistening silver and reflecting crystal glasses. Everything shimmered. And it was there I drank my first martini, pretending to be Simone de Beauvoir—the epitome of French intellectual sophistication.

The rest of the evening remains a blur. I was so nervous that my eyes kept wandering about the room, watching all the other people as they ate and drank. I know I drank two martinis, I think I ate a steak, and I remember Lucius told me outrageous stories about Virginia City. He told me that any child born in this town was called a "hot-water plug." Water in the mines can get as hot as one hundred eighty degrees. When the water breaks through into a mine, the miners stop it with a wooden plug. I guess if they didn't have wood they would use babies. . . .

Lucius walked me back to my room at the hotel, and with a bow and a doffing of his hat, my dinner companion wished me a good evening at the door. The next morning I left for Chicago. I never saw him again.

❧

On the twenty-third of September, 1960, while I was en route to Chicago, Simone de Beauvoir wrote to Nelson Algren about Jean-Paul Sartre. Her "most dear little being," Sartre, had a new love—a redhead. She suggested that this redhead was simply a new addition to Sartre's coterie of brunettes and fake blondes. She also told Algren that Sartre, besides the redhead, had started an affair with a much younger woman, an upper-class innocent from northern Brazil.

Next to me, on the seat of the car, sat two books. The first was de Beauvoir's *The Mandarins,* which was dedicated to Algren, and had crocheted France, the existentialists, and Chicago into my dreams. But de Beauvoir was so nonplussed about her lover's lovers that it confused me. Where I came from, no one dared smile at another woman's boyfriend, much less husband. Here, in *The Mandarins,* a whole other life had emerged. I was befuddled—and intrigued.

And finally I was on my way to live in New York. I had saved my money for this move by working at boring jobs and eating noodles with Crisco oil, salt, and pepper. I was determined.

So it seemed fitting that the other book on the seat was *America Day by Day,* also by de Beauvoir, which chronicles her travels in 1947. It was during those travels that she met Algren. I wanted to see 1928 West Evergreen Street, Chicago, Illinois. I wanted to walk down the street to the old German restaurant where they took most of their meals, and then on down to Lake Shore Drive to watch the fishermen—and the stars above them.

Late in the afternoon on the twenty-seventh of September, I pulled alongside the curb on Division Street, on the South Side of Chicago. Straight in front of me was a dilapidated hotel with a bar downstairs and rooms on the second and third floors. I chose it because it was around the corner from Algren's flat. The hotel register was on the bar. I was a nineteen-year-old girl trying to look like an older woman. The bartender asked me if I was sure that I wanted a room. I told him, yes, I really wanted a room. He asked if I wanted it for the hour rate or the evening rate. I told him the evening rate. He shrugged. I took the key and walked upstairs to the first room on the left. It was a simple room, very clean, with the lumpiest mattress I had ever slept on. Outside the window was a *cliché*—a broken red-and-yellow neon light that blinked on and off all night—OTEL, in red, OTEL, in yellow, OTEL in red. I was comforted by the light—and its nearness to the street.

I left the hotel and walked to Evergreen Street. It was still warm enough for the children to be playing a uniquely Chicago street game called tenner in which tennis balls were aimed against the steps of the stoops. One-a-tenner to the first step, two-a-tenner to the second step, three-a-tenner to the third step, four-a-tenner to the fourth step—and then, bingo, you were a winner! But if you hit a cracked step and the ball veered off in another direction, you lost.

The street was noisy. People were sitting outside on the gray stone stoops, visiting. Telephone wires were strung along the street, sometimes caught in the branches of the tenacious urban elms. Cooking smells came from the kitchens of Italian and Polish blue-collar folks. I didn't see Algren, although I tried to look through his second-story window—and I didn't see de Beauvoir, who was back in Paris. But I did eat in his neighborhood German restaurant, and I did glance into all the bars—looking. Looking for Algren. Actually, I had no idea what I would have done if I had found him.

On the corner of his street was a newspaper stand. An elderly man was sitting on an upside-down milk crate reading one of his papers.

"Excuse me," I said, "could you tell me which way to Lake Shore Drive?"

He pushed back his cap and looked up at me. "Lady," he said, "Lake Shore Drive is a very long walk from here. You'd better drive or take the bus." He began to read again, shaking his head.

"But sir," I persisted, "how far is Lake Shore Drive?"

"Lady, you want water? Walk down that way three blocks."

I walked to the water. Not to Lake Shore Drive, as de Beauvoir had said, but to the considerably closer Chicago River. De Beauvoir was being fanciful; Algren was not the strolling type.

❧

Today, as I sit in my studio in New Mexico, I see hundreds of butterflies, orange and black with glimmers of pink, painted ladies, or *Vanessa cardui*. I understand that, because of the abundance of rain last year, they multiplied as never before in recorded history. The air is silent, and if I stop moving my pen across the lines of the page, I can hear their whispering flutters, their silent announcements. Here is a blooming lilac, there is a blooming honeysuckle, they tell each other, flying in colorful pairs against the deep blue sky of this high desert land.

One of Mme. Leduc's most admired writers, André Gide, wrote, "Whoever studies himself arrests his own development. A caterpillar that set out really 'to know itself' would never become a butterfly."

I think for a long time about Gide's statement. I am struck by his narrowness. If he really believed this, there would be no journals of André Gide, no autobiographies of Violette Leduc. And I would not have read those writers who have guided me throughout my life with their self-explorations, their questions, and occasionally, their answers.

The next evening in Paris I walked up the Boulevard Saint-Germain to André Gide's favorite café, Les Deux Magots. I was looking forward to seeing Lili again. Would she bring her journal and her notes?

Lili had not arrived yet, so I found a table in a corner away from the door. The night before, my tape recorder had picked up too many of the sounds of the café. I needed to be more careful.

Les Deux Magots sits beneath four stories of interlaced iron balconies in Montparnasse. Its awning still hovers over the pavement, but now there is an enclosed sidewalk café, glistening with glass and brass. Until the end of the war, and the invasion of tourists, Les Deux Magots was one of the hearts of literature in Paris.

Lili walked in and saw me immediately. Smiling, she approached the table and held out her hand. She was carrying a tiny handbag—there would be no letters or notebooks tonight.

"How are you?" she asked.

Before I could answer, the waiter arrived.

"Madame Jacobs!" he said, and proceeded to speak much too quickly for me to understand. Lili laughed and answered him, and then he left.

She explained: "This waiter is Paul, whose father, Victor, was an old friend of my husband's. The family has been working here for years. I used to leave messages with Victor for my husband—this was all before answering machines. He delivered them to Alain on the back of *les additions*."

Paul arrived at the table with two coffees and two cognacs, all on the house.

"Last night was very interesting for me," Lili said. "I had not thought a lot about what I would tell you. Actually, I wasn't convinced I would talk to you at all!"

"What convinced you?" I asked.

"I suppose it is because you are just as nervous as I am."

We laughed together.

"It seems to me, and correct me if I'm wrong, she continued, "that you are searching for the part of Violette that is *not* newsworthy. People have been attracted to her eccentricity, but they have overlooked her seriousness, her beautiful use of language, her commitment to art. I like the idea that you are trying to understand her from an instinctive point of view."

"Yes, you're right," I replied. "I'm writing this book using intuition rather than precision. But this means that I'm not sure where it will take me."

"Well, I appreciate that uncertainty," Lili said sympathetically. "Now, where did we leave off last night?"

"We were talking about you and Violette and the war."

"Ah, *oui*," Lili said, and she continued. "I think one of the reasons I was attracted to Violette was my own history. I met her a few months after returning from prison. Do you mind if I tell you a little about myself? It will help you to understand Violette better, I believe."

"I would like to hear more," I said.

"I had just spent sixteen months in the Cherche-Midi prison, which was then run by the Germans. In prison we were all forced to do anything to survive, no matter what we were in for. Prostitution, stealing, murder—it made no difference. We had to find ways of living together, of making deals with ourselves, and one another. If I get through this day, I thought, I will be nicer to so-and-so. If I find something to eat, I won't forget hunger when I get out, and so on."

With relish, we took sips of our delicious cognacs and smiled at each other.

"I was starving," Lili said. "When I finally looked around at my situation, I realized that most of us were there because we had committed crimes against the Nazi system. It was obvious to me that we women did not fit the passive role assigned to us by history."

"Why did you have to go to prison?"

"It was strange. The Cherche-Midi prison was just around the corner from the Rue Mayet. I had grown up and still lived on the Rue Mayet. Some of the sounds I heard during the day were the same sounds—from the same people and places—I had heard all my life.

"I was in prison because I had been caught delivering a suspicious-looking package to a bookstall alongside the Seine. You see, I worked with a group helping stranded British soldiers escape into the free zone of France. One of my jobs, along with many other Frenchwomen, was of a *passeur*, a 'ferryman.' Because of my English, I was able to communicate with these soldiers. My job was to translate for my colleagues and to determine whether any of these airmen were German plants."

"I didn't know there were British soldiers stranded in France," I said. "Were there many?"

"Hundreds," Lili replied. "They were caught behind enemy lines in occupied Europe. Many of them were stranded in June of 1940, when British forces withdrew from France. Tens of thousands of men crossed the channel from Dunkirk in small boats, but many were left behind, trapped, scattered in groups throughout the forests of France.

"So there I was, locked away in my own neighborhood. It was ludicrous. We were awakened at six-thirty every morning by the growl of *'Aufstehen, Schweinehund'*—Get up, pig dog. We were then given a cup of vile liquid that they called coffee. We had to make our beds, dress, and use the toilet by six-forty. Then the guard, with an outrageously normal wedding ring on his stubby hand, would shout, *'Kübel raus, du Scheisskerl'*—Bucket out, you shit. If we were late or slow, we were punished by being thrown into solitary confinement for five days. Of course, we were also beaten whenever the Nazis felt like it. They didn't need a reason. And the toilet was nothing more than a tin can that was emptied only once a day. The smell, the lack of ventilation, the heat in the summer, the cold in the winter, all were a constant nightmare."

Lili looked about the crowded café. "There were always six eyes trying to leave you in privacy," she said quietly. We tried to be supportive of one another, but we knew that one of the four put into each cell was an informer. You could count on this. And since we were constantly being moved from cell to cell, you were never able to tell who was who, so you learned to trust no one. This distrust, the psychological isolation, it was terrible."

Lili's voice was getting quieter, becoming almost a whisper. I nudged the tape recorder closer, trying not to interrupt her story.

"Picking the maggots from the infested bread took time, and then there was nothing to do. No books, nothing to write with. You could not lie down on your cot at any time during the day. So we just sat. And the more I sat, the more I withdrew and lived in my head, until the real world faded away. I was left with a numbness that was like death. It was like suffering from an interior malnutrition . . . impossible to describe."

Violette tried to describe this same feeling in a novella, *The Woman with the Little Fox Fur*, in which she told the story of a destitute woman who finds a mangy fox boa in a refuse bin. This outcast woman treasures her fox, and it allows her some pleasure in life. It is her lover, her child, her friend forever—it is the mythological figure of the trickster fox, Reynard. Alas, poor Reynard was always hunted for his pelt.

One day the woman realizes that she has to sell the fox for money to buy food. She chooses a merchant, walks into his shop, and offers her fox for sale. The merchant looks with disdain at her bedraggled prize and shows her the way to the door. Back on the street, she finds herself with her hand out, begging. And into her outstretched hand fall coins, more than enough to buy food. She returns to her dismal garret elated with her friendly boa, her dignity restored.

· IV ·

Completing my inaugural long-distance car trip in 1960, I arrived in New York to look for an apartment and a job. After I was somewhat settled, my grandfather Eli asked me to have dinner with him. We went to a fish restaurant on Eighth Street in Greenwich Village. Again I was nervous, aware that I lacked any semblance of sophistication. I wore the light-green wool coat I had made, and flung my grandmother's gift of a red fox boa around my neck—the fox with its head still on and its tiny stone eyes staring straight ahead.

My fox boa was not mangy, it still had all its hair, yet it had the appearance of an embalmed mummy circling my neck. Eli seemed to recoil from it, yet I assumed this was because he was so kind-hearted. Indeed, when my grandparents sat in the evenings to read and listen to the radio, taking the same chairs by habit, a tiny mouse would appear and stay behind my grandmother Rosa, scampering around. Eli looked forward to seeing his friend every night. After many weeks of this visitation, Rosa happened to move and see the mouse. She picked up a book and slammed it down on the poor creature.

My grandparents had arrived in America not yet having met each other—and both holding on to their European culture with uneasiness, but with a great deal of style. Eli was a tiny man, at most five-feet-three, but large in presence. He was a teacher, an intellectual from the old school, and a bona fide, card-carrying communist. I thought he was the ultimate bohemian.

He took me very seriously.

As a girl I occasionally tried to move conversations in my family toward discussions about the world and all its whys. My family would rise up as a unified clan and denounce me as "always philosophizing" or being "too intense." Only Eli encouraged my seriousness.

Eli was the one person everybody listened to, for a few minutes at least. If he went on for too long, Rosa would tell him in Yiddish to be quiet—or she would just look at him with that awful maternal ancestral scowl. Although he was tiny, he stood his ground. He also clung, just as tenaciously, to the few strands of hair still on his head. He combed and patted them and endured somberly the constant teasing about someone's cutting them off in his sleep.

Eli was born in 1897 into a highly educated family. One family story says that his father was a physician to Nicholas the Second. I inherited a small blue china vial supposedly given to him by the czar. Another story is that my great-grandfather was a wealthy businessman who paid for the building of the first hospital in Kraków.

I prefer the first story.

In his youth, as a student and intellectual, Eli was deeply involved in the political branch of Zionism. And then came the Revolution.

"Drown the Revolution in Jewish blood!" screamed the government's voice.

With the mounting threats of pogroms and the increase of police activity against Jewish Zionist intellectuals, Eli, at the age of seventeen, was imprisoned for a year on a trumped-up political charge and then exiled forever from his homeland.

Eli and a group of friends were part of an exodus from villages and towns in the Pale of Settlement to the Middle East. These people, mostly young, were seeking a way to heal the wounded Jewish heart. They wove their paths to the pre–State of Israel, to the land of blue skies, constant sun, and soft breezes from the sea.

They traveled across Europe to discover a small, desolate, and swamp-infested valley sitting on both sides of the River Jordan. Entering the Jordan's mouth, they were startled to see in front of them the Sea of Galilee.

In 1915, Eli and his friends built one of the first kibbutzim in a fertile valley in northern Palestine. Very few of them had any agricultural training. They learned from books and from their Arab neighbors. Earnest in their wish to establish a safe home for the besieged Jews of the world, they persevered with fierce determination. They spoke an assortment of languages, but settled on Yiddish while beginning to resurrect the ancient language of their new land, Hebrew. The kibbutz they called Degania, from the Hebrew word for "grain," *dagan*. In honor of Eli's pioneering work, a little street in Tel Aviv was named after him. The map says it is off Ben Yehuda Street, but it must be as tiny as he was, because I never found it.

Two years later, the settlers of the kibbutz were forced to flee when a small army of Turks lurked and threatened nearby. With only an hour's warning, they saddled horses, loaded guns and food, and left Palestine in a trail of dust. It is difficult for me to imagine my grandfather on a horse, much less holding a gun, yet I have seen a picture of him and so it is true.

After his escape, Eli traveled in a circuitous and mysterious way, going first to London and then to Paris. He settled in a tiny garret room on the Rue Flatters in the Latin Quarter, on the Left Bank. This area was one of the hubs of the Russian intellectual community, which had grown considerably after the Russian Revolution in 1905. He refused to live on the Right Bank, although he was offered a room there for almost nothing. He wanted nothing to do with the petit bourgeois. Still, he admitted that he missed the working-class community and the *pletzyl* there. I remember asking him, "The pletzl. You mean the bread that is a cross between a bialy and a small challah?"

"No, no." He laughed. "A pletzyl. P-L-E-T-Z-Y-L."

The pletzyl is a small area, south of the Seine, traversing the Fourth and Fifth arrondissements. In the early part of this century it looked like a neighborhood in an Eastern European city. There were kosher markets, kosher bakeries, and the traditional delicatessens smelling of brine. It was here that the religious Jewish community lived, attended shul, and strolled on the Sabbath. I have always felt that it was because of my grandfather's love of Paris that I fell in love with it too. I could easily imagine him with a beret and his amber cigarette holder, talking with friends in a café, because I often saw him like this in a coffee shop on Broadway.

Eli studied at the Sorbonne for a year, enhancing his French. This he added to his inventory of languages—Russian, Polish, English, German, Yiddish, Arabic, and a little Turkish. It's not clear when Eli landed in America, but it seems to have been about 1919. There were many Jewish organizations helping newly arrived immigrants settle in the New World, under the auspices of various political and religious groups. Eli was directed immediately to his political name-tag, the socialists, later to be called the Communist Party of the United States of America.

Once in America he became a teacher, teaching Jewish history, literature, and language. In his office hung portraits of Lenin and the writer Gorky. There was another portrait of Gorky, hanging in my grandparents' apartment, but Rosa would not allow Lenin or Stalin to live in her presence.

We visited the New York branch of our family every summer—and it was from these summers that I remember loud and boisterous arguments around the kitchen table. Glasses of schnapps, cups of coffee, and cigarettes littered the table, and would suddenly bounce into the air as a heavily applied fist hit the wood. I didn't understand very much of this, because the arguments were in Yiddish, but Eli's sheer force of will put me on his side.

The bad times for our family came with the House Un-American Activities Committee investigation and the persecution of known members of the Communist Party.

On East Eighth Street in Greenwich Village, in an old Civil War–era building with enormous rooms, a dumbwaiter, and questionable plumbing, lived my aunt, uncle, and two cousins. The Alger Hiss family lived on the floor below. When we visited I would often play with Tony Hiss, the son. We spent a great deal of time on the stairwell or in the backyard adjoining the Washington Mews.

The summer of 1948, when I was seven years old, everything changed. We were not allowed to talk in the stairwell, and when we played outside we had to stay away from the trees and telephone poles. Our families thought they held listening devices. I remember a man with a tan jacket and a fedora leaning against a tree, watching us. I knew he was bad, and I was frightened. Tony's mother was very nervous and stayed sequestered in her darkened apartment with her cats. I felt sorry for her and was drawn to the mystery of her house. Only once do I remember being invited in to pet the cats. I whispered "Thank you" while she sweetly watched me with the cats, and then I tiptoed to the door.

My entire family was being threatened by Joseph McCarthy. Redbaiting was woven into the fiber of everyday life. In 1953, the students in my school district were given a slip of pink paper to take home and have signed by parents. The slip asked the question: Are you, or have you ever been, a member of the Communist Party?

My father, a teacher, was considered a public servant. Any hint of a left-wing history would be grounds for dismissal. Both my parents were serious assimilationists and stayed away from anything considered too Jewish or too foreign. They were guilty only by association, not by membership.

But they refused to sign the pink slip. Every day I went to school empty-handed. Every day I was forced to lie about the missing paper. I remember the embarrassment, the chagrin. The matter was resolved, roundabout. When it came time for the "squealers" to testify, for some unexplained reason, the names of members of my family were not mentioned.

Eli, though, was fired, never to be reinstated. He ended up teaching in a tiny room above Mays department store on East Fourteenth Street. He had two rows of old, worn red theater seats and a desk. Only a few determined students continued in this much-maligned yeshiva of higher learning. He kept the school going until his retirement, when he was able to collect Social Security.

❧

On the evening Eli and I were dining in the fish restaurant on Eighth Street, he asked me if I would like a drink. I answered with sureness, "A dry martini, light on the vermouth, and two olives, please." He was a bit taken aback, but seemed delighted and ordered a scotch on the rocks for himself. He told me that he usually ordered schnapps and threw it back with one movement, but this time he would behave like a gentleman.

"Now," he said, "I have a gift for you."

Out of his pocket he handed me a long, amber cigarette holder, which had belonged to his father. He showed me how to insert the cigarette, how to hold the holder, and then the trick of keeping it steady between my lips while I talked.

A large white plate covered with sharp-ridged shells arrived at the table. The shells had been pried open to reveal gelatinous gray lumps floating in slimy brine. I had never seen oysters before and wondered how I was going to eat them without getting sick all over the tablecloth. Eli squeezed a little lemon juice on one, picked it up, and placed it sideways on his lips. In one quick sluicing movement, he emptied it into his mouth and swallowed. Then he squeezed a little lemon juice on another one and handed it to me. I closed my eyes, placed it in my mouth, threw back my head, and gulped. Although I am not a slimy-food eater (forget aspic, forget loose boiled eggs), to this day I love oysters.

· V ·

I couldn't imagine Lili wearing a red fox boa—but I smiled each time she inserted her cigarette into her holder.

"How did you get out of prison?" I asked.

"It was the end of the war!" she answered, as if I should know better.

I was in a muddle and started to stutter.

"I am sorry for being rude, please. . . . I guess I am jumping around a bit." She smiled.

With a deep breath, I asked, "So what happened after you left prison?"

"My family placed a *loving* prison around me. Velvet bars, floods of sunlight, and soft, down-feathered silence. They were always watching me, catering to my needs. There was very little food at the table. Every bite I took was savored by my mother. Each swallow was aped by everyone else's gullets. They gave large portions of their own rations to save my life.

"After three weeks, I could not bear their witness and moved to an apartment at number twenty, Rue Paul-Bert, second floor. My windows had wrought-iron *fioriture*—curlicue, yes?—and faced Vins Berthe, a tiny food shop formerly called Florale. On either side of my building were a *charcuterie* and a chemist. There was a *pâtisserie* on the corner, and the Nicholas wine store on the next street. I settled into my freedom.

"The two entrance doors to my building reminded me of two perching owls. They were ten feet high and carved in traditional French patterns. Where there was a crack, you could see the wood was dark brown through and through. The doors were simple and quite grand. Two fluted columns were carved into the center of each door, ending at the top with two small round windows. At night, when the inside light was on, the owls' lit eyes beckoned me to enter.

"I loved going home to the Rue Paul-Bert. The lodge belonging to Madame Moutiere, the concierge, was on the street floor straight in front of the entrance. Two beveled glass doors led to her headquarters. When the always starched, clean-white lace curtains were pulled across the doors, you knew that Madame was not available. When the curtains were open, you could enter without knocking, by pulling on one of the brass handles and pushing hard on the other.

"The smells from her lodge! As soon as you entered the vestibule, you knew what she was having for dinner. Sometimes her peasant cooking reminded me of our country home in Saint-Désiré when I was a little girl. When she made sauerkraut from an old family recipe from Alsace, I found excuses to go in—a minor request, a tiny complaint—and departed with a full plate.

"The first time I met Violette Leduc, I was returning from the *poste* on the Rue des Boulets. I was climbing the stairs, daydreaming, and didn't see the woman on my left descending.

"I collided with a tall lady with tiny little eyes set over an enormous nose. Her blond hair was twisted with multicolored rag curlers. What a sight! She looked like an inmate in a de Sade story. I had to control myself not to draw back.

"'Excuse me, Madame,' I said.

"'Excuse *me*, Madame,' she answered with a voice like musical bells. Then she smiled and her face was transformed. Simone de Beauvoir described Violette perfectly: 'A tall, elegant blond woman with a face both brutally ugly and radiantly alive.'

"We introduced ourselves and chatted shyly, and discovered we lived next door to each other. I didn't see her again for another five weeks.

"Although there was only a wall between us, I rarely heard noise coming from her apartment. We both worked at home. I learned later that she was completing her first book, *L'Asphyxie*. And I was editing, for a series of French police novels that were supposed to be both bloody and humorous. It was a simple task and I was grateful just to have a job.

"One day, I heard a terrible commotion next door. After a few minutes it ceased. I listened and waited, then went on working. Ten minutes later it started again, and it continued for a long time. I couldn't concentrate on my work, yet I didn't want to interfere. Finally it was too much, and when the next period of calm began, I went next door and knocked. She flung the door open. Standing before me was Medusa. She was fury letting loose her rage upon herself. It was frightening just to look at her.

"She asked me sharply what I wanted, her tone implying that I should mind my own business. I was mute—my voice had remained in my apartment, sitting on my chair. And then, right before my eyes, her body was suddenly drained of its electricity—her power went out. She apologized with tears running down her cheeks.

"I looked behind her, and the only things that appeared out of place were two cooking pots sitting in the middle of the hallway floor. She had obviously been warring with them.

"'May I make you a cup of tea?' I asked.

"She moved out of the way and I walked into her kitchen. Sitting down at the table, Violette placed her head in a nest of long, gangling arms. I busied myself putting on water to boil and looked around for the tea and teacups.

"Her apartment was simple and free of any extra furniture. The layout was similar to mine. You walked through the front door into a short hall with a small toilet on the right and a clothes closet on the left. At the end of the hall, turning left, you entered the kitchen and living room combined. In her kitchen area were a table and four chairs in the center, and the buffet, stove, and sink on the right, along with shelves holding her dishes and some food. Neither of us had a refrigerator—we shopped each day for fresh food.

"Behind the kitchen-and-living-room was the bedroom. This was where she worked, either sitting at the simple table or with a tray across her knees in bed. Her bed faced the windows, which looked out onto our street. And the windows were perfectly clean, with lovingly tended window boxes of geraniums and begonias outside on the sills. Inside, potted plants sat on deep window ledges. I recall a bronze bird perched on the edge of her favorite gardenia pot, poised ready for flight. The floor shone with hand-scrubbed care."

I remembered that a friend of Mme. Leduc's once said, "Violette liked to wash things, to clean things. It was as if she were washing and cleaning her words."

"In the left corner of Violette's kitchen–living room," Lili continued, "was a small enamel Godin stove. Alongside the stove was another work area, against the longest wall, the one with windows. On the worktable was a copy of Beckett's essay on Proust, a lamp, a walnut shuck, a paperweight, a white Japanese vase with two branches of *chatons,* and her writing materials."

At the table next to Lili and me sat a couple, their heads resting on their hands as they leaned toward each other. They were passing words—whispering—with barely a ribbon's space between their lips.

"The photographs, I almost forgot!" Lili exclaimed, drawing my attention away from the neighboring table. "Hanging above her worktable were many photographs of de Beauvoir and Sartre, including the famous portrait of de Beauvoir by Cartier-Bresson. Her favorite photo of the writer Maurice Sachs, standing in a white open-necked shirt with rolled-up sleeves, already quite bald at thirty-five, hung between a picture of de Beauvoir and one of Greta Garbo. In a frame on the table was a picture of her grandmother Fidéline—there were no photos of her mother, there never were.

"To the left of the table were the bookshelves. I had bought the same kind at the same market on the Place d'Aligre. The tops of her shelves were clear of objects but the other shelves were neatly jammed with books, even an old copy of the Bible. Tucked into the corner of one shelf were a bottle of Granvillons and a packet of Gitanes."

Lili laughed. "I just remembered something I had completely forgotten! Years after we met, Violette was given a Cocteau drawing of Genet. It hung above her bed for the rest of her life. In my files at home is a letter Cocteau wrote to Violette. I will show it to you before you leave Paris.

"Anyway, it was February 1945. Paris was liberated. But here I sat, waiting for the water to boil, waiting for Violette to stop crying. We were liberated, yet not freed from our worries.

"More and more food was appearing on the market shelves, fuel was a little easier to find, lights could be left on, and soon windows would be left open to allow in our first free spring.

"Finally Violette stopped crying and raised her head to smile at me. The kettle began singing its long, steaming whistle, and Violette rose from the table to make the tea.

"I didn't want to pry into the reasons for the private tantrum I had interrupted, but I was curious. Sitting with our hands wrapped around our hot cups of tea, I was saddened by the slouch of the tall woman sitting across from me. The silence continued for a long while, but I didn't mind.

"Before I heard a word, I knew Violette was preparing to speak. I learned very quickly when the words were about to leave her mouth. She would move her head to one side, look right past me, and make a tray of her hands, palms up.

"She said, 'I'm sorry for bothering you, I lost all sense of where I was—I am ashamed.'

"I could only try to reassure her with a smile.

"She continued in a dramatic voice, 'This evening I have the most important meeting of my life. I am meeting with Simone de Beauvoir at the Café de Flore and I am terrified.' Imagine!"

Many years ago, my husband, Joe, and I were in Paris and sheepishly couldn't resist the traditional literary pilgrimage some tourists indulge in—an afternoon at the Café de Flore.

Picasso used to sit three tables from the door, along the windows on the left.

Simone de Beauvoir used to sit every day on a red banquette at the back of the café, alongside Sartre.

And Violette Leduc spied on them all from the table behind the door on the left.

Joe and I waited until one of these distinguished tables was available. Picasso's was first and we sat down. I told Joe obscure stories about the Café de Flore, about the poet Apollinaire, who lived almost next door and met his friends here every day. It was here, probably at this table, that the famous review *Les Soirées de Paris* was born. It was here, certainly at this same table, where Giacometti sat too.

"The Café de Flore was a different sort of place during the occupation from what it is today," Lili said. "It was very popular because of its nearness to the Métro and how easily one could find the entrance during blackouts. Most of this time, the Flore was an oasis of silence, allowing writers to work undisturbed, despite the

Gauloises Bleues smoke, which made an already dim café even dimmer."

Lili paused, smiled, raised her eyebrows, and lit a cigarette. "Violette thought that real writers sat in cafés to work and that make-believe writers sat in cafés to be seen. When the war started and these writers, make-believe or not, were faced with the harsh reality of subsistence, the cafés became more a home to artists than ever before. Fuel was rationed. Cooking at home, even working at home, was difficult. It was warmer in the cafés, and the writers could take their meals here too. Many writers used the Café de Flore as their living room. Sartre, who was not in Paris during much of the war, was able to send mail to Simone at the Flore as if it were a home address.

"I remember a letter from Simone I was shown many years after the war. It has always seemed so very funny to me. It was sent from the Café de Flore in October of 1939. It said, 'Dear little being: I reread your philosophical letter. You're a splendid philosopher, my little poppet. You must begin to construct a system, since you have the time. . . . Your charming Beaver.' It was sent to Sartre while he was in the army!"

Lili sat there smiling while I looked around the mystical café. It was difficult to imagine what it was like during the war. I suppose it was dingy gray. Today it glistened with prosperity.

"Let's have one more cognac?" I said. "A nightcap."

Lili laughed. "We call it a *pousse-café*, somewhat like a chaser. The last drink, chasing the others away."

Her friend Paul arrived to take our order.

"We would like two cognacs," she said in English.

"Writers sat down to work about eight-thirty in the morning and continued until noon," Lili resumed. "Then they left the café, to search for a bargain lunch, or go home to their families, and returned around two to visit with their friends. This visiting went on until four, and then they worked again for another four hours. Dinner, for those who ventured home, was at eight, and then they would come back to the Flore. When there was an air raid, everyone would move as if to leave, but many would just climb upstairs where it was warmer and continue working. Even when the electricity failed, the glow of the acetylene lamps and a seat near the stovepipe were luxurious compared with the cold and dampness of one's own hotel room or garret. Boubal, the proprietor of the café, once remarked, faintly irritated, 'When they die—de Beauvoir and Sartre—you'll have to dig them a grave under the floor.'"

Lili drank the last of her cognac and signaled Paul.

"I must go now, it is late." She looked tired for the first time.

"Lili, why don't we meet somewhere more quiet, and maybe a little earlier?"

"Yes, that will be fine. Tomorrow I have a busy day, but I can meet you for an hour, at four let's say, in the lobby of your hotel?"

"The hotel lobby is quite small."

"Yes, I know the hotel. But it will be fine. We can sit at one of the tables and talk without being bothered."

Lili shook my hand and was gone.

The next day I wandered around Paris with my camera. I wanted to photograph the various places Mme. Leduc mentioned in her books. This was also a wonderful excuse to learn the city. I barely made it back to the hotel by four.

Lili had already arrived. With her was the hyperactive poodle belonging to the woman I called "Madame of the Front Desk." The poodle was lying calmly in Lili's lap.

"How did you get that dog to calm down?" I asked. "Every morning when I come down for breakfast, she is almost hysterical." All Lili did was laugh and shift the poodle on her lap to make it more comfortable.

"Now, where were we?" she said. "Let's begin. I am afraid I have only a short time."

"I understand. Why don't you tell me what you thought about Madame Leduc's writing?"

"Of course. That same day, you remember, when I saved her pots from being destroyed, I asked Violette if she wrote for a living. She said she started to write for women's magazines during the war and wrote mainly for Lucien Lelong, the famous couturier—flowery descriptions of clothing and perfumes reeking with optimism. It being wartime, and everyone worrying about where to buy a meter of cloth, much less a warm coat for the winter, I was always a little dismayed when I came across those silly fashion magazines. But I reminded myself that women left behind on the home front still had to eat. Plying one's needle to make clothing or dreaming about a pretty dress was neither criminal nor treasonous.

"As I told you, the evening of the day I made her tea, she was taking her manuscript to an arranged meeting at the Café de Flore with Simone de Beauvoir. When Violette told me about this meeting, about her respect for Simone, her face was transformed by her smile, similar to when I first met her on the staircase. I was fascinated by her ardor, not realizing that this passion was Violette's everyday behavior."

I learned that Mme. Leduc's infatuation with de Beauvoir began when she read *L'Invitée. A woman writing on behalf of millions of other women,* was how Mme. Leduc described her. She was so possessed by de Beauvoir that during the war, when she sold food on the black market, Mme. Leduc ran her schedule accordingly. She would leave Normandy for Paris at whatever time was necessary so she could visit the Café de Flore.

"Strange to think that while I was sitting in my prison cell, Violette was peddling butter in Paris and watching Simone at the Café de Flore, no?"

It was in 1942, when Violette was living in Normandy, that her friend Maurice Sachs forced her to write about herself. "You're being eaten alive by your unconscious. . . . Write down your childhood memories. . . . Your unhappy childhood is beginning to bore me to distraction. This afternoon you will take your basket, a pen, and an exercise book, and you will go and sit under an apple tree. Then you will write down all the things you tell me."

This command from Maurice came after an evening when I screamed and sobbed after talking to him for three hours about my unhappy childhood. And so I began to write.

I realized that a life is so much slower than the tale we tell in an exercise book. Yet the solution to my unhappiness may lie in working, in writing; this way I may give birth to myself. So off I went the next morning to write, to fill pages as a homework assignment for Maurice.

Sitting beneath an apple tree laden with green and pink apples, I dipped my pen in the inkwell and, with my mind a blank, I wrote the first sentence of L'Asphyxie: *My mother never held my hand.*

Light with the lightness Maurice had given me, my pen had no weight. I went on writing with the carelessness and facility of a sailing ship blown by the wind. The innocence of a beginning. He told me to "tell the paper about your childhood."

I told the paper.

I said to Lili, "Madame Leduc's writing seems endless. She turned the corner of her years, circling the block of her life, again and again, so often that I feel as if I know her more intimately than any other writer I've ever read."

I fondled my coffee cup, around and around. "We remember, for instance, going to the seashore when we were little. We remember this every once in a while during our life. This seashore memory helps string us to our past. Madame Leduc accomplishes this in her work. The same thing happens in my paintings—I dredge up memories and reflect upon them again and again. Leduc convinced me that repetitiveness is helpful in understanding one's own psychological situation."

"Well, she certainly did repeat her life in all her books," Lili replied. "She avoided straight lines of time. Her words wandered through the circumstances of her personal life, over and over and over. As if she had to keep jabbing her finger into her heartache in order to feel it.

"The death of her grandmother, her illegitimate birth, the coldness of her mother, her love affairs with Hermine and Isabelle, her alienation, her ugliness—time and time again, and then once more. She embraced writing the way some people embrace religion. She was a convert, totally dedicated to the redemption of her soul.

"Every day she had the same routine. First she cleaned her apartment and cleared her table. Everything had to be in order. If it was warm and the windows were open, I could hear her quietly moving about. A concert would be playing softly on her radio, preferably Bach. Then she would put on her *blouse-tablier*—her beloved smock of blue and white checks. When she was sixteen years old, she saw a photograph of Cocteau in a newspaper and was fascinated by the cuffs of his smock. She could see that these cuffs were very tight around his wrists. Years later, after she started to write seriously, she bought herself a smock with tight cuffs and wore it while she worked. And just in case, she always kept an extra one folded in a drawer.

"Then she would place an ordinary school exercise book on the table, dip her Blanzy-Poure pen into the ink, and write exactly three pages."

"She had her own sorrow waiting behind her to dip into privately," Virginia Woolf wrote, and the line has always reminded me of Violette. *Once the exercise book is closed again, I accuse myself of living,* Violette wrote, as if in response.

· VI ·

B ecause I live in the high desert, far away from cities, I rise with sunlight and lie down in darkness. Nature is my alarm clock. But in Europe, at sea level, I get a second wind that allows me to eat at eleven in the evening, have a cognac at one a.m., and go to bed still full of energy at three in the morning. Scientists say we have more oxygen-carrying red corpuscles at higher altitudes. I don't know what the reason is. Perhaps, by carrying the sand from the desert on the soles of my shoes, I am safely guided upon the sidewalks of Paris into the small hours of a new day.

When I left my pink room on the Avenue Rodin I lost my entire month's nonrefundable rent. So when I began staying at the Hôtel Senlis, I was far and beyond my allotment. The proprietor offered me a reduced rate for the month of my stay. I asked him to include *le petit dejeuner* in the amount, but he refused. My face must have revealed disappointment, for he said, as I was walking to the elevator, *"Oui, oui, café, café,"* and smiled.

The next morning I went downstairs with my portable larder—health food cereal, vitamins, and grapefruit juice. Madame brought my coffee in a nice-sized pitcher, along with a pitcher of milk. With my back turned to Madame at the desk, I poured the cereal into my coffee cup, added the milk, and tried to keep the crunching sound as quiet as possible. Then I wiped out the cup and poured the grapefruit juice, drank, and took my vitamins. I wiped out the cup once more and had my coffee. This way I saved seven dollars a day, two hundred ten dollars a month, the equivalent of one week's rent.

While this morning ritual took place, I also wrote to Joe. These letters were my way of staying connected to myself, to my home, to my family. "My dear heart," I would begin, and tell him about the previous day. This small but pleasant task helped ease my isolation.

Violette Leduc had suffered the feeling of being cut off from her world, and it is this loneliness she writes so much about. Whether I am in Berlin, the middle of the Sinai, or Paris, I feel loneliness so profoundly that I ache with a rock-hard pressure in the solar plexus, that space between the pillars shielding my heart. It is difficult to find the exact words for this feeling, so I bow low with respect to the unnamable and loiter around its definition.

To writing letters I added other daily routines, including watching American news on television at seven in the morning, and doing the crossword puzzle in the *International Herald Tribune*. How mundane this all sounds—how ordinary—how necessary.

After the morning ceremony I would set off to the Bibliothèque Nationale, sometimes imagining I was a student from the Sorbonne going to do research. My route was to walk down the Rue Soufflot, with the Panthéon at my back, down the Boulevard Saint-Michel to the Rue de Médicis, around the Place de l'Odéon, and past the Théâtre de l'Odéon.

Once on the Rue de l'Odéon, I would walk slowly past number 12, where Sylvia Beach was the proprietor of Shakespeare and Company. It was James Joyce's permanent mailing address and a safe haven for Ernest Hemingway, Ezra Pound, Aldous Huxley, and many other well-known and not so well-known writers. The Rue de l'Odéon empties into the bustling Carrefour de l'Odéon, where I would buy my newspaper, and in the evening, a hot crêpe with butter and sugar from an outdoor vendor.

From the *carrefour*, the intersection, I would explore the various ways to reach the Pont du Carrousel, which took me across the Seine to the Right Bank. One of my favorite routes was the Rue de Seine. Rainer Maria Rilke described it: "Sometimes I pass small shops, in the Rue de Seine. . . . There are antique dealers, small bookshops, or windows overcrowded with watercolors. No one ever enters these shops and apparently they do no business. But if one looks in, one can see the owners seated, always sitting, reading, unconcerned; not a thought about tomorrow, no worrying about success."

Today, the atmosphere is quite different. The shops are still there—the bookshops and the art supply stores—but the business competition is fierce, the rents are outrageous, and there is certainly no time for the proprietors to sit and read. Yet if you walk this street in the evening, in the dead of winter, you can easily imagine the dim interiors existing not so long ago, the cobblestone road lit by gaslights, and the smell of coal in the air.

On this same street, at number 31, George Sand first appeared in public in men's clothing. At number 60 still stands the Hôtel de la Louisiane, where Simone de Beauvoir lived. Baudelaire lived at number 57, venturing out only at night for fear his creditors would nab him during the day. As when I sat at Picasso's table at the Flore, sometimes walking along this street, I would catch just the slightest glimpse of the ghosts of my teachers.

From the Rue de Seine, I would walk to the Quai Malaquais and over the Pont, past the courtyard of the Louvre, to the Comédie-Française. In the nineteenth century this theater was the seat of the Classicist movement, although Victor Hugo's play *Hernani* was first performed there on a famous evening in 1830. His fellow Romantics, including Stendhal, Alexandre Dumas *père*, Théophile Gautier, Gérard de Nerval, even Balzac, were in the audience that evening. The audience was split in its response to the work. The Romantics, thrilling at the rousing success and crying out, "Racine is buried," celebrated in the lobby. The other half of the audience, the Classicists, jeered the play, and a riot ensued. Waistcoats were torn, top hats toppled, eyes were blackened, and noses were bloodied. All for the cause of art.

When I finally reached the Bibliothèque, I would hasten indoors, along with the rest of the researchers, and receive my card with the day's seat assignment. I didn't like sitting too close to the entrance, nor did I like facing the entrance, so I often had to ask for another seat. If there was one, the library staff was obliging; otherwise I would have no choice. If I came too late for the first rush I would have to take a number and sit outside until someone gave up his seat.

I worked until twelve-thirty, or until my stomach grumbled enough to embarrass me. Then I would leave my belongings on the table and pick up a pink card, the *fiche de sortie provisoire*. This card allowed me to return to my seat after lunch.

I found a small *bar-tabac* a few doors down on the Rue de Richelieu. For thirty-six francs I could get the cheapest but most filling meal possible—a baguette with hard salami and cheese, along with a carafe of water. After eating, I would order an espresso, do my ritual crossword puzzle in the *Herald Tribune,* order another coffee, and then return to work. Every day the same rotund, pink-faced man waited on me. By the end of the first week I learned how to order *en français familier,* with almost the correct accent, tutored by this friendly waiter.

I would leave the library at about six-thirty. Because this was February, the lights of Paris were already on and my walk home had a very different flavor from the morning walk. Quite often I would go down the Rue Bonaparte, past Sartre's old apartment at number 42, and turn left on the Rue des Beaux-Arts, the Rue Jacob, or the Rue de l'Abbaye. The Rue des Beaux-Arts reminds me of the nineteenth century. Indeed, the old Hôtel d'Alsace at number 13 remains, whose wallpaper was so ugly that Oscar Wilde proclaimed, "I can't stand this wallpaper. One of us will have to go." Oscar Wilde died. The wallpaper stayed, and is there, I have heard, even today.

· VII ·

The night of the next meeting, I arrived at Le Dôme before Lili and sat down at de Beauvoir and Sartre's banquette. I took out my tape recorder and my notebook and sat watching people. By now I had my perennial European sore throat. Tonight would just make it worse. The room was filled with smoke and the banquette was in the back—the perfect place to corner the grime!

It was good to see Lili again. She looked very handsome, with a black beret hugging her head at a rakish angle and a deep-maroon wool cape that slipped off as she approached the table. She was carrying a large satchel. The letters? The journals? I hoped. I rose to greet her. She kissed me on one cheek, then the other, and then an extra kiss on the first cheek. I found myself becoming very nervous again. What did three kisses and a bulging satchel mean?

We sat down next to each other on the shiny red banquette, and Lili folded her cape on the seat. De Beauvoir and Sartre saved their serious discussions for when they met here. Now it was our turn. Lili seemed prepared for a long evening.

"I would like coffee and a cognac," she said. "We have a lot of work to do!"

The waiter arrived, and she asked him to clean out the ashtray. We ordered. This was serious business.

"So, I will continue where we left the story yesterday. Okay?"

1942. Maurice Sachs—writer, dilettante, homosexual—was also a Jew who converted to Catholicism. In fact, Cocteau arranged his baptism and was even his godfather.

"Sachs often used people to satisfy his appetites for food, drink, luxury items, and for young—*very young*—men," Lili said.

Sachs was voracious for control over life's situations, and he performed outrageous acts of both malice and tenderness, dazzling the people he conned and tantalizing the people who did his bidding. He was paradoxical, he was fascinating, and Mme. Leduc had been very much in love with him, that was obvious.

In the early autumn of 1942, Leduc and Sachs moved to the village of Anceins in Normandy. It would be safer and cheaper in the countryside, Sachs proclaimed. Paris was still living on a hopeful song that autumn, desperately trying to ignore the anti-Jewish directives.

A few months before, on May 29, all Jews had been ordered to wear the Star of David, according to the Eighth Ordinance: "It is a six-pointed star having the dimensions of the palm of a hand and with black edges. It is to be in yellow material and is to carry in black lettering the inscription 'Jew.' It must be worn from the age of six years old and be quite visible on the lefthand side of the chest, carefully sewn onto the item of clothing." The star was to be sewn on with only a needle's width of space between stitches—just in case anyone tried to sew it on loosely and temporarily. Maurice Sachs never wore the star. And a number of Jewish artists and café inhabitants dodged this stigma as a way of thumbing their noses at the occupation.

On July 15, Jews were forbidden to enter any public building. The next day at dawn, mass arrests of foreign Jews took place. Almost thirteen thousand were rounded up in the largest arrest of civilians recorded in French history. The purgatory of diaspora was quickly becoming hell.

"During this time, Maurice was arranging for Jews to be smuggled out of the country for exorbitant prices. And Violette was writing air-filled articles for women's magazines," Lili said, shaking her head. "And Simone de Beauvoir was writing at the Café de Flore, along with her 'family' of friends."

De Beauvoir later wrote about this time in Paris: "Yet, though their [the Jews'] suffering remained alien to us, it is also true that it poisoned the very air we breathed." The statement always surprised me with its apparent frigidity. Now I could ask someone to verify my intuition.

"Lili, is it prickly on my part, or does de Beauvoir sound condescending, even dispassionate?"

"You are not being prickly, your response is fitting," she replied dryly. She paused, looked toward the far side of the café, and lit another cigarette. "They were . . . strange and painful days."

Lili sat quietly for a moment, then continued. "One day Adrienne Monnier sat with Colette over lunch at Souty's on the Rue de Babylone. They were served a fresh omelette and a lovely steak with 'lots, really lots of sautéed potatoes, beautifully crisp,' said Monnier. Their conversation was about good food, where to find chocolate, and who still had coffee.

"That same day, eight thousand Jews, who had been rounded up the day before and stuffed into the Vélodrome d'Hiver, were passing the first of many days without food and water. Also that same day, four thousand Jewish children were deported from Paris. I will never forget it. Lili paused again. "For me, on that day, the war exploded into my life."

Under the German occupation, much to the surprise of the reading public, 7,008 books were published in France—among them Camus's *The Stranger* and works by Raymond Queneau and Paul Claudel. No living, or dead, Jewish author was published, no matter from which country or which century. So while the great French publishing houses were continuing to publish, they were drawing a thick red line through the lives and careers of their Jewish writers. This exclusion caused Stefan Zweig, the great biographer of Balzac, and a Jew of the world, to commit suicide when he was exiled in Brazil.

The greatest publishing houses of France had acquiesced to the Nazis' rules on censorship. Along with many other French companies, and not a few French people, they agreed to be closet collaborators under the banner of "saving France." They agreed to look the other way, for a little while at least.

Amidst all this chaos, Violette Leduc was writing.

"And by the end of 1942," Lili said, "Violette had become an expert black-marketeer. Code name: Paris Beurre."

"You see," she said, leaning back, "Violette was famous for her butter. She always kept her promise to deliver the best butter available. It sold for more than four hundred francs per pound, and remember, this was a lot of money. She did sell other products, but butter was her specialty.

"It all started when Maurice Sachs ran out of money and people to swindle. He dared not show himself in Paris, having left behind a trail of debts and a history of very unhappy acquaintances. And so, in Anceins, after a midnight dessert of baked apples covered with fresh cream, Maurice announced, 'My dear Violette, if you want to go on living here, you will have to go out and make us some money in Paris. I haven't a penny left.'"

Paris Beurre loved the black market. She loved the danger, the suspense, and she especially loved the money. This new occupation gave her a sense of well-being and pride, both of which she sadly lacked. For the first time in her life people needed her, were even willing to pay her. The war gave her a perverse sense of pleasure.

Her first sale was a half-pound of butter placed on a cabbage leaf. This was to go to a person named on a list that Maurice had given her. She packed the precious item and set off walking to the *poste* in the village of Notre-Dame-du-Hameau, a little less than two kilometers away.

The late autumn of 1942 was unusually warm. The grass lining the road was still a fine silky green, leading her past open meadows and small woods—drowsing toward auburn.

"Every so often," Lili continued, "Violette would stop to listen to the waters of a stream as it made its way to meet the Risle River and on to the sea. Rarely would there be an automobile, although there was the occasional farm cart being pulled by a single horse or by someone on a bicycle. She knew she was approaching the village when she saw an old timber house in the distance that had probably been a carriage stop in the eighteenth century. Finally she passed over the river on a little bridge and went directly to the *poste*.

"Standing behind her in line was a local woman with an armful of small packages. The woman suspected Violette was sending a parcel of food and advised her to register the parcel and lie about its contents. She explained that this way the person would receive the package the next day—without the contents' having been confiscated. Another woman came in and said that a rabbit skin should be draped over perishables before mailing because it helped prevent spoilage.

"The women's advice worked. Two days later, a money order to Violette arrived, and she sent more butter, as well as eggs, meat, and dead ducks to Paris."

"Lili, where is Anceins? I have looked on all my maps but I can't find it."

"Anceins is a small Norman village sitting beside the Charentonne River. I have never been there, but Violette often described it to me. It sounded lovely."

Lili's eye caught someone across the room. "Excuse me a moment," she said. "I must say hello to my friend. Would you order another coffee for me please, decaffeinated?"

Oh dear, I thought, how do you say "decaffeinated" in French? In all the times I have been in France, I have been too embarrassed to ask for decaffeinated coffee. Not only was I nervous about saying the word, I was afraid it would seem terribly gauche asking for a bourgeois American drink, even if it wasn't for me.

I signaled the waiter.

Bluntly, decisively, staring him straight in the eyes, I said, *"De-caf-fein-at-ed café, s'il vous plaît."*

"Oui, Madame, décaféiné. Crème?" He smiled sweetly.

Lili returned and settled into the banquette.

"Violette and Maurice lived at Monsieur Mottier's house, which was up the road on the left of the church," Lili said. "Violette told me that Monsieur Mottier charged a very large amount of money for rent."

Leduc's room was on the second floor in the old granary, next to the chimney. This warm spot was a great comfort in the winter. She and Sachs had twin rooms, each with a cherry-wood bed and a satin, feather-filled comforter. Each room had two windows, one looking out at the road and the other onto the kitchen garden. The windows were framed with starched white curtains, slightly dusty, but clean. Below her was a wonderful garden of blackcurrant bushes and rose trees sitting among cabbages, endive, parsley, and chervil. The path was lined with a border of flowered luster tiles. When she raised her eyes from the kitchen garden, Leduc could see the back of the village. Pasture land and stubble meadows, outlined with poplar and willow trees, cast hundreds of shades of green. Beyond the fence was the black octagonal steeple of the church—and in the winter, across the plain was the hazy Ferté-Frênel forest. Because she did not like to go outside to the toilet, she would urinate into a blue bottle and shyly empty it each morning. The villagers knew she did this, but they never let on—they didn't want to embarrass her.

She accumulated great rolls of francs and spent them on books and more books, paper, and food. She was generous to her suppliers. They were always paid fairly—she never took advantage of them.

In November, Maurice Sachs disappeared into Germany. Some accounts say that he was rounded up in a sweep by the Nazis. Others claim he was a Gestapo informer who was discarded when he was of no further use. The truth seems to be that, under pressure, he enlisted in the Service du Travail Obligatoire.

The posters for the Service read, "They are giving their blood. Give your labor to save Europe from Bolshevism." In a letter to a friend, dated December 28, 1942, Sachs spoke of signing a contract to work for one year. The Germans shipped him to Hamburg, where he lived in a barracks and ran an electric crane, "alone in a glass cage sixty feet above the workshop floor. It keeps my spirits high," he wrote.

For a little more than two years, Leduc worked the black market while writing her first book, *L'Asphyxie*. She wrote every day, with very few deletions, unlike her mentor, Gide, who said, "It is thought that I write slowly. The truth is that I go for rather long periods without writing. As soon as my brain is in good form, my pen or pencil cannot go fast enough."

"Violette continued to amass a small fortune as Paris Beurre," Lili went on. "She always carried her money in a bath glove attached to her slip with two safety pins. Between writing and running food, she hung about with other people in her trade. She had a special friend named Zoucous who had fascinating gold teeth. Every evening close to ten o'clock she would meet her friends at

Monsieur Boungasse's café. They would sit around, all men and Violette, drinking calvados and playing *banc* until the late hours of the night. Violette won as much as she lost. She told me she loved the comradeship of her village—she was comfortable there. For the first time in her life she felt at home."

Toward the end of the war, Violette was forced to carry the black-market provisions to Paris herself. The *poste* system had crumbled, along with every other semblance of normal human exchange. So she rose before light in the morning and set off for Notre-Dame-du-Hameau, where she caught a bus to the train station, carrying two old and worn suitcases weighing more than twenty pounds each. They were stuffed with sausage, pâté, cream, lamb, eggs, and of course her famous butter. She had to move quickly into crowds of people, melt her identity, and fade her suitcases into her stride to avoid the Germans and dodge the informers. These expeditions wore her down. But she was too captivated by the bath glove rubbing against her skin, too attached to the euphoria of being part of the world ever to say no to the next train. Yet she admitted, *The more food I sent to Paris, the more I lost my appetite.* Finally there was excess money in her life.

"What did she do with all the money she made?" I asked, wondering whether Lili knew of a secret cache or a never mentioned recipient.

"For twenty thousand francs she decided to have her nose fixed! She battled with herself for a full week before the surgery. Then she realized she liked her nose. But it was too late, she had already made the commitment.

"It was obvious to Violette that the surgeon didn't like her. She found herself apologizing, groveling. She felt humiliated, but determined. She literally walked into the operating room and lay down on the cold metal table. When the surgeon walked in, she said, *I'm here.* He didn't answer."

I've suffered so much, she said. *If you knew how much I've suffered...*

"Don't talk," the surgeon said, slicing off her confession.

She prayed during the days following the surgery, prayed that her new nose would make her beautiful. It didn't.

When the dressings were removed, she said, *I didn't recognize the old woman before me, the old woman with a big nose, the same nose as before. A little less long? A little less ludicrous? It made me look older and harder.*

Afterward she complained to the surgeon, but he dismissed her firmly and complained about the smallness of his fee.

A year later she met her friend Alice Cerf at the Montana Bar, a jazz club in the Eleventh Arrondissement. The poet and screenwriter Jacques Prévert sat down at the next table and whispered loudly to his friend, "It's her mouth, her eyes, her cheekbones, they should have fixed." Prévert was known for his mockery. Violette overheard him, and once again her self-esteem was pulverized.

Lili took a sip of her coffee. "*Pouah,* this has become cold," she said. "I think I'll stick to cognac!"

I held my glass to hers and smiled. I didn't want to interrupt, afraid she would stop before we got to the contents of the bag.

"Le Dôme has been here since the beginning of the century. Until the Second World War, it was the main café and meeting place for Left Bank bohemians.

"I remember when the war began and the people at Le Dôme were forced by the Nazis to black out their windows if they wanted to stay open in the evenings. They mixed blue powder with olive oil and applied it to the glass. A little later, blue curtains were installed. It made the café warmer in the winter but stuffy in the summer.

"After the war was well under way, many of the regulars moved to the Flore or the Deux Magots. Not only was Le Dôme too far from the Métro station, which made it impossible to find in the dark, but the Germans had begun to take over the seats. They would bring in their own coffee and tea, insisting it be prepared under the noses of the French. Of course, since we were forced to drink imitation coffee and tea, the smells were tantalizing. We took pride in being able to sit and ignore the aromas.

"Finally, Simone and her friends stopped frequenting Le Dôme when the Nazis demanded they show their identity papers before using the telephone. This was just too much."

Lili leaned back against the red banquette. She was tired—she said her throat was scratchy—and then I noticed my red battery light was on.

"Oh no," I told her, "I can't believe this has happened. The batteries in my recorder are dead."

I rewound a little and played back the tape. Her words were there, almost to the end.

"Lili, this weekend my friend Anna and I are going away. Can we meet again on Monday?"

"Yes, I think so, but let me check."

She reached into her satchel and after searching around pulled out a brown leather notebook. Is this the notebook I've been waiting for, I asked myself. No, I saw with disappointment, it was only a calendar.

"Yes, we can meet in the afternoon at my friend's bookstore, Les Livres de Campagne, on the Rue Racine. It's very close to your hotel. My friend has an appointment, so she has asked me to tend the shop. It should be quiet on Monday, and we will have the entire afternoon."

I paid our check and we wound our way around the tables to the street. We said good-bye, and before I knew it Lili was in a taxi with her bulging satchel, still bulging.

· VIII ·

Two days before, I had received a note from home with a letter from an old school friend enclosed. I hadn't heard from Anna in years; coincidentally, she was now living in Paris. She wrote that a friend in New York had shown her an exhibition catalogue of my work and she was interested in what I was doing.

When I called her, she thought it was a joke. "Here, in Paris? No!"

"Yes," I answered, "and Anna, how would you like an adventure?"

"I'm too busy, I have a deadline on this article I'm writing."

"But I need you."

"Ah, I thought so," she crowed. "You need my *français*! Still too shy, uh. Okay, okay, I'll do your translating. It'll be a good excuse to take a break." We made plans to meet at her local café, next door to her flat on the Rue Saint-Louis-en-l'Île.

A couple of hours later, after catching up, we were poring over a Normandy map. We couldn't find the village of Notre-Dame-du-Hameau, so we went to the post office, where Anna held a lengthy discussion with the clerk.

He said there was only one village in Normandy with a name resembling Notre-Dame-du-Hameau, and that was Notre-Dame-du-Hamel—probably but not certainly the village we were looking for. I discovered later that Mme. Leduc changed the name to protect the people in the village.

We decided to chance Notre-Dame-du-Hamel and rented the cheapest car we could find, a bright-red Renault. We stopped briefly to buy a baguette, salami, and a wedge of cheese, then set off in search of the village. All we knew was the zip code. As we drew near the area the postal clerk had suggested, it was obvious this village was even smaller than we had imagined.

Anna, who is an expert at directions, especially in French, flung our Renault up close against a green metal fence in the village of Couvains, slammed on the brakes, and announced that she was going to ask the *gendarmes*.

It was noon on Saturday and it seemed that the *gendarmerie* was closed for lunch. Anna held down the button of the bell until two men dressed in green came to the gate. She asked them where we could find Notre-Dame-du-Hamel. One man said he had never heard of it and the other thought it was maybe that way; he arced his finger in a vague direction.

Back in the car, Anna was more stubborn than ever. But in ten minutes we were lost again. Up to another green metal fence and another gate with a bell, though this time we were in luck. The *gendarme* drew her a map that was clear and correct. In five minutes we were in Notre-Dame-du-Hamel.

We stopped to speak to the first person we saw—a woman with a dark red apron wound around her sturdy body, sweeping her porch. At first, she was shy and didn't want to talk. Anna, fluent in French and once again undaunted, convinced her. She introduced herself as Mme. Roland and said that even though she was only ten years old at the time, she remembered Mme. Leduc as having gray hair, being shifty and distant, and going from door to door buying food.

Mme. Roland pointed down the road with her broom—Mme. Leduc had lived in Anceins, the next village, she said.

We returned to our car and drove down the D252 to Anceins. I didn't have to see the sign to know where we were. I recognized the steeple in the distance from the description in *La Bâtarde*. It was the ugliest church she had ever seen, Leduc wrote. And I agreed. The front was flat, except for two out-of-scale brick buttresses, two arched windows surrounded by a brick trim, and an arched door trimmed in stone. Circling the church was a cemetery whose focal point was a rococo monument to the men who died for France in the Great War. Leduc said there were always flowers placed at the top of the monument, but no one knew who put them there. We followed Leduc's directions and found the house in which she and Maurice Sachs had lived. We also found the present owners at home.

The Mottiers were friendly people. The house had been passed down to them from the grandfather, whom Mme. Leduc called M. Motté, in reality M. Mottier. When we arrived, in the afternoon, they had just finished eating lunch. Monsieur was dressed in a red sweater with blue farmer's overalls. Madame was elegant, even in her slippers.

They invited us into the kitchen and we all sat down at a red Formica table. The kitchen was not a bit old-fashioned—I was disappointed. I was so determined to see this house that I had imagined it already—forgetting the passage of time. We were not invited to see the rest of the house, and it would have been terribly impolite to ask.

My disappointment passed quickly when both M. and Mme. Mottier said that they remembered Violette Leduc. They described her as blonde and very polite. M. Mottier said he was a little boy at the time, and he remembered looking up at a very tall and skinny lady and seeing only her large nose. Giggling, they told the famous story about her urinating into a bottle. "They still talk about it in the village!" Mme. Mottier said.

After a tour of the garden we left the Mottiers' and found a room for the night in L'Aigle. I was exhilarated by the day and couldn't sleep. I stripped off my bedding, tiptoed into the bathroom, and molded my bed into the tub. While Anna slept, I struggled with the *Herald Tribune* crossword puzzle and drank cognac, finally falling asleep toward morning.

· IX ·

Back in Paris on Monday afternoon, I walked to the Rue Racine through a downpour, skirting great puddles of water and weaving through an undulating sea of umbrellas. I had forgotten to get the exact address of the bookstore from Lili; I knew only the names of the street and the store. I walked up and down the street but couldn't find the store. The rain was so heavy that it was difficult to see much of anything. I stood against a wall trying to figure out what I wasn't seeing, wondering if I also had the wrong street. Juggling my Paris *Plan* under my umbrella, I searched for the nearest *poste*. I was frustrated, nervous, and shivering. Okay, I said to myself, one more time. And then, from behind my back, came Lili's voice, "I am here." And there it was, Les Livres de Campagne, its name in minute gold letters on a glass door.

I entered a dark room, made darker by the storm. The walls were lined with shelves of old books. The room smelled of damp stone, old paper, and ancient inks.

"Here, let me take your coat and umbrella," Lili said. "I suggest you remove your boots and put them next to the heater. We will sit in the next room, where it is warmer."

By the time I unbundled myself and walked into the other room, my shivering had ceased. This room was smaller and also filled with books, but here everything was light-colored. The shelving was painted white, most of the books were new, and in the corner was an old, thickly painted yellow table with two comfortable-looking blue upholstered chairs. On the table was a bouquet of white and pink tulips, along with a teapot and two cups and saucers. It felt like a country sitting room.

"I'm sorry I'm late," I told Lili, "but I walked past the door a few times without seeing it."

"It is fine, don't worry. This store has been here for almost one hundred years, and I forget that everyone does not know where it is. My friend Colette Villon and her family have always owned it.

She carries books by writers from the provinces, like the poet René Char, and books about the countryside of France. It is well-known to Parisians, so Colette doesn't feel the need to hang a large sign."

Although it was storm-dark outside, the little room made it seem as if spring had arrived. Lili poured a cup of tea for me. My hands and damp body warmed up and we began to work.

"How was Normandy?" she asked, and I told her about my adventure.

"It is amazing you found the village. You are a good detective," she responded, smiling. "Violette would have been pleased with your tenacity!"

For a moment I felt a flush of contentment, even a little accomplishment. I still wasn't sure how I was going to approach this biography. But I sensed I was on the right track—and I was accumulating courage.

Now I wanted more details about Lili and Paris during the war.

"Lili, I can't get the story you told me about your imprisonment out of my head. Most of my generation in America has no idea of what it was like to live in a country where there was a war. Could you tell me more about what you did that put you in prison?"

"But we are talking about Violette, not me. . . ."

"Yes, I understand. But I'm trying to put all this in some sort of context."

She smiled, hesitated, spoke.

"I called myself an urban partisan. Another of my jobs was to overhear what the Nazis were saying. In school I studied German, so I was using it in the best of possible ways—to fight the enemy. I listened to their complaints—listened for information—and passed on what I heard to comrades in the underground network. We used it to counter their propaganda activities, sabotage their plans, and play havoc with their morale.

"I also carried false passports and papers to people in the Resistance. You know, war can only be written about in black-and-white, painted in black-and-white. Anyone without the proper identification loses his membership in the world. I took this job very seriously.

"Yet as a young woman I had to be very careful. If a German

soldier showed any sign, any sign at all, of noticing me, I pretended not to see him. But I would see and hear everything, absolutely everything—and I didn't need unwanted attention.

"Day after day, I would sit in cafés, especially Le Dôme, drinking the awful colored water, dressed like many young people of the time—as a *zazou*."

"A *zazou*?"

"A *zazou* was like . . . a zoot-suiter in the forties. You have to understand that Jewish groups were no longer legal—except for a few phony ones the Germans set up as a front to try to convince the rest of the world that everything was still normal in France. So when surplus clothing was sent from American Jewish organizations, it ended up at the Saint-Ouen flea market. The male *zazous* bought baggy suits with jackets down to their knees and straight, full-legged trousers, and platform shoes. The female *zazoues* bought black skirts, tight black sweaters, and platform shoes too. Their hair was long, straight, and dyed as black as possible. Sometimes, especially in the summer, they wore it in a pompadour. They wore no makeup, except for on their eyes, which were lined with kohl and finished with mascara. Both men and women wore a cross hanging around their necks, not a de Gaulle Lorraine, but a Christian cross. They spent all their time in cafés and seemed never to work. In all seasons they carried umbrellas hooked over their arms—this was a ludicrous and provocative symbol of the *passé* civilized days of history."

"Where does the word *zazou* come from?" I asked.

"A song sung by Charles Trenet. It went, *'Je suis swing, zazou, zazou . . .'*" Lili accompanied the snippet with a sort of seated jig, pointing her index finger toward the sky.

"Then, one day in 1944, my chief told me to stop by Monsieur Clotis's bookstall near the Pont Neuf. I was to pick up a package wrapped in newspaper and tied with string and bring it to an address on the Rue Lagarde. When I picked up the package, Monsieur Clotis said he was sure I would like these books, and wished me a good day. I walked slowly, nonchalantly, to the Rue Lagarde.

"Although I put on a brave front, I was always terrified on these missions. I was continually reassuring myself that everything was under control. But I was tired and my weariness was not allowing me to think clearly. Also, I was hungry—all of Paris was hungry. Actually that is not quite true, *most* of Paris was hungry. If you had money, there was, of course, the black market, but even that food was becoming scarce.

"That day was particularly grim. Violence was random. In Paris alone, at least a hundred people a day were being assassinated by the Milice, the French special police, or by the Gestapo. As the Resistance grew, these brigades of Milice, who were in fact collaborators, had been raging through the city following the orders of the occupiers. Individuals who had been assassinated were walked over, passed by, as they lay dead or wounded on the streets. Out of nowhere would appear men with stretchers, lifting a body, taking it away. Then out of a doorway someone would appear with a bucket and a mop, clean up the spilled blood, and disappear through the same doorway.

"People would pass, lower their eyes, sink as far as possible into their shoulders, and walk on. It was useless to take a backward glance.

"On that dreary day, as I was passing the Sorbonne, I heard people running behind me, and before I could move out of the way, I was thrown to the ground, the package was wrenched from my arms, and I was kicked in the side. I remember trying to get up, but a furious boot kicked me again and I lost consciousness. When I came to, I was on a cold stone floor in a room with very little light. I was experiencing such physical pain that I was convinced I had died and this was hell.

"I found out much later that the package I was carrying contained twenty-two counterfeit French passports and ten books of illegal food-ration coupons."

My face must have turned gray, for Lili paused, then said, "I am sorry, my dear, I got carried away. You want to hear about Violette Leduc, not my war stories."

"Oh no, please," I insisted. "I want to hear as much as you'll tell me."

❧

I was confused. I was upset because Lili was upset. I was beside myself with the nearness of such terror. The panic I was feeling was familiar, but the realities were becoming all mixed up.

While Lili was lying on the floor of a Gestapo prison, we had already moved from Nevada. I was two months short of three years old, living on an ordinary street in the ugly and conventional town of Compton, a suburb of Los Angeles.

Cyprus Street ran from the high school, two blocks east of the railroad tracks. The street was lined with small, low houses. They had useless front yards carpeted with the inevitable middle-class grass rug.

But the trees, flowers, and shrubs were luscious—the wild mustard turning the hills across the river into reverie. Great jacaranda trees fluttered their lovely lavender blossoms onto the broken sidewalks. Bougainvillea vines with paper-thin cerise flowers dripped over chain-link fences. Great pink and white hibiscus, which, surprisingly, are related to okra, refused to be cultivated as a flower store commodity—wilting as soon as they were cut.

Mediocrity was my milieu. The Los Angeles River was my countryside, lined with cabbage fields and mustard, and roaring with menace during thunderstorms. By the time I had entered high school, there was no need for the sandbags and the rowboats—the Los Angeles River had become a concrete gutter leading to the sea.

California is where my father's mother drove in 1920, across the vastness of America on rutted roads that ran into pavement when entering a town, and then back again into the ruts. She drove alone with my father to make a new life away from New York, away from Russia.

My father was a teacher at a school that sat flat-out in the middle of nowhere. A good percentage of his students were Asians whose parents owned flower farms in the San Pedro Hills. Occasionally I would accompany my father to visit a student's home. It was like a dream.

Rows upon rows of flowers divided by color and by size. Red carnations, eyed Shasta daisies, clouds of baby's breath. The fields were huge pieces of patched fabric thrown onto the ground for God in heaven to see. The fields swayed with the movement of the wind. I would stand in the middle of this vastness and smell the musks of flowers sliding on my skin like a touch of perfume.

The people on my side of the tracks were white people from the very poor farms of Oklahoma. They had come to Los Angeles to work in the shipyards during the Second World War. They were widely unread and mighty proud of their ignorance. They had met few, if any, Jewish people. Not one of them knew that Jesus was a Jew. We were known as the "kike family with them colored friends." They were brutal to my sister and me.

Two times I was ambushed by a gang of abusive white boys. Each time they jabbed at me, called me "nigger lover," shoved me down, and left me with my dress pulled up and my panties showing. I finally got smart. I sharpened the corners of my black lunch pail and swung at anyone who came too menacingly close. After a couple of bloody encounters, I was left alone.

Violette Leduc also lived on the *dismal fringe of town. The boys at the school ganged up on me,* she said. *At five of four every afternoon, I could sense them getting ready to chase me along the roads. I was afraid of being afraid. . . . Their hate hit me harder than their missiles.* The abuse stopped when her aunt complained. She was finally left alone.

"I was released from prison on the day Paris was liberated in 1944." Lili eyed me thoughtfully and lit a cigarette. "With my tiny bundle of belongings I walked around the corner to my home. The whole day was bizarre. My family didn't know what had happened to me—and then suddenly I was there. They couldn't believe that I had, all along, been so near."

· X ·

"Violette was writing furiously," Lili said after pouring us another cup of tea. "Simone de Beauvoir offered her courage and encouragement. Violette would meet with de Beauvoir every two weeks and reveal her newest writing. She took Simone's advice. But the fractured part of Violette's psyche was becoming more apparent.

"Here, I'll show you an example."

Lili got up and walked over to the other table. She opened her satchel and brought out an envelope stuffed with papers. This was stunning! This was what I had been waiting for! My heart raced. At that moment, I understood why people are sleuths of history. Archaeologists, scientists, historians, they're all looking for the missing pieces to complete an idea, prove a point. (When I walk in the desert, I always look at the ground and not the mountains or the sky in the distance. I am always hoping that I'll find the elusive pottery shard—that special one—or that, when I carefully brush the dirt and dried grasses from the area, a complete, unbroken, ancient pot will be revealed.)

Lili walked back to the table, sat down, and placed the envelope next to her on the seat.

"Ah, here." She put on her reading glasses. "I have a copy of a letter that Violette wrote to Simone one Friday in 1945 after pestering her the day before." She began to translate. "*Dear Simone de Beauvoir. You had asked me to find a bicycle, I haven't done it. You asked me to take care of your sister and I did it badly. I cry everywhere. I believe that you despise me and this paralyzes me. I continue my little trips [for the black market], as a robot. What to do? Speak to me strongly. Advise me. I will obey. I ask for your forgiveness for the awkwardness of this letter but I can't find words. I shake your hand with all my heart. Violette.*"

"What happened? What was this about?" I asked.

"Simone had become tired of Violette as a person, but not as a writer. She resisted Violette's uncontrolled passions. But she didn't struggle when Violette brought her fresh butter, fresh vegetables, or fresh poultry from the country. She didn't resist when Violette took her to expensive restaurants and paid for her meals. People have said that the relationship was *de guingois*. You know what that is?"

"No, but I can look it up."

"No, no, you know what I mean—more one way than the other."

"Lopsided?"

"Yes, lopsided. But it was not. Their relationship went both ways. Violette was able to give a lot to Simone when Simone had very little. We must remember this."

"From her writings," I said, "it seems that the black market provided Madame Leduc with her first real experience of camaraderie."

"Please excuse me for interrupting," Lili said, "but I need to ask you a favor. I know you are trying to be polite, but I would like it if you called Madame Leduc 'Violette.' And I am sure she would like it too."

"Thank you. Actually, that would be a relief! But the black market—even though it created a sort of camaraderie among smugglers, it was a convenient form for Violette's own brand of rebellion, especially because it brought her close to de Beauvoir."

"This is true," Lili said. "When I met Violette in December of 1944, all of Paris was still hungry. The Nazis had plundered our country, and our shelves were bare. But Violette and her friends never lacked for food.

"On the other hand, there was a general philosophical aversion to people who charged inflated prices in return for saving lives. Yet Violette thought of herself as a patriot. She comforted her disturbed self-esteem by making a fortune in money and a fortune in friends. According to everyone I have spoken to about this period, she was extremely generous."

In Germany, Violette's friend Maurice Sachs was coming to the end of his life. He didn't know it, so he continued to be optimistic. He seemed to be more concerned about his friends in France than he was about his forced labor in Germany.

"Just a minute," Lili said, "let me find something." She opened the envelope and went through the papers. "I have a copy of one of Sachs's last letters to Violette." Lili took out a sheet paper. "Here it is. He is writing from Hamburg—from the labor camp. It was the twenty-fifth of February, 1943."

"But Sachs was Jewish," I said. "Why wasn't he in a concentration camp?"

"Because he signed up to work in the labor camp before they began rounding up the Jews outside Paris. He probably thought he would be safer there—blending into a thousand-man workforce."

She looked at me as if to see whether I understood. Pushing her reading glasses further up her nose, she continued to read.

"'It's suddenly gotten very cold again, and there's been a veritable invasion of vermin which I try to get rid of by taking baths.

"'I'm rather tired of being with working-class people all the time: they have all our defects without our good qualities.

"'En masse, it goes without saying, they suffer from the usual contagious stupidity. But the local doctor we go to for treatment has invited me to stop and see him once or twice a week. He speaks a little French. A charming man, with all Balzac, Proust, and Stendhal there in his really excellent library. On Saturdays he gives me brioches and preserves.'"

Lili put down the letter. "Before Maurice and Violette went to Normandy, Maurice introduced her to his friend Madeleine Castaing. Madeleine and her family became an important source of companionship for Violette. And then after the war, Violette introduced me to Madeleine, and then *we* became friends!" Lili shrugged in that French way. "One of Maurice's last letters was to Madeleine." I settled back to listen.

"'Eight September 1943. Dear Madeleine. I have just seen around me so many deaths and dramas under the bombing when your letter reached me. Your letter caught my breath.

"'Soutine dead! I had not felt anything in the same way since the death of Proust. My body feels empty and my head fills with tears.

"'At last he achieved a life without glory and his work will begin in his glory. . . .

"'Everything is in the cruel order of this world. This suffering man could die only uneasily. May he have died conscious of the prestigious survival to which his genius called him. . . .

"'I will speak often of this great man, the only error that I can observe during his lifetime was a discretion that is not in my nature.

"'I am thirty-six years old this week, my face has changed much (I weigh 68 kg now) and the first white hairs are apparent. It is time, it is very much the time that I write a beautiful book. All the elements are living in me. The form is the only thing that is missing, the frame, the expression, if one will. A constant and tormenting thought.

"'I owe this book to my friends, it will be the only excuse for my bad habits and I want it for the friends that it will bring me. And then, one must say that what one has seen expresses what one has suffered. It is the way for men to be ants.

"'I kiss both of you with all my heart. Maurice.'"

"Later, Violette felt terribly guilty about Maurice's death. He had written her near the end of the war and asked in a cryptic fashion if she could forge an official document saying that she was pregnant with his baby. He was looking for a way to get a leave from his labor assignment. She tried—she even went so far as to obtain a fake birth certificate from a doctor. But she was tired of being used by him and then so coldly discarded. After circling this piece of paper for three days, she burned it. He died shortly thereafter, and of course, she felt responsible."

"No one knows how he died, right?"

"As far as I know," Lili said, "he simply disappeared. People still claim to see him in different parts of the world now and then."

She got up and went to the bookshelf, where she picked out a volume. "Violette felt that she had taken a healthy stand to protect herself from Maurice's manipulation. After he died, she read what he wrote about the character Lodève in *Tableau de Moeurs de Ce Temps*, and she was devastated. She knew he had based it on her. I have a copy here."

And she read from the volume.

"'She bears a cross, the most terrible of all, that of being incredibly ugly and of knowing it.

"'Ah, that grotesque nose which, above a sunken chin, makes her look like a gargoyle, that low forehead, those large and protruding cheekbones, that thick skin, that indiscreetly sensual mouth, those prominent, bulging eyes—what vicious fairy assembled all of these features in one single face as if creating the caricature of a character. A preposterous example of what nature herself would never be sufficiently cruel to reunite in one face.'

"Violette was deeply hurt. Who wouldn't be? Years later, when his book *The Hunt* was published posthumously, I felt that Violette's decision to abandon him had been somehow redeemed. At the end of the book he had written another devastating piece about her. From then on, I never said anything nice or complimentary about him or his work. I am furious when I think about him!"

"I agree," I responded with ardor. "I just read Sachs's books, here in Paris, and wanted to toss them across the room! But like

Céline's, they are well written and engaging—philosophically you resist, but you read them anyway."

Sachs wrote, "Three months spent in the company of a woman whom I look on only as a friend, but who is high-strung and in love with me, has confirmed for me many of my opinions about women—they have such cowardly minds, are so hardened in their materialism, so devouring by nature. They are life, if you like, but nothing to do with the higher sort of life, unless they happen to provide you with pleasures."

Sachs wrote this in November 1942, while living in the room next to Violette in Anceins. His reputation was dismal. He stole, he pandered to the rich, he ingratiated his way into the lives of many fine writers. He even stole manuscripts and rare editions from Cocteau, and then turned around and in a cavalier fashion auctioned them off at the Hôtel Drouvot in Paris. Two of the rare editions were invaluable—one by Proust, the other by Apollinaire with a lengthy autographed inscription to Cocteau.

In his memoirs Cocteau wrote, "Beware of Maurice, he is a charmer: he charms God himself." Soon Cocteau forgave him, admitting, "I have always preferred thieves to policemen. . . . He gave more than he took and he took in order to give."

"Maurice got away with many of his capers, with audacity," Lili continued. "I have never really understood why he wasn't in prison from the time he was an adolescent. People were beguiled by his bad behavior. He seemed to represent to Violette everything she felt she was lacking. He was an eloquent speaker with an elegant air. He loved the good life. He worshipped writers, as she did. She was tremendously impressed with him. And he was a homosexual, which was usually true of the men with whom she had relationships. Except, of course, for Gabriel Mercier and a lover named René."

"How long was she married to Gabriel Mercier?" I asked. "It is unclear in her books."

"I'm not sure either, but I think they were married in 1939. I do know they were divorced in 1947. She did not live with him for many years. In fact, she left him to live with Maurice in 1942.

"Maurice and Violette lived pleasantly in Anceins. But by the beginning of 1944, things were becoming very bad in all of France, particularly in the large cities. People were not able to buy clothing, no shoes were being manufactured. The Germans had confiscated everything from bolts of fabric to spools of thread, even twine to wrap packages. Indeed, the shabbier we all looked, the more proud we were. Only collaborators could afford nice food and new clothing. We all knew who they were—they were fat and colorful, in a black-and-gray time.

"The black-marketeers were the *franc-millionnaires*. But when the war was over and their francs were almost worthless, they found themselves in the same bind as the rest of us. Even the farmers were almost starving.

"Every week each family of three received a ration of one-half pound of fresh meat, three-fifths of a pound of butter, and two inches of sausage. Bread was nearly impossible to buy."

"I don't understand," I said. "By this time the Germans were gone."

"Yes, but a large food-producing region of France was still under German occupation after the armistice," Lili said. "The lamb-grazing, egg- and butter-producing areas above Bordeaux and up into southern Brittany were still being forced to send all their food to Germany."

Violette came out of the war alone. She had lost her community, her francs had very little value, and she thought she had been labeled an informer by her friends at Anceins.

The Nazis had confiscated a château in a nearby village which they used as a headquarters. They were aware that Violette was selling food on the black market. Her primary contact was a M. Boedec, who was arrested for his dealings and tried, but only fined in the end. One day the Nazis arrested Violette and questioned her. She was brusquely body-searched by a *thickset one [as he] finished lighting an army-issue cigarette. He blew the first puff in my eyes,* she wrote in *Mad in Pursuit.* He found twelve kilos of butter tied around her waist.

Violette would knot several handkerchiefs together to form a belt, then pin on four burlap bags, each one containing three kilograms of butter, spacing them around her waist so that she wouldn't sit on any of them. It was a heavy and uncomfortable load. If the handkerchiefs came loose, her knees would bang against the blocks of butter as she walked.

The Nazis, in their threats for the names of farmers who supplied her with food, fingered all the shadows of Violette's pathology. They threatened to lock her up with *her deranged imagination.* After twenty-four hours she was finally coerced her into giving up the names of the farmers. She crawled back to Paris in disgrace—mortified about her behavior, forever suffering this shame.

"In later years she could talk about this time only when she had too much to drink," Lili said. "Her mask of well-being would deteriorate into one of self-loathing. She would be inconsolable." *My feelings were as long as the night,* Leduc wrote. Eventually she suffered two serious nervous breakdowns.

"But no one in the area was arrested because of her," I said to Lili. "According to the Mottiers, the village remembers Violette with fondness. They appreciated her fairness in her dealings with them. They remembered the funny nose—they were grateful for the rounds of calvados she bought in the café. She didn't cause anyone harm."

Lili stood up and went to the back of the room where water was boiling on a hot plate. While I gazed out the window at the rain, I could hear her preparing a new pot of tea. She returned, poured it into our cups, and sat down.

"This information you give me makes me happy, but also very sad," Lili said. "If only Violette had known this, it might have made her life much better." Lili sat for a few moments looking out the window.

"Violette returned to a Paris enveloped in gloom," she resumed. "The city was liberated, but there were still eight hundred thousand Frenchmen working as slaves in German factories and the north of France was still controlled by the Germans. Everyone was trying to find ways to survive.

"Violette continued to barter. She now knew the sources of food from her black-market work. So she would supply someone with a chicken and then that person would pay her with a leg of the chicken. Once I craved a lemon. I don't know whom she traded with, but she got me the lemon for a tenth of a kilo of sugar and two cigarettes. She would buy real coffee from the restaurants she had supplied during the war and brew some for me, then walk around her apartment and make sure all the windows were closed so the smell would not be detectable. Usually, only informers could get real coffee. It embarrassed her to be indulging in this whim, but

I was pleased to have the treat. At that time, the only hot drinks you could buy in Paris were Viandor, a meat extract; *tilleul,* lime tea; *verveine,* verbena tea; or the ubiquitous Bovril. We all yearned for coffee and cigarettes more than anything else."

My stomach was growling. We laughed, it was so noisy. It was time to leave. Lili walked with me into the dim front room of the bookstore. It took a moment for our eyes to adjust, and then I put on my boots and coat.

"Lili, those letters you have—would it be possible for me to copy the two you just read? They would be very helpful for my book."

"Of course, take them all to copy."

"Oh, no," I answered, "I can't be responsible for them. You're taking a great chance—"

"I know, I know," she interrupted.

"Look, let's go to the nearest copy shop and I'll make the copies. It won't take long."

Lili gathered everything into her satchel, put on her coat, locked the store, and led me down the street.

"Make two copies of everything, while you are doing this," she said.

I had her sit nearby while I copied the forty letters, twice. When I was done, I put the letters and copies in the satchel, minus my two copies, and handed it to Lili.

"No, my dear, you take an entire set of the copies," Lili insisted.

This is what I had wished for, never thinking she would give them *all* up. My hands were trembling as I put them in a bright yellow Livres de Campagne plastic bag, which I placed carefully inside my backpack. We walked out into the rain and said good-bye. When I turned to wave, Lili had gone behind the shadow of a mountain of buildings.

The first thing I did was go to another copy shop and copy the letters once again. Then I walked to my hotel and put the second-generation copies in my suitcase and stored it in the closet.

I liked eating alone in restaurants with a book and my note pad. I was always trying new restaurants, on either a whim or a recommendation. My favorite was on the Rue Saint-Jacques, around the corner from my hotel. It was not fancy, and every evening they had a special menu for that day only. As long as they weren't serving pig's feet and lamb's heads, I was happy there. And so, not long after leaving Lili, I was seated in the back of the restaurant with a carafe of wine and the copies of the letters. First I put the letters in chronological order, and then I began to read. It was slow going. My tolerable French, combined with the handwriting, made it difficult, but I was immediately engaged in the material. There were letters from Maurice Sachs, from Simone de Beauvoir, Madeleine Castaing, Serge Tamagnot, and even Clara Malraux. To translate and eat at the same time was a juggling act—and this material was too valuable. I stopped trying, finished my dinner, and went back to my room to work.

· XI ·

The next day the weather turned beautiful. The sun made a rare curtsy and opened its arms to a pure blue sky. I decided to go to the Luxembourg Gardens and sit in the fresh air. The Gardens have long been a favorite park for artists. There are wide gravel paths, with hundreds of green-painted hard-slatted benches and chairs scattered about. People brood among the trimmed lime trees. Even the children played quietly.

When Hemingway was starving in Paris, I remembered reading, he came here to capture corn-kernel pigeons for dinner.

When Alfred de Musset wrote of his affair with George Sand, he described how the meandering gravel paths of the Luxembourg Gardens made his heart leap while he waited for his beloved.

All of the allusions to art, women, and romance make the Luxembourg Gardens a woman's place, a garden of the heart, an oasis when she is in turmoil.

As I sat at the foot of a statue of George Sand, I reread Violette Leduc's description of coming to the Gardens for the first time, when she was still a schoolgirl.

The gates of the Jardin du Luxembourg stood guard over a garden unlike any I had ever seen. I plunged through them and after some difficulty found an empty bench near the Sénat. I ate my dinner. The statues among the foliage stood with their great uncluttered bodies prophesying the coming of night. This contact with antiquity refreshed my spirits. . . . Now I was there.

Here, where I was sitting, was the center of an area where the Germans dug trenches and built concrete blockhouses to defend themselves against the Allies. In fact, two days after the Americans moved into Paris, the Germans fought a fierce battle here. Their snipers continued to fight for a week after the liberation.

It still startles me that I was alive while this catastrophe was happening. In America we were protected by distance; war was only a black-and-white newsreel.

During the war, I was very young. But I remember the floor lamp in our house with the milky white glass at the base that was turned on during blackouts. Since we lived two blocks from the railroad tracks, I could hear the lurching and screeching of the midnight trains. They often woke us. The trains were camouflaged with army-green-and-ocher fabric, wrapped around them like tea cozies tucked around a warm teapot.

And there were other things—dreadful things. The time a woman and her little girl were living with us while waiting for the woman's husband to return from the war. The girl would cry out at night in terror and I would cringe into my pillow as a dark rush of air traveled up my spine.

And I remember a young woman hanging above a chair in the middle of an enclosed porch. She was wearing oxford shoes and socks that were not white. The wooden chair below her was tipped over—and her feet were dangling too far above the floor.

· XII ·

They met in line at a cinema on the Champs-Élysées.

"Violette, I would like to introduce you to my friend Simone de Beauvoir," their friend Alice Cerf said.

At long last, it happened. Violette had been watching de Beauvoir for months, adoring her from a distance, dreaming of this meeting. Yet all Violette managed to say now was *"Bon soir,"* and then she retreated into the familiar brown collar of her coat.

Later in the week, another of Violette's friends, Bernadette, arranged for her to give de Beauvoir her manuscript to read. Violette carefully placed the manuscript in a cheerful orange folder that she had bought at Mme. Aubijoux's book and stationery store. It cost her four francs. She chose it because it unfolded like an orange. Violette met Bernadette at seven o'clock at the Café de Flore. She put the orange folder on the small round table and gripped the edges of her seat. Simone de Beauvoir arrived twenty minutes late and Violette was panicked. *The conversation was brief. No, she wouldn't sit down. She took the orange folder from Bernadette's hands. "I shall read it. Good-bye."*

Simone de Beauvoir read the first line, *My mother never gave me her hand,* and was captivated at once.

❧

When I first read *La Bâtarde,* I skipped de Beauvoir's preface and read through to the end. I was dazzled. Then I returned to the preface and read de Beauvoir's blessing.

I searched for the rest of Violette Leduc's books. I found them in musty bookstores, one in the dank Shakespeare and Company in Paris, with the store's stamp of "Kilometer Zero Paris" on the inside front cover.

I became infatuated with her use of language. I understood her alienation and created a fictitious friendship with her. My last visual arts project had been a series of twelve woodblock prints. Each print was a narrative piece about a woman—a vision of my imagination—and Violette had been on my mind. Yet as I sat on a bench in the Luxembourg Gardens, I had no idea what this friendship with Violette meant, or where its ghost would lead me.

I was also confused by my attraction to such a psychologically unattractive person. Violette revealed her presence in the world in a most perverse way. She antagonized Natalie Saurrate, she offended Colette Audry, she irritated Genet, she exasperated Cocteau, she quarreled with Camus, and she provoked her friendship with de Beauvoir interminably. Curiously, all these friends were dedicated to her.

De Beauvoir wrote to her lover in Chicago, Nelson Algren, about her visits with Violette. She described how Violette often broke down in tears, piteously, in resignation about her lonely existence.

De Beauvoir and Algren referred to Violette as "the ugly woman." Algren, in his pedantic way, said Simone should not continue to see her.

Nevertheless, de Beauvoir persisted in her commitment and responded that she would continue to spend time with the ugly woman, who both loved and needed her. Leduc had been reading to her from her diary, and de Beauvoir was moved by the beauty of her language and impressed with her literary courage. Leduc's writing was "as daring as anything written by a man."

How and why does this "ugly woman" transform language into fluttering angels whispering in my ear? What is enticing me to follow her for so many years—through research shelves in libraries, to Paris, to Lili, and back to New Mexico, to my desk at the window, my fountain pen filling this notebook with these words?

It is simple, and it is one of the most complicated events of my life. Violette said it all. I have *to work if I want to give birth to myself.*

❧

The clouds rolled their great carpets across the sky and it started to rain softly. At first, I ignored the inconvenience—only put away my notebook. Then, without warning, without even a clap of thunder, an enormous bucket of water overturned on my head. I got up and ran to the Métro, then down the steps into its shelter.

❧

The following morning I received an unexpected phone call from Lili. She asked if I would like to go with her to a concert—a little Haydn, a little Ravel, a Mozart violin piece. I was delighted. She said to meet her at the Amphithéâtre Richelieu at the Sorbonne. The theater was just a few blocks away from my hotel. After a late lunch, I walked to the rue de la Sorbonne and entered the courtyard. All French movies about students must be filmed in this courtyard, I thought, it was so familiar. Its austere beauty of stone was warmed by the late-afternoon light.

Lili was leaning against the wall near the arched entrance and she beckoned to me. We followed the crowd across the courtyard into the theater. Where were Sartre, Malraux, Gide? They were gone, of course, but the aura of their presence lingered upon the wooden benches climbing upward into larger and larger semicircles under a faded and peeling blue dome ceiling. The paled ceiling captured the sounds and, most of the time, returned it to our ears with grace.

Seated below us on the stage was a small orchestra composed of young adults and very old people. The first violinist, an elegant elderly woman in a white blouse with a lace collar and a long black skirt, walked over to get her instrument. Then I saw her fall, flat-as-a-board frontward, not even bending at her ankles. Miraculously, a gentleman, the second violinist, was standing there and caught her by the shoulders. She didn't bend in his arms either. She lay upon him like a plank of wood, with her heels on the floor, and smiled. Then, regaining her balance, she reached straight down and lifted her bow and violin out of the case. The kindly gentleman stood her up, walked her to the first violin's chair, and helped her sit down. It was difficult not to break out laughing. Lili had her hand over her mouth, her body shaking. I felt tears welling from interior laughter. And all along, the violinist had the sweetest smile on her face. I had the distinct impression that the orchestra had been through this performance before. Two young bugle players took their seats, gulping huge bellyfuls of laughter.

Finally the conductor, who was already onstage, blithely chatting with her friends and ignoring the first violinist, left the podium and walked back up the stairs—just to be able to walk down again and make her grand entrance. She had a shock of very white hair, which flowed proudly over fuchsia silk shoulders. Her skirt was the traditional long black, ending at a pair of sensible black shoes.

The conductor bowed, raised her baton, and the music began. I couldn't believe what I was hearing—and seeing. The baton went only two ways, left and right—no flourishes and definitely no musicality. The orchestra couldn't follow her. The musicians would lose their way and then look embarrassed. The bugle boys laughed behind their music, and then the music stopped flat. I was afraid to look at Lili.

Bravely, the conductor raised her baton once more, and the musical comedy was reenacted. The solos were beautiful. The elderly first violinist played well—the buglers were outstanding, performing a duet from Ravel—but as soon as the entire group tried to play together, there was chaos. It was the most remarkable, funny-bone performance I had heard, and it continued to the end of the program. There was great applause and many bows. The first violinist was helped to her feet and she bowed too.

Lili took my arm as we went up the stairs to the exit, then across the courtyard and out onto the rue de la Sorbonne. We walked without a word—until she turned to me and we both burst out laughing.

"I have never seen anything like that before," she said. "The woman conducting used to be very well-known, what a shame."

When we reached the Métro at Cluny, Lili said, "You know, I will be at my country house for about ten days. Would you like to visit for a couple of those days? Next week, maybe?"

My shyness stepped forward and stood in my face. I bumbled through excuses: "I don't want to bother you." But Lili in her good-natured way just ignored me.

"Here, write this down," she said. "Take the number four seventy-one train at ten from the Gare d'Austerlitz. You will arrive at one-seventeen at Châteauroux. I will meet you at the station there, and we will drive to my home in Saint-Désiré."

Meanwhile, I continued my research both at the Bibliothèque Nationale and throughout the city of Paris.

I made plans to interview another of Violette's friends, Françoise d'Eaubonne, the French feminist writer. But my French had improved only a little—so I hired a young woman, Nina, who taught French to English speakers at the Alliance Française, as my interpreter.

Mme. d'Eaubonne lived in the Tenth Arrondissement on the Boulevard Bonne Nouvelle. To get to her flat, we had to pass through an alley leading to a storehouse of women's clothing, then climb two wide and apparently once elegant flights of stairs. There was no French spoken here, just the singsong cadence of Turkish.

She welcomed us and showed us into a small room. My gift of a jasmine plant was promptly placed outside on the ice-covered windowsill, alongside a frozen pair of white knickers.

Mme. d'Eaubonne was a round woman with short-cropped gray hair and a perennial cigarette living between her lips. Her hands were elegant, decorated with many rings, and always gesturing, insisting. Her face moved through as many expressions as a crowd of people catching your eye.

Françoise d'Eaubonne was born in 1920 in Paris. She was born at an opportune time, when writers such as Gide, Colette, and Valéry were still alive and creating. She was fortunate enough to have encountered the best of two worlds of literature— the nineteenth and twentieth centuries. Mme. d'Eaubonne had written more than twenty books, including two autobiographies, *Drôle de Jeunesse* and *Les Monstres de l'Été,* a book about Simone, *Une Femme Nommée Castor,* and many articles on feminism and ecology.

In her apartment, on my left, was a desk covered with books and papers. In the center of the desk, almost buried by paper, was a typewriter. On the wall behind it were a photograph of Mme. d'Eaubonne with Simone de Beauvoir, and a poster of the Alvin Ailey American Dance Theater at City Center in New York. Above an old and weary sofa with a paisley shawl thrown over the back was a reproduction of part of Michelangelo's Sistine Chapel ceiling: Adam was almost touching the fingertips of God, while Eve was already embraced. To the right of God and Eve were small shelves holding Mme. D'Eaubonne's treasures—necklaces, bracelets, brooches, lying and hanging about, mixed with snapshots and snippets from magazines. Papered, willy-nilly, around the room were more photographs, notes, newspaper clippings, announcements of art exhibitions and readings, with an entire area devoted to Katharine Hepburn. Each wall was a shrine with pictures of famous writers, among them de Beauvoir, Leduc, Gide, Dostoyevsky, Woolf, Yeats, and Sartre.

She sat in the middle of this small room at a small table, draped with a lovely piece of silk, engulfed in books. Directly facing her was a television set whose screen was much too dusty for viewing.

She spoke English at approximately the same level at which I spoke French, so Nina translated.

Mme. d'Eaubonne told me that Violette Leduc had always been respected by the writing community, *l'avant-garde, les poètes maudits*. Her friends put up with her erratic behavior because her work was not to be denied.

"If you look at this photograph of Violette with her dear friend Serge Tamagnot," she said, pointing to one wall, "you can see their friendship reaching through the emulsion. There is no rancor—and her smile, while minimal, makes it clear that she likes the photographer."

Mme. d'Eaubonne handed me another photograph of Leduc and Tamagnot and said it was for me. When I protested at her giving away an object of value, she laughed and said she had many. Like Lili, she is resolute in keeping Violette alive in literary history. Mme. d'Eaubonne gave a copy of this photograph to every writer interested in Leduc. On the back she wrote, *"Avec le meilleur souvenir d'une écrivain amie, Violette Leduc"*—with the best remembrance of a writer friend.

❧

Now, looking out at me each day is Violette with her blond pageboy Carita wig, small eyes squinting into the sun, wearing a turtleneck sweater and heavy white tights, and bundled in an enormous lambskin coat with rabbit fur trimming the collar and cuffs. Her hands are elegantly crossed and resting on her lap, holding the predictable cigarette. Serge Tamagnot is sitting beside her speaking to the photographer, engaged. Violette is calm, staring straight into the lens. I know that pose. Trying not to smile, opening your eyes wide, not letting the lines of your face fold any further, keeping your chin up and forward.

· XIII ·

Thursday morning. I boarded the train to Châteauroux. When I arrived Lili was waiting for me at the platform. As I stepped off the train she handed me a small bunch of violets. I was moved by her graciousness; I understood that she wanted me to be comfortable. Then she led me to the best car in the world—my favorite—an old maroon-and-black *deux chevaux*, a Citroën 2CV. This is the quintessential automobile of France, the symbol of bohemia and the beret-topped intellectual. It is teasingly called a sardine can—but I love its design, with the sloping front and severed rear fitting snugly into flared bumpers.

When we got into the car Lili asked, "Did you have a nice trip?"

"Yes," I said, "I love traveling on trains. It's a pleasure not having to drive. Someday I'll tell you about my train trip from Berlin to Warsaw."

"You couldn't eat, could you?" Lili laughed.

"That's right, how did you know?"

"I have heard the same complaint many times," she said. "They tell you that there will be a food car, but once the train leaves the station, you find there isn't one!"

"Yes, I found out the hard way too," I said. "I got on the train without any provisions and noticed people in both the first- and second-class compartments with baskets of food. At dinnertime I knew I had a problem when the baskets were opened and everyone started eating. No one got up to go to the phantom dining car. Finally I managed to communicate to the conductor that I needed food. He smiled and beckoned me to follow him.

"We swayed through two cars, both second-class, and both containing compartments with hammocks and tiny coal-burning stoves. The air was filled with coal dust and smelled like pickles and whiskey. In the third car was his cabin. Here, on a portable tray, he made me a greasy hot dog on a piece of Polish Wonder bread. It looked dreadful but I was so hungry that I ate it, with a load of mustard on top. It cost me ten cents."

Lili laughed as she pulled onto the road and drove toward Saint-Désiré.

The smallest roads in France, those not indicated on conventional maps, are remarkable. They are smooth and well-maintained—they are a pleasure. The French add plastic to the top layer of the macadam, and this binding extends the life of a road to about forty years. In America we don't add plastic because it's too expensive. Our roads last twenty years, if we're lucky.

We took the D927 to Culan and then the D4 to Vesdun.

Vesdun is one of the three claimed navels of the body of France. Every country has a navel, a spot at its center. Some say this is where the soul of the country resides, others say the heart. The other two navels are Saulzais, north of Vesdun by nine kilometers, and Bruère-Allichamps, another twenty-two kilometers. Vesdun takes its location so seriously that the village has constructed a garish mosaic map at its main and only intersection. The village is lovely—but I had the distinct impression that come summer there would be racks of gaudy postcards and coffee mugs decorated with hearts and "Vesdun" in old French calligraphy.

I mentioned this to Lili and she agreed.

"Not only is the village preparing to sell tourist items but they are actually encouraging tourist buses to stop here. Huge two-decker buses from all over Europe arrive every day in July and August. Some days the fumes are so stagnant that the people of the village are forced to stay in their homes. I wish they had not insisted on this awkward distinction, and let Saulzais or Bruère-Allichamps be the winner."

We drove on through Vesdun and turned right on the D479. This area of central France sits on a semiarid plateau, the Champagne Berrichonne, which is mainly a cattle-raising region. It is very beautiful, with rolling green hills and small forests scattered over the terrain.

This is George Sand country—filled with midnight nocturnes and proud gravel drives winding toward châteaux and simple country farms.

∞

A year after meeting Lili, I was back in France to complete some research. On a bleak day in March, my eighteen-year-old daughter, Naomi, and I visited George Sand's land—her beloved home in Nohant in the Vallée Noire. Naomi was going to school in England, and I missed her terribly. I knew the best way for us to travel was to let her do the driving—which was fine with me. We drove from Paris to Saint-Désiré and stayed at a *gîte* that both Lili and a friend in New York had recommended.

The next morning we set out to locate George Sand's house. It was not easy, and we found ourselves going about in circles. Then, there it was in front of us, looking smaller than we had expected. We parked and entered through a gatehouse, and crossed an open, paved central area to the front door. No one was there, absolutely no one. The door was open. We had a little map, which we followed from room to room, ending at George Sand's bedroom. Still, there was no one in the house. No guards, no tourists.

We photographed each other standing at her desk, then took turns sitting at her desk.

We photographed each other standing by her bed, then took turns lying on her bed.

We looked in her drawers and through her books.

We looked for her imprints on the desk blotter, her shadows in the closets.

We leaned against her mantelpiece and talked about her books, feeling that she would arrive in the room at any moment and ask us to join her for dinner.

Strange. So much freedom in such a famous place. We were careful not to abuse it.

When we sat on her chair, we did so gingerly.

When we lay on her bed, we pretended to be feathers.

Naomi and I shared a few very special hours. It was a rite of passage in our relationship. We went from parent and child to two women sharing our love of literature.

I was grateful to the guard who wasn't doing his job.

❧

At Saint-Désiré, Lili drove around the village church and turned up a wide gravel driveway. Her home had ornate white iron gates, which stood open in greeting. There were no flower beds or lawns at the house, just the beige gravel skirting its walls.

We curved around the driveway and stopped at the front door. The house was two-storied, made of whitewashed stone, with a brick cornice running around it under the eaves. It had a slate-tiled roof, with dormers every few feet. There were brick chimneys everywhere, some with double flues and others standing alone. The front double-door was painted a deep gray with leaded glass windows across the top. The door was capped with a stone lintel.

All the windows had white metal-louvered shutters. The look was austere, and yet the house was welcoming and warm in its traditional style.

We gathered sacks of food and my overnight bag and went inside. Everything in the house was old and inviting. There was no sign of an interior decorator. Lili had told me earlier that her husband had died a few years before and they'd had no children—but she was pleased that her nephews and nieces used the house for occasional holidays.

After getting settled, we cooked dinner together. Actually, Lili did most of the cooking and I took directions. When we finished eating, we sat by the fire and I gave Lili my house gifts—a box of Debauve et Gallais chocolates from the Rue des Saint-Pères and a bottle of old cognac.

"Now we are set for the evening ahead!" Lili said.

I turned on the tape recorder and placed it between our cognac glasses. Lili sat on the sofa and I sat across from her on a soft mauve upholstered chair. We had decided that she would tell me more about this area, the war, and her life.

"During the war," Lili began, "I brought people here to hide on their way to Spain, Portugal, or Gibraltar. My identity card carried my Paris address as my permanent domicile. What the Germans didn't know was that I had another identity card with the Saint-Désiré address. With this, I could pass between the occupied and free zones.

"A real border between the two Frances didn't exist. There was no barbed wire, no fence along the line of the two zones. In some places the imaginary demarcation followed a stream, in other places it meandered along a country road. But you could always count on German sentries and their vicious dogs to be somewhere in the vicinity.

"You see, Châteauroux was an important center for the Resistance. Although the area is mostly open plains, with few woods, we had some semblance of control over the Germans because it is so hilly. They could trench themselves in, but we could fight them from the hills. It was a bit of a standoff."

And in this area Lili met Alain Jacobs, her future husband. It was February 1943. She was in the middle of a rendezvous with a Resistance liaison in Châteauroux. They needed to get some of their people to Marseilles to meet a British submarine. While Lili and the liaison were making plans, a man walked into the café where they were sitting. Lili knew he was Jewish, she just knew— and she was anxious for him. He took a seat at the rear with a good view of the front door and ordered a coffee. His face was haunting—haggard and thin, with round silver spectacles perched against his ashen skin. Lili's colleague, Henri, saw him too, and she motioned him closer.

"You know, the Germans patronize this café, especially after the afternoon sentry duty," she whispered to Henri anxiously. "We have to get him out of here."

"But how do we know he's one of us?" Henri asked.

Lili nodded impatiently and put up her hand to quiet him. "Listen," she said.

Coming toward them was a low rumble in the air.

"Another air raid on the railroad terminal," Lili said.

The café owners, the Allard brothers, kept their goods and a black-market supply of bicycles in a shed behind the building. This shed was familiar to Lili and Henri because they used it for clandestine meetings. The shelves lining the walls were mostly bare because of the war. There was a window, just large enough for a normal-sized person to get through. This window let out into a narrow cul-de-sac. They knew the doorway across the alley opened to a passageway that led to the fields. Their only chance was to get the man out the back door of the café to the precarious safety of the shed.

The café was quiet. Everyone was listening. The hum became a roar. And finally the sirens rang out.

Lili and Henri knew what to do. They headed for the rear of the café and placed themselves between the man and the aisle leading to the front door. Before he knew what was happening, they had him by the arms and out the back door. He resisted, but they gripped him tighter and almost lifted him off the ground. When he turned to speak, Lili cut him off. "Be still," she said.

"I must have sounded firm, because he didn't say a word," Lili told me. "We pushed him into the shed, crowded in behind him and closed the door, then crouched where no one could see us. We pulled him down to the floor and sat huddled as the bombs dropped. Finally the planes left, with the wind blowing toward England. We didn't move.

"Henri and I had acted very quickly. Now we looked at each other nervously. Then this man said to Henri, *'Les caoutchoucs,'* and Henri nodded."

I interrupted. "What are *caoutchoucs?*"

"It means 'galoshes,' you know, overboots. It was a safety password. Passwords were often slightly insane." Lili shrugged. "So there we were, huddled together in a flimsy lean-to, whispering to the stranger.

"'Where have you come from?' Henri asked.

"The man clamped his mouth shut, and Henri and I laughed with relief.

"'You're going to have to trust us,' I said. 'You really don't have a choice.'

"He looked at us keenly, drew in his breath, then slowly told his story."

He was a member of a partisan group in Paris. When the fighting became too intense and the partisans realized they didn't have enough weapons, they fought their way to the outskirts of the city. There, they found and joined a Maquis group whose primary job was to sabotage and ambush Germans in the woods around Paris. By August 1942, the Resistance group had been forced above the demarcation zone at Vierzon and their fatalities were increasing at a horrible pace.

The Germans moved into the unoccupied zone and patrolled their territory. The partisans knew there was nowhere to run. To slip across the border was almost impossible. So they decided to split up and try to contact the underground in different parts of France. Those who were Jewish thought it was best to travel alone.

After hiding with several families in the Loiret area, the man headed south, where it would be warmer. Four days before, he had found himself a safe house in a church. Father Lanier, the church priest, suggested that he contact a friend of his.

Then two days later, while the man was hiding in the church basement, Father Lanier was arrested and taken away by the Gestapo.

As soon as it grew dark, the man left for another safe house, a farm outside town. The people who owned the farm told him to go to a café and ask for someone named Henri R. They gave him a password to give to the proprietor, Allard. They told him that Lili would be there, and gave him a description. He went to the café that evening but there were too many people. He was afraid to risk the approach until the crowd was smaller, so he sat in the back.

"I am traveling without any papers," he told Lili and Henri. "I know this is taking a chance, but if I am caught I would rather go to a work camp in Germany than to Bergen-Belsen, or even Beaune-la-Rolande, right here in France."

"I asked him only for his first name and he answered 'Alain,'" Lili said. "For the time being we chose to transfer him here, to Saint-Désiré, fifty-two kilometers away. We decided that I would move him overland starting that night and Henri would remain in Châteauroux."

"But," I interrupted, "how could you move him through your underground? The way you describe him makes him seem so conspicuous."

Lili laughed, leaning back into the sofa cushions. She took off her shoes. "He was actually no more conspicuous than most Frenchmen. He was dark-haired, yes, but so are many French people, and he was slim, average height, as are many Parisians. No, the only thing that made him look different was his glasses, which assigned him the label of 'intellectual.' He needed to look more ordinary, like a shopkeeper or a lorry driver.

"I was nervous about our decision for other reasons. It was bitterly cold, and wherever we stepped there was the danger of snapping a frozen twig and alerting the Germans, who were continually on patrol. Of course, no automobiles were allowed out after curfew, so driving was not a possibility. And even if we could hitch a ride with a farmer, their wood-fueled lorries always drew attention because you could smell them before you heard them. Also, they were desperately slow, especially on the hills."

But there was no choice. Lili and Alain planned to follow the Indre River to Champillet and then cut across to Saint-Désiré. Going this way would be longer by fifteen kilometers—but they thought it would be safer in the long run.

And the weather really worried them. It felt as if it was going to snow. Alain was dressed shabbily and wearing worn army-issue boots. Lili needed to find him some warm clothes. She knew decent boots would be impossible, but she had to try to find him something. Father Lanier's church was probably under surveillance, so this source wasn't available. It was growing dark and Lili had to beat the curfew hour or risk being stopped. Henri stayed with Alain while Lili went to a convent—where, she knew, she could count on the sisters, who had helped her before.

"They kindly supplied me with heavy, dark clothes and two loaves of bread. No boots. I didn't have enough coupons to buy a pair, even if they were available. Wooden sabots would have made too much noise and were too uncomfortable. After asking around, I gave up and went back to the shed without the boots.

"Alain was now dressed in proper clothing but I was still worried about his feet. On checking his boots we found that he had worn large holes through both soles. I could see that there were sores on his feet, and they were becoming infected. The nuns had tied up the bread and extra clothes in a piece of heavy canvas, so I folded this canvas into rectangles and Alain put them in his boots. It worked."

Night arrived. Alain and Lili crawled through the small window of the shed, and she led the way to the river. They had to travel all night and sleep by day. They hoped to cover the area in about twelve hours.

That night they got to an area just north of Champillet. They found a place to sleep next to the river, on ground that had been hollowed out by the rain. Above them, in fact right over their heads, was a path used mainly by farmers. Lili was nervous about this path, but the sleeping area was dry and a little warmer than she expected.

The next day, Alain slept deeply, never moving, never making a sound. Lili slept lightly, anxious to hear anything that might indicate danger. In the evening they each ate some bread, drank some water, and left the banks of the Indre, edging the village of Châteaumeillant.

They arrived at Culan around eleven. Lili was tempted to stop at a friend's house for something hot to drink, but as they drew near the village she spotted smoke and realized that there must be a group of German soldiers bivouacked on the outskirts. Rather than take the risk, she and Alain pressed on by cutting across the rolling plain, then going around the lake at Souperons, and right up to the side entrance of Lili's house.

It was three-thirty in the morning. The house was closed for the winter, Lili's family was in Paris.

"I quietly led the way. On the floor, below the windowsills, I placed blankets and pillows to make us comfortable. We needed to be near the ground, so we could hear movement on the road. We could have no light. I remember yearning for something hot to drink but not daring to light the stove. Instead I found a bottle of whiskey, and as we finished the bottle I got to know Alain."

"I'm amazed that you could travel all the way there in the dark," I said.

Lili laughed. "I had made the journey many times. My parents loved the outdoors, and walking this path was an annual expedition. When I was a girl, we would hike along the Indre and stop for the evening at an inn in Champillet. The next day we would continue on to Châteauroux. Each year a different person would come to fetch us and drive us back to Saint-Désiré. Now Châteauroux is an industrial city, but when I was little, it was a small rural town identified from afar by its church steeple."

"So what did you learn about Alain?" I asked, getting back to the story.

"Well, I learned that he was a newly appointed professor of literature at the Sorbonne. His specialty was nineteenth-century British literature, but he had a serious interest in contemporary American literature. So, of course, he spoke to me a little in English. His accent was terrible, and I tried not to laugh. He seemed good-natured, though, and laughed at himself. When we finished the whiskey, I went to my father's closet and found Alain a pair of boots and some better clothes. We shook hands and said good night. I pulled up my blanket and fell asleep.

"In the late morning I awoke to find Alain gone. He had left a note on the table, weighted down by the empty whiskey bottle. I had to destroy it, but what he wrote remains in my memory: 'Dear Lili. I am told that there is a place on the other side of the world where grief and sorrow never wander. I hope we will meet there again. Alain.' I didn't see him again until 1946.

"Let's go to sleep," Lili said abruptly. "I am tired and I want to show you around tomorrow."

I kept forgetting that she was seventy years old. I jumped up from the sofa and collected our dirty glasses and her ashtray heaped with cigarette butts.

"No, no," she said, "we will do that in the morning. Let me take you to your room."

The next day, we drove south through the beautiful Berry countryside to the medieval town of Aubusson. It was noon and the ancient narrow streets were empty. All the people were at their midday meal. We found a small restaurant for lunch.

"During the war," Lili said when we were seated, "in this area of the Creuse, the French communists seized upon the opportunity of general bedlam and took control of every municipal building. Then the Germans conquered them and massacred whole villages, burning most of them to the ground. Meanwhile, the communists did nothing to help protect the people—they went into hiding and literally abandoned them. Luckily, Aubusson was not destroyed. Do you want to see the tapestries while we are here?"

"Lili," I said, "what I most want to see in Aubusson is not the famous tapestries, but to see number one, Rue Jules Sandeau."

"Why?" she asked.

"George Sand," I replied.

When Jules Sandeau was a student he had a romance with a young married woman, also a writer, named Aurore Dudevant. During this affair they collaborated on a novel, *Rose et Blanche,* written under the shared pseudonym Jules Sand. Afterward, Jules Sandeau wrote *Mademoiselle de la Seiglière,* and was soon forgotten. Aurore went on to become the famous George Sand.

When we finished eating we walked to number 1, Rue Jules Sandeau, where the writer's birthplace was identified by a small brass plate on the stone wall. But there was no romance or history left on the doorstep—for the building had been reconstructed. So we turned the corner and strolled farther along the next old cobbled street. This street was renamed in 1945, the Rue Déportés-Politiques—to honor the men and women who had been deported for their political beliefs.

We were so involved with our sightseeing that I did not pay attention to the time. "Lili," I said, looking at my watch, "we'll have to leave if I am going to catch the evening train for Paris tonight!"

We quickly walked back to the car and left Aubusson. About halfway to the station in Châteauroux, we stopped for gas, and finding we had made good time, decided to have a coffee. The café was no different from most in rural France. There were no plaques distinguishing a tourist place, no blue stars proclaiming the quality of its food, but there was a feeling I experience only in Europe. Even though this was merely a café, it had an atmosphere that filled me with a desire to belong to an ancient country.

We were quiet as we left the café. I was tired and I could see that Lili was ready for solitude. We had another hour's drive to Châteauroux but continued to avoid the main roads by driving north through tiny villages. I enjoyed reading the old-fashioned small stone road markers. Sometimes a marker designated a village with only one house.

We arrived at the station with fifteen minutes to spare. I bought a chocolate bar and the *Herald Tribune;* then Lili walked me to the platform and kissed me formally on both cheeks. I felt sad about leaving, but I didn't want to burden her with my feelings.

"I have enjoyed this visit very much," she said. "Please don't be shy about spending time with me. This reminiscing has been good for me too—it eases my loneliness. I miss Alain so deeply I have no language for it. Call me during the week and we will make plans. I have a translation due to my publisher, but otherwise I am free."

"Thank you. I will call on Tuesday," I said, relieved. This time I kissed her on both cheeks, then paused, smiled, and kissed her again.

· XIV ·

All the way back to Paris I remembered the many days and nights that I had spent on trains in Eastern Europe.

When the Berlin Wall fell, I wanted to go to Eastern Europe as quickly as possible. I told a friend about my plan, and she said,

"Go, before the pollution from the have-a-nice-dayers and aerobic zealots invades."

I went alone.

I conjured, like magic, the courage to do this from Violette. Her wits, her notebooks, and her Blanzy-Poure pen would carry her to a new place. She was an adventurer into the psychological unknown. I was trying to walk her path.

Berlin was a turning point for me. I wanted to understand this part of the world that had destroyed so many members of my family. I wanted to feel their terror. Somehow this trip was necessary for me to nurture my roots in America.

I landed at the Berlin airport one afternoon in March and took a bus directly into the city. At the intersection of Budapester Strasse and the Kurfürstendamm was the Verkehrsamt Berlin Center, which helped budget travelers find a room for the night in someone's home. I waited in line, along with many young people, feeling jet-lagged and out of place.

When my number was finally called, I approached the woman at the desk. She asked me if there was anything special to describe me to enter in the computer. I told her I was Jewish. I thought it would be interesting to stay with a Jewish family, if possible.

After waiting around for two hours, I was handed a slip of white paper and told to go to a flat on Damaschke Strasse. When I arrived I followed her instructions to ring the bell five times. An elderly gentleman answered the door.

I am hypervigilant. When I walk into a room full of people, I know within thirty seconds where the exits are, which people seem safe, and who is Jewish. This man was definitely not Jewish, and his flat gave me a queasy feeling. But I was suffering from lack of sleep and the general malaise of a new journey, so I decided to ignore it.

My room was very nice, spotlessly clean, with a beautiful satin-covered down comforter on the bed. I made myself comfortable, took a walk, had dinner. That evening I slept on a feather bed. It felt like I was sleeping on top of my dreams.

Part of my fee included breakfast, so the next morning I went upstairs to take my meal. The elderly gentleman greeted me and introduced me to a young man who he said was a friend. I sensed that this young man lived in the flat and was my host's lover. My host showed me to a table alongside shelves and shelves of books. As soon as I sat down, I sensed danger. He told me he was a retired professor of philosophy. I looked around the shelves, haphazardly, and my skin started crawling. Lined up in front of me were Nietzsche's *The Birth of Tragedy* and *Beyond Good and Evil,* Gobineau's *The Inequality of the Human Races,* Sir Halford John Mackinder, Haushofer, Rosenberg's tracts, *Der Völkische Beobachter* of the National Socialist Party, Treitschke, Göring's *Four Year Plan,* and directly over my coffee cup, *Mein Kampf.* Obviously the man was a Nazi, and I was caught in a strange and upsetting setup. I felt trapped. The two men's smiles turned to smirks. But I refused to give them pleasure. I remained calm, ate my breakfast, and said good day.

I didn't know what to do. Even before I had met these two men, I didn't like Germany. It was now obvious to me that the woman at the Verkehrsamt was mean-spirited, an antagonist. I knew the hotels in Berlin were filled. So I decided to stay, to try to confront this cunning declaration of anti-Semitism.

I spent the day sightseeing, drinking coffee at the Kaffee Einstein, and trying to understand Berlin. In the evening, rather than return to the flat, I went directly to dinner and to hear the Berlin Philharmonic. I heard Mischa Maisky perform Dvořák cello concerti. His playing transported me to a place of beauty, away from ugliness. Maisky gave me hope.

I came back to the flat after one in the morning. I had to go upstairs to use the bathroom. As I entered the hall, the two men came to the door. In front of me they stood, legs apart, arms folded across their chests. They were wearing the tiniest bikini underwear and they both had obvious erections. I turned away from them and walked back down the hallway. The hairs on my neck were being blown by cold air. I closed the door to my room and quietly drew the latch, and decided to use the sink as a urinal. Behind the door I heard laughter and sex and Wagner. Three hours later I heard my doorknob being rattled—they were trying to get into my room. I quickly dressed, packed, placed the money I owed on the table, and left by my private entrance. By now it was almost five in the morning. I stood and waited another hour for the bus to take me to the train station. A funny thought crossed my mind and made me smile—I recalled reading about Violette Leduc's urinating into her blue bottle during the war. I was glad to be leaving Germany.

I got on the next train to Warsaw.

❧

Because I live in a world where threats of destruction are often realized, I feel the ever present menace, or freedom, of death as a visceral possibility. Anxiety and trepidation attend my theater of time lost, time wasted, time emptied onto the backstage of the endless dark.

I remembered the book *Hitler Terror,* with a white swastika and its black shadow on the brown cover. Actually titled *The Brown Book of the Hitler Terror and the Burning of the Reichstag,* it was prepared by the World Committee for the Victims of German Fascism and published in 1933. My father bought it in 1934 and signed his name twice inside the front cover. I don't know why he signed it two times. Did the subject require a double proclamation of selfhood?

I found and read the book when I was ten years old. I read it outdoors in a shaded corner where the fence met my house and where the smell of dirt was stronger than the smell of grass. The book states that in Germany, as of the fifth of May, 1933, any non-Jewish woman who was seen consorting with a Jewish man would have the initials J.H. branded on her face. *J.H., Juden-Hure,* Jewish prostitute.

Brainwashed by the covert anti-Semitic media, I confused the branded face with herds of branded cattle going to slaughter.

On the day of my birth, May 5, 1941—the same day that the French Resistance began in earnest—Florczak Franciszka, number 26780 at Auschwitz, a Polish prostitute, was murdered there.

Florczak Franciszka died in Poland—I was born in America.

Five thousand miles is a long time.

I found her photograph neatly framed, hanging on a barracks wall at Auschwitz. It was not presumptuous to think she had been used up by the Gestapo and was considered no longer attractive, no longer a viable utility. Was she ill from the Nazis' sexual persecution—had she been starved to annihilation? Was she pregnant by one of her tormentors? Did they kill both Florczak Franciszka and her baby? There were numerous scenarios, all brutal.

A copy of her photograph hangs on the wall of my studio. Her head is shaved, with just the slightest shadow of hair. She stares beyond the camera, one eye looking as if it's already dead and the other still preserving hope. The picture was taken upon her arrival at Auschwitz, on December 12, 1940. Winter is in the photograph. Her nose is darker than the rest of her face, she is cold. She must have just begun the starvation diet of watered-down soup and maggot-infested bread. Franciszka's mouth has a lopsided and cynical warp.

The mass destruction of millions of human beings in my lifetime creates nightmares, malignant with despair. It is difficult to find light in our world. Every day the media remind us of our inhumanity. Sometimes they toss onto the page a tidbit of promise— a child saved from a raging river, a chicken laying red eggs, a country electing an intellectual president. Most of the time I row around the negativity about the human condition, pleading for redemption, checking for the beating of my heart.

❧

Auschwitz is German for *Oświęcim*, the name of the Polish railroad town that lives alongside the camps. During the Second World War the railroad carried those millions of people to their deaths in both Auschwitz and its neighbor, Birkenau. The citizens of the town of Oświęcim ignored the camps. Oświęcim was a railroad junction, on the main artery through which most trains traveled to Prague, and on into western Europe. The area now manufactures chemicals, leather, and agricultural implements. During the war the trains carried gold from the teeth of human beings, to be melted down and made into money. They carried hair from the heads of human beings, to be made into pillows. They carried skin from the bodies of human beings, to be made into soap. It didn't matter what the trains carried, as long as they continued to run.

Forty-nine years after Florczak Franciszka died, I journeyed to Auschwitz to try to understand this perplexing involvement with my inherited memory—to try to understand some part, however small, of this suffering, to try to understand the craving to obliterate human beings.

I arrived on the morning of the first night of Passover. The sun was trying to push through a dense wall of smog, but the day was brooding and smoky nevertheless. The only color was along a well-worn path outside the camp—a few yellow tulips living in a bed of overgrown weeds. Because of the cramping, the tulips had diminished in size and color to almost nothing. Inside the camp occasional flowers, now limp, had been placed in the barbed-wire fence as a remembrance to a ravaged people.

My people, the people of the Old Testament, the people of the desert, and all people who are forced to pay for man's inhumanity sliced themselves into my reality. The destruction of unfinished histories left me silenced.

Auschwitz is now a museum, a monument to history. I lament all the suffering perpetrated by the stupidity and pathology of those assassins. When I try to imagine what it would be like to survive the violence and insanity of an entire nation, it is hopeless. I bow low to those survivors. They are the archetypes of our contemporary mythology.

Walking up and down the camp's narrow streets, I was shoved back in time, trying to identify the feelings echoing there—of the Jews, the Romany, of Florczak Franciszka. These people were not allowed a last visit with themselves—there was not a natural cadence to their lives. No matter how hard I tried to fuse myself into their pathos, I failed. I was an intruder in their life story. I whispered for them to ignore me as arrogance in their landscape.

Because it was both Passover and Easter week, the camp was empty. I was glad there were no tourist buses, no guides homogenizing the experience into a digestible thirty minutes. I wandered the camp in an eerie silence—which made me edgy and acutely aware of the ghosts whose relics lay heaped under hills of earth.

One barracks had thousands of eyeglasses; another, thousands of shoes; yet another, thousands of suitcases once filled with personal and hopeful belongings—now mummified into history. All of these objects, at one time, were held by human hands, walked in by human feet, looked through by human eyes.

The enormity of the heaps hammered me to my knees.

After exiting each barracks, I had to sit outside for a few minutes to touch my face, straighten my hair, brush lint off my black jacket—to remind myself of who I was and labor with my revulsion. Sometimes, when I have a nightmare, I struggle to wake up and then the struggle becomes part of the nightmare: this was the same experience.

There, in the last barracks I entered, I walked toward the heart of the nightmare. Here was the house of the children.

Lining the walls were photographs of thousands of children. Every child was photographed three times. One picture of the right side, one picture of the left, and one picture straight on. In all cases their heads were shaved. In one of the three photographs each child wore a head covering—the girls a scarf, the boys a striped hat. Each photograph was identified with a number, not a name. The children were dressed in the familiar striped uniforms, buttoned up to the neck, with straight, pointed collars.

The children had a look of detachment. They were not there, sitting in those chairs. They were not posing for the documentation of the regime of Cain. The children had left for elsewhere— their spirits were gone. They had seen too much violence and death to be able to feel any longer.

There was a term coined during the war, *mu*ʒ*elmen*, which referred to the fact that once people lose their desire to live, they will soon die. These children had no hope in their eyes, and soon after the photographs were taken, so were the children. Why the Nazis had bothered to photograph everyone was beyond my grasp. The systematic assassination of children went further than I could comprehend.

A large number of children were gassed upon their arrival at the camps. For inexplicable and inhuman reasons, some children were given a little more time. From the photographs it was hard to tell to which ethnic or religious group these children belonged. There were no obvious Semitic features, no circumcisions, no horns. The one thing I did understand, upon seeing those faces, was that it set me hard against some Germans and Poles.

The helplessness of the people brought to Auschwitz, as all camps, had been deliberately and cleverly choreographed since the beginning of the 1930s. By the time these people were rounded up

in the 1940s and transported away in cattle cars, they
eased, distressed, disheartened, dis-everything that it su.
anyone survived. When I saw Auschwitz, when I felt Au
when I swallowed that vile place, I was numb with fury.

I had to sit down. But wherever I sat I felt the ghosts of peⱼ
rising through me. I vomited their bile into the dirt, along theⱼ
paths—to their ovens. I forced myself to stay in Auschwitz for the
entire day. By early evening, as the light was falling, the first night
of Passover had begun. It was quiet. The town outside the barbed-
wire fence returned home for supper, not a seder, I was sure.

But would the villagers be sitting before their meals, saying
"Prɀepras zam," which means, "I'm sorry, forgive me for anything
I may have done to hurt you." Would this word be said for all of
us—for the Jews, the Romany, the socialists, the Resistance, the
prostitutes, Florczak Franciszka, the children? Or would this word
be reserved for their own little world? One would hope they could
no longer ignore the barbed-wire fences—lined on their side with
yellow tulips. But I was not convinced.

· XV ·

When I returned from the Bibliothèque Nationale on Monday
evening, I found a message from Lili. "Please come to lunch
at my apartment on Wednesday. Call only if you can't come."

On Wednesday I left the library at noon and walked along
the Rue Étienne-Marcel into the Marais district. This area was
once a marsh, separated from the city, and attractive to robbers
and rogues. When the Seine overflowed, this was where it flooded.
It was also where Parisians settled in the thirteenth century as
the city grew. The Marais went through many transformations—
from being a home for aristocrats to being the center of the fash-
ionable world, then plummeting to the depths of poverty at the
beginning of the industrial age. Now there is a revival of the
district.

Lili lived on the Rue du Temple, almost exactly between the
numbers 42 and 122, formerly the homes, respectively, of Flaubert
and Balzac. Her apartment was in a beautiful seventeenth-century
building, once home to a famous salon, quite grand.

Lili answered the buzzer, and I walked up a large circular stairway whose wooden banister was rubbed with centuries of use. On the second-floor landing I looked up and saw Lili waiting for me outside her open door. My eyes traveled further to the ceiling, where an enormous dome was painted in subtle colors, to give the climber a sensation of reaching toward a vault of sky.

Lili explained, "For the past century, these buildings were largely neglected, until people started moving here in the 1950s. Paris had become very expensive and this was all we could afford. Alain and I bought the lease and lived in this room and a pasted-together kitchen while we renovated the rest of the space. It took five years of living in plaster-filled chaos for us to complete the task. By the time we finished, we had a six-room apartment."

The rooms were spacious, with high ceilings, and elegantly proportioned windows looking out upon the Jardin Saint-Aignan.

"Come this way, this is where I spend most of my time."

Lili led me down a hallway to the opposite end of the apartment. We entered another large room, but smaller than the main salon. Between the windows and around the walls were floor-to-ceiling shelves with a ladder running along a track. There were thousands of books. Placed here and there on the shelves were small framed prints and various objects. On the polished wood floors were beautiful Persian rugs.

In the center of the room was an old wooden table covered with papers, books, and journals. It reminded me of the Collier brothers on legs. Lili's chair had wheels that coasted along a worn path. There were no file cabinets, only stacks upon stacks of paper. Floor lamps glowed beneath green or milk-glass shades. It was just one in the afternoon, but the day was dark, contemplative, and the lamps cast a friendly warmth about the room.

"Alain worked in this room until his death," Lili told me. The only change I made was to store his papers in boxes."

"But how do you find anything?" I asked.

"Oh, it is simple. Here, look. Each pile is a letter of the alphabet. When the pile becomes dangerously high, I start another pile behind it. Someday I will have to go through everything—but the task is so daunting that I always lose my courage."

I marveled at her system, thinking too of my husband and his nutty way of filing papers. Joe and Lili would probably like each other.

We sat on the sofa, facing the desk.

"Remember when we were at Les Deux Magots," I asked Lili, "and you told me about having a copy of that letter to Violette from Cocteau?"

"Yes, of course!" Lili exclaimed. "Let me see if I can find it."

She went to one of her piles of papers, lifted the pile intact, and placed it on another table. After much rustling and dropping of sheets of paper on the rug, she seemed to give up.

"I can't find it, what did I do with it?" She stood, leaning her hands on the table, thinking hard. "Ah, I know where it is!"

She went to the shelves and pulled out a book, opened it—and there was the letter.

"Where was it?" I asked.

"Why, where it *should* be," she answered confidently. "In Cocteau's *Les Enfants Terribles*!

"I think the letter will give you a bewildering view of Violette that many people experienced but could not articulate. I will read it to you. Listen.

"'The true forces of spirit, of gaze or heart become commercial only if one delivers them to the public diluted with a lot of water, so as to prevent too violent a fall between innovation and habits.

"'Violette Leduc represents for me the bitter and acidic stone of an epoch in which a number of novelists triumph in more accessible and, I will say, more amicable domains.

"'But if you look for what distinguishes modern letters and gives them their rank of nobility, you will find it in the work of a woman incapable of making concessions and with a robust handshake.

"'Violette Leduc does not *what is done*, but what will be done. It is the secret and mythology of true artists. Jean Cocteau.'"

Lili handed me the letter. "You are welcome to take this to copy," she said, and sat back against the cushions.

Clipped to the letter was a copy of Cocteau's drawing of Genet that had been torn from an old magazine. It was in Cocteau's characteristic style—one long, thin line, migrating, reeling over the paper.

"This is a lovely drawing," I said. "It makes Genet look quite pleasant! Do you know where the original is?"

"Sadly, I have no idea," Lili answered. "I suppose it could be with Violette's only remaining family, her stepniece, Claude Dehous. When Violette died, and then Alain, I lost track of some of our friends. They may know where Claude is."

I was curious—and now that Lili had brought up Alain again, I felt it would be a polite moment to ask: "Lili, would you tell me more about your husband?"

Lili gazed down at her clasped hands. She wore her wedding ring. For a moment, she retreated into herself.

"It has been six years, and I still miss him very much," she said finally. "Since we didn't have children, we were closer than was probably healthy. Sometimes in the middle of the night I wake and hear him walking softly toward the bedroom—the way he used to do after working late in our study, afraid he would wake me. My heart floats away when I realize he isn't coming. It takes me until dawn to get myself back—to find real time again.

"He died slowly, over three years, of heart disease. He didn't suffer. His body just got slower and slower. One morning I woke to find him asleep next to me. When I reached for his hand I felt his death. It was over—just like that."

Lili lit a cigarette and stood and walked toward the tall windows. Turning to me, she said, "It took a long time for me to—as we say in French—*trouver le goût de vivre*, find the taste for life." She stepped out of the room, then reentered after a few minutes and sat down, composed.

"Is it okay to continue the story about Alain?" I asked.

She smiled and nodded.

"How did the two of you find each other again?"

"As I told you before, when Alain left my home in Saint-Désiré in February of 1943, I didn't see him again for three years. One day when I was sitting with Violette at our neighborhood café here in Paris, La Mandoline, he walked by. We recognized each other instantly.

"'Monsieur . . . it is Alain, yes?' I asked him. 'Please come and join us.'

"Alain sat down, in the warming sun, on a lovely spring day, in free France. He looked as if he had been ill for a long time. I had often thought of him, but assumed he had been devoured by the war.

"You know, Nietzsche stole a phrase from the seventeenth-century mystic Jeanne Guyon: 'the wrapping of the body by the soul.' When I saw Alain that day, this metaphor came to my mind."

Violette was very gracious to him. She had an uncanny instinct for detecting a sensitive soul. With all her craziness, she had a selfless humanism that was touching.

Violette reminded Alain of his grandmother. Her name was Nikhoma and she had lived in Odessa. She was an impossible woman but he loved her. She had two sons and one daughter. The sons were members of a Jewish self-defense group at the University of Odessa. On May 3, 1881, a mob of thousands attacked Jewish homes, schools, places of business. Her sons' group tried to protect the Jews.

After many hours, the police arrived and arrested six hundred fifty rioters, plus one hundred fifty Jews. All of these people, all eight hundred, were loaded onto barges and towed out to sea. For six days Nikhoma waited on the shore of the Black Sea. For six days she prayed for her sons. For six days she made promises to God, while the *malach hamaves*, the hovering angel of death, waited with her.

Then the barges were brought back to shore. Neither of her sons was on board.

Nikhoma, her husband, and their daughter emigrated to France. Nikhoma was still young, but she was already an old woman in her heart. She had one more child, a son, Alain's father. "Heaven is beneath the feet of women," she used to tell Alain. She became odder and odder as she grew old. When Alain was a little boy he tried to protect her from the judgments of adults. For so many years she raced toward *olam haba*, the next world—she was in a great hurry—but it took another sixty years.

Violette was a natural friend for Alain. He had great empathy for her. The day Lili and Alain were reunited, the three of them sat and talked well into the evening. They spoke of the war, of France. Alain did not talk about himself. The conversation moved from politics to literature to food and back again. None of them wanted to leave the table. But it finally grew too cold and they had to go. They made arrangements to meet again.

Later Violette told Lili that the conversations had made her realize that she was . . . *the apprentice of pain.* She had . . . *its halo in [her] stomach.* She sensed the same sorrow in Alain. Her friendship with him lasted, not without storms, until she died. The two shared a unique understanding. Lili was slightly envious because Violette would come to her with her external miseries, while she sought counsel with Alain in a quiet fashion, prepared to listen rather than rant.

"Why don't you bring your tape recorder to the table," Lili said to me, "and we'll have some lunch." She showed me into the dining room, where a cold lunch was already prepared. We sat down to eat, with the tape recorder on the table between the wine and the dessert.

Alain Jacobs was born at the Hôpital Rothschild on the Boulevard de Picpus in Paris. His father was a businessman and his mother a pediatrician. He grew up in a family that wandered in and out of the Jewish intelligentsia of Paris and Berlin. His mother's family were secular Jews who had been assimilating since their arrival from Berlin in 1916.

At the start of the Second World War, there was an enormous discrepancy between the Jews who had been living in France for generations and those newly emigrated. The older Jewish community called themselves Israélites, the younger emigrants were socialists. Before Paris fell, this socialist Jewish community organized itself in the Resistance. Indeed, at the memorial to the French Resistance in Mont-Valérien, sixteen percent of those remembered were Jews—at a time when only seven percent of the French population was Jewish.

On June 14, 1940, the German occupiers entered Paris in two formations. One advanced toward the Arc de Triomphe, the other toward the Eiffel Tower. The heart of Paris was trapped in parentheses, and the flight of Parisians began. La Grande Peur, the Great Fear, drove almost one-quarter of the population to the roads. Thousands were killed by strafing and bombardment by German shelling—a massive catastrophe.

Alain and his parents did not leave Paris. The family was divided. Alain thought his parents should go to America—he was safe because he had been born in France. But they were reluctant to leave Alain and their home, so the three of them came to a compromise. His parents would remain until friends could safely ease the whole family out of Paris into the free zone.

For the next year the elder Jacobses led a hidden life. They rarely socialized—they wrapped themselves in a flimsy shroud of hope. Alain was trying to purchase documents for his parents that said they had been born in France. He felt as if his family were being held by the neck and slowly strangled. Yet he continued to hope because of the intense resistance among the Jews of Paris. He became intricately involved in the clandestine Jewish Solidarité movement. Although his group was not armed, they performed minor but irksome forms of sabotage—puncturing the gas tanks of German officers' cars, for instance, and crowbarring rails from the train tracks leading into Paris.

Then, on September 27, 1940, an order was announced for all Jews in France to register at the local *poste de police*. M. Jacobs, as head of the family, arrived to place their names in the census of the Jews of Paris that resulted in an official legal distinction: the Germans labeled Alain's parents immigrants, while he was French-born.

But almost two years later, at the end of May 1942, this distinction made no difference: all Jews were forced to wear the yellow Star of David, and the deliberate isolation of the Jewish people began.

On July 4, 1942, Bastille Day, the Jacobs family took an unusual summer-afternoon stroll to the Luxembourg Gardens. On their way home they passed the Chambre des Députés. Alain told Lili he would never forget the unified shiver the three of them experienced. There, draped over the portal of one of France's most sacred buildings was a banner reading *"Deutschland siegt an allen Fronten"*—Germany is victorious on all fronts.

Two days later, Black Thursday, the French municipal police, along with members of the French Fascist Party, were handed lists of 12,884 Jewish immigrants. And within two days, nine thousand Frenchmen dressed in comforting French uniforms rounded up every one of these people. The men were shipped to Drancy, an unfinished public housing project, the women and children to Pithiviers or Beaune-la-Rolande.

Alain did not have time to warn his parents. His group of partisans had been told to "warn the Jews of Paris . . . knock on the door of every known Jewish family. Do away with the usual precautions. Every Jew must leave his home on the night of the fifteenth." Alain was ordered to cover the Fourth and Fifth arrondissements. A friend assured him that his parents, in the Eleventh, would be informed immediately.

But M. and Mme. Jacobs were taken.

Alain learned later that his friend, the one who promised to contact his parents, had been caught in an identity control check by the Gestapo; he was never seen again. His intuition had alerted him, Alain told Lili after the war, but his orders were firm. It was a tragic lesson. From then on, an indelible emptiness was stamped upon his heart.

And yet, Lili believed, he survived the war because of this tragedy. After that Thursday, whenever he felt the slightest quiver of danger, he acted upon it. His survival instincts were honed for any signal of catastrophe. For the rest of his life, he would start upon hearing a telephone ring, jump at the sound of a door bell, grab Lili's arm when he heard a siren.

He frantically tried to save his parents. Every week he went to Drancy to yell encouragement to his father through the wire fence—and try to hand him food and cigarettes.

His mother, he was told later, was taken to Buchenwald, where she tended sick women and children. Within three weeks of her arrival there, she was dead. She was found next to the bodies of a mother and child, wasted by overwork and starvation.

His father was transported to Auschwitz in a cattle car. When he arrived, he was told to go right. His two best friends, two of the finest minds in France, were told to go left. These two were murdered that day, gassed. His father lived for two more months, working at clearing land on which more crematoriums would be built. He was one of a group of six men who were shot one day in retaliation for not fulfilling their daily wheelbarrow quota of stones—they were used as an example. By the time Alain's father died, the Jews remaining in Paris were in hiding.

Not one Jewish deportation train was stopped and saved by the French Resistance. Not one. Alain felt bitterness for some of the things that the Resistance *didn't* do.

After Alain left Lili in Saint-Désiré, he moved through the nights until he reached a unit of partisans outside of Bourges. He fought alongside this group, through the end of 1943, traveling in southwestern France as a courier, carrying information from one unit to another across the area.

One day in December, his unit was met by a farmer who said he could help. In the evening, after promising to return with food, he returned with the Germans instead. Alain's group, four women and nine men, were rounded up and herded to a railroad line, where they were loaded onto cattle cars. Along with hundreds of others they were transported to Ravensbrück. Alain remained in this concentration camp until it was liberated by the Allies. He never spoke about his experiences. Lili had no idea how he survived. It didn't matter. We have no right to judge the people who lived through this horror—it was beyond human comprehension.

Alain refused to have children because of his experience. He couldn't bear the idea of loving his children and then perhaps losing them. Lili couldn't argue with him.

❧

"GOOD NEWS STOP WE ARE PREGNANT STOP MORE LATER STOP LOVE SON," read a telegram sent on September 30, 1940, from my father in Virginia City, Nevada, to my grandparents at 643 Maltman Avenue in Los Angeles.

That same day, my grandfather Jacob left the family's small grocery store in Boyle Heights to buy a bottle of wine. It was time to celebrate. Their first grandchild was going to be born. He crossed the street in a state of distraction, and was hit head-on by a utility truck.

On October 8, 1940, at nine in the morning, at Los Angeles County General Hospital, Jacob died of a basal fracture of the skull and maceration of brain tissue. He never regained consciousness. Seven months later I was born. His death, I have always felt, was my fault.

❧

Violette found herself pregnant in the middle of the war—at the end of her marriage to Gabriel. The idea of rearing a child was unimaginable and impractical.

Before the war, one of Violette's many jobs was selling lace. She remembered that a customer had spoken about a "good" abortionist. Violette approached this woman, who made the necessary arrangements. The abortionist was an unmarried woman who took pride in being so. She was also a midwife.

The woman had Violette lie down on a narrow bed. She placed an orange rubber glove on her right hand. Violette was then subjected to an exam. No explanations. The woman just told her to lie still. A probe was pushed against her uterine wall.

Violette returned to the woman fourteen times to be probed. Nothing happened. The probes cost a lot of money. Violette was becoming worried about the passage of time. Finally, Gabriel, from whom she had just separated, got the name of another abortionist, which he wrote on a piece of paper and slipped under her apartment door.

This one was a female obstetrician. She told Violette to take sulfonamides regularly to induce a miscarriage. Violette was terrified of dying. All she wanted was to be herself again. That night, she went to bed with a warm brick, an orange, and her sulfonamide. She stayed in bed, waiting, for three days. Nothing happened.

And then she did what we all yearn to do at times like these. She went to her mother for solace.

Her mother, for the first time in memory, showed compassion. She put her to bed and made her comfortable. Violette was freezing and refused to take off her eleven pieces of clothing. She was still carrying all her black-market money on her person, in her coat pocket, in an old sock. She refused to take off her coat.

Her mother went for help and returned with a doctor. He ordered an ambulance to take her to a clinic. Violette didn't want to leave her mother. She was starving for Berthe's attention—she had this hunger until the end of her life.

Berthe promised that if Violette went to the clinic she would go with her and sleep on a cot in her room. Violette gave her consent. She arrived at the clinic with a temperature of 103.2. She was ravaged by infection, septicemia, bordering on septic shock—it could be fatal.

It was against the law to have an abortion in France. If Violette admitted to an abortion attempt, the clinic would have had to do anything possible to save the fetus. Then Violette could be arrested and sent to prison. The doctors and lawyers would insist on the name of the obstetrician, and she would be punished too.

Berthe begged Violette not to tell the truth. The doctor prodded her for a confession. She was not a criminal. She was obstinate. She was heroic.

Violette was placed on a gurney and wheeled into the operating room. Her clothes, all eleven pieces, were removed, and she was left lying nude on a metal surface. No one heeded her pleas of being cold. She was ordered to place her legs in rings hanging from the ceiling as if she were a circus act. The rings tortured the skin behind her knees. She was humiliated.

Into her vagina, hard up against the cervix, was packed *Laminaria japonica*. Harvested in Japan, the gnarled but smooth branches attempt to absorb moisture in the vagina and thus dilate the cervix. No matter how flexible these twigs can be, they are never soft enough to forgive already tender tissue.

After this procedure Violette was returned to her room and ordered to begin taking tablets of propydon, a smooth-muscle contractor. Every fifteen minutes, throughout the night, she had to take a pill. She was told she could not sleep, she alone was responsible for staying awake, no one would remind her. Berthe cried that it was inhuman. She said she would spend the night and help Violette. The administration replied there were not enough cots. This was their revenge on Violette's refusal to admit to an abortion attempt and give up the name of the doctor.

Violette kept herself awake by turning the light switch off and on, off and on, off and on. Somewhere in the dark the contractions found her, and it became easier to stay awake. At seven in the morning a nurse examined her. She claimed Violette was holding back the birth. She held her hands over Violette's body and with all her weight came down on her belly. Violette said . . . *the slaughter yard inside me* was finally cleaned out.

But this wasn't the end. Violette's temperature was now 105.7.

She was dying. Within seconds she was taken to the operating theater, where a hysterectomy was performed. It took three weeks for her to recover enough to walk.

"A week after the surgery I went to visit her in the hospital," Lili said. "She was so thin that I shuddered with remembrances from the war. She told me that during the night of the septic abortion she had an awareness that changed her life. She admitted to herself that she wanted to live alone, be alone. She didn't want husbands, and now she couldn't have children, which was fine with her. She forgave herself this understanding. She was alone. *Finally alone.*"

Maurice Sachs berated her in a letter: "You were wrong. A child! You could have given it all the affection you so much need to give. You were being given an opportunity to love. And you rejected it." To Violette, a child grew, a child left you, and that in itself was a tragedy.

❧

When there is the promise of life, we forget death—we forget that dying is just as natural as living. Violette Leduc said that having a child meant *cosseting a life* forever. Lili and Alain Jacobs chose not to have children. They saw too clearly the terror of loving—and then the unimaginable horror of dying.

I lived in America, protected from war, protected from the burdens of want. But the veil of protection was a façade. I wanted a child and was blind to this reality. I was almost twenty-nine years old and had been told I didn't have much time.

So there I lay with an enormous belly—a mountain of stretched skin protecting the unknown, a mountain to conquer, the savage pain—and photographs were being taken of me. One nurse told me one thing, another nurse something else. I was an animal and did only what I intuited, no matter what they said.

And then, in one mysterious moment, the emphasis in my life was irrevocably changed. The camera moved away from the belly and focused on the head of the emerging child. My son's birth was recorded frame by frame. Blood, fetal leavings, moisture soaking the white sheets. Pushing, stopping, pushing again. This time I was taking directions, wanting only to do the right thing. And suddenly, there he was—large, so beautifully formed, not one bit fragile.

But a few days after his birth, I began to worry, and I haven't stopped worrying, twenty-seven years later.

Lili, Alain, and Violette Leduc are correct. This disquiet never ends. I call it daymares, horrific reminders of the delicacy of life. This newborn body was stronger than my faith in life. I had to stand beside myself and offer instructions. In those early days I stood and shrilled at myself. Let him crawl, let him walk, *let him be.* It wasn't easy. I suffered this pain far more than the pain of the birth of a nine-pound baby from a one-hundred-five-pound woman.

The books said to feed my baby every four hours—I nursed whenever he murmured. I don't think he ever touched the ground; he never left my side. I believe in the ways of animals and how they raise their young. I don't believe in how human beings rear children—I have seen few triumphs.

I suffered grief from family, friends, and neighbors. You will spoil him, they said again and again. How do you spoil a new human? I asked. To hell with the lot of you. I held him and rocked him and told him stories. I even sang to him and he loved my singing until he was old enough to discern that my voice was always off-key. "Where did you come from, baby dear? Out of everywhere into the here."

❧

"Alain came home," Lili continued. "When he was liberated, he returned to Paris, to the same apartment where he grew up. It had been cleaned out. The only traces of his life were the unfaded areas on the walls where paintings had hung, scratches on the floor where his father's desk had been, and his mother's examining table in her dispensary, turned on its side. He couldn't stay even one night. He immediately put the apartment up for sale.

"A few weeks before we met again, Alain found a job in a publishing house. He read manuscripts and made recommendations to the publisher. But his real trade was his writing. He was a brilliant writer, who took great risks. He was considered avant-garde, and his following grew over the years. He became a kind of cult figure."

There was great conflict during the war about publishing. Some writers refused to publish during the occupation, claiming they would be contributing to the German cause. Others felt that if they didn't publish during this time they would be contributing to a crime against the human mind.

"You have to understand," Lili said, looking directly into my eyes, "we were prisoners in our own country. I knew if I cooperated in any way with the occupiers, it would appear as though I thought of myself as a free person. I was clear in my position—I was not free. I refused to participate in any form of legal publishing. So along with my voluntary work of moving illegal people through France, I also voluntarily wrote for the Resistance. I just couldn't find a rationale for doing anything approved by the Germans."

When the war was over, a new literary generation was born. This was an exciting time, full of hope and possibilities. For many, the sun was finally emerging from behind the storm clouds.

"Our courtship was short," Lili went on. "After that first meeting, Alain and I never doubted that we were going to spend the rest of our lives together. We were married two months later. There was no time for a honeymoon, there was barely time for an evening alone together! We were both hard at work and loving every moment of it.

"While continuing his reading duties at the publishing company, Alain helped establish a literary magazine. This magazine was published by the company to test new authors, to see how the public responded to them. He complained that he had an easier time finding new works by talented writers than he did getting paper to print it on.

"I was asked to translate a series of American and English mysteries into French. This was a new genre for our country. The more bloody the books were, the better they would sell. Occasionally I would have other free-lance translating jobs."

But life was still difficult in Paris. André Maurois, writing about his return to the city after the war, observed that people spoke about the price of chickens and apartments rather than about literature and art. People had not stopped suffering. "The women in particular are immeasurably exhausted," he wrote—and this was true. Everyone was constantly searching for food. When they found it, they would share it with their friends.

"I prepared many odd stews to feed many people," Lili told me. "Violette often brought us extra food. She, Alain, and I would eat together at least once a week. Violette told stories that had Alain doubled over with laughter. The more wine she had, the funnier she was—and the funnier she was, the more relaxed Alain became. She was a healthy tonic for us.

"One evening in 1945, Violette excitedly told us that Simone de Beauvoir had arranged for her short story 'Le Dézingagé,' to be published in a new review, *Les Temps Modernes.*"

This was a literary magazine named in part for Charlie Chaplin's film and conceived by Sartre as a positive response to the liberation. He felt a deep hunger among the French intelligentsia for an intellectual review. *Les Temps Modernes* encouraged emerging writers and commented on important topics. Its second issue featured another of Violette's stories, "Train Noir." By the time the third issue came along, Violette's name was listed on the masthead alongside those of de Beauvoir, Sartre, and Genet.

De Beauvoir believed so strongly in Violette's talent that she took her first book, *L'Asphyxie*, to Camus, who was editor of the Série Espoir. His aim was to publish books that were risky, but which he felt had tremendous merit. His publisher, Gaston Gallimard, supported him. Violette's book sold only 840 copies, Raymond Queneau's first book only 744, both below the average. Nevertheless, both of these writers continued to write and eventually repaid their editor's belief in their work.

Camus's friends teased him about printing Violette's book as the first in his series. He had named the series Espoir, hope—and *asphyxie* means "suffocation."

Lili paused from her narration, leaned forward and lit another cigarette, then sat back and said, "I know, I know, I smoke too much! Americans! I can't disagree with you, but I love my habits too dearly to worry now, especially at my age." She laughed, then resumed her story. "Even after we moved to this apartment, Violette continued to come often to have dinner with us. These were hard times for her. She was experiencing a serious depression due to the failure of her book."

Nevertheless, she persevered and finished a second book, *L'Affamée*. She completed it while staying in Jean Marais's room at Cocteau's house in Milly-la-Forêt. She couldn't believe she was actually sleeping in a movie star's bedroom.

Plain Jane, you're going to snore in the bed of an idol, Violette wrote. She worried about the *spectacle of an ugly woman . . . wearing a flannelette nightdress.* She worried about putting in her curlers. She sighed for a hot-water bottle.

This book too was strongly championed by de Beauvoir. But Violette was nervous that the previous failure would be repeated. And it was. There was only one review, not bad, in *Les Lettres Françaises.* De Beauvoir said again and again, "Just have confidence. It will all work out."

Violette tried to comprehend the lack of critical attention and sales through her understanding of other artists—artists who were, or had been, considered failures during their lifetimes. Because she saw art through her perceptions of the heart, she had a special rapport with the painter Soutine, experiencing a feeling of intimacy with his images. In her book *Mad in Pursuit* she wrote: *I think of that Russian who understood and could feel the despair of the trees, the convulsions of their branches, the agonized pauses of the dead leaves. He was taken over, he was possessed by the tree's grief and torment, this Russian, when it was being tortured by the hurricane, when its topmost branches were bent down to sweep the earth in which its roots were riveted.*

"Let's have some coffee," Lili said.

We walked down the hall into the kitchen. It was tidier than the one in Saint-Désiré, with more chrome and stark white surfaces. Behind the stove and the sink was the only color in the room— lovely hand-painted tiles with deep-red flowers and bright-green leaves.

"This room is more practical," I said, "compared with the kitchen in Saint-Désiré." I remembered copper pans swinging from the rafters, open shelves of dishes, dried flowers and garlic ropes hanging everywhere.

"It is easier to clean. Paris is grimy," Lili replied. "To me, this is one of the warmest rooms in the apartment. Alain and I liked to cook together, so we built the extra-long counters and twin sinks. This is where we would catch up on the news of the day. Sometimes Alain read his work to me while I prepared the food. I love being read to."

We sat down at the long counter and Lili poured coffee. I served the lovely *tarte aux prunes* I had brought from La Mère de Famille on the Rue du Faubourg-Montmartre.

"I'm interested in Violette's friend Genet," I said. "They were both outlaws!"

Lili laughed. "You are right! But Genet was a real one, having spent years in prison. Violette was only a minor criminal. She once was caught shoplifting and released with a warning. In France, both of them were referred to as *'passéistes.'* This doesn't really translate—it's someone who is not consistent with contemporary life, one who doesn't follow the rules."

Violette and Genet always seemed to be balanced on the edge of disaster. They tempted and maligned the establishment. They enjoyed being outlandish and on the margin of society. They both wrote of solitude, of their sad, singular isolation. And they knew they would continue to be outsiders because of their unfortunate childhoods.

Neither of them cared to construct a coherent book of narrative writing. They were more interested in salvation through their work, not in traditional composition.

Their love lives weren't coherent either. They were either bisexual or homosexual, depending on who is telling the story. Violette's love affairs, in her most intimate descriptions, flow with the smell of flowers and shimmering rivers of passion. Genet's descriptions are rough, tough, with a proprietary posture, erected on concrete, smelling of excrement and sweat. The sexual realities of these two were distinctly different.

While Genet exposed himself to the degradation of accepting evil, at the same time he reached for redemption in his writing. He may well have found it. But Violette had a more difficult problem. Outcast women were not acceptable—there were no schools for outlaw women writers, as there were for men. Her preposterous view of the world exiled her. Violette may be the first woman to write in the absurdist tradition. She was stubborn in her writing, without reason or mannerism. She was proud of being logically contradictory.

Violette met Genet on an autumn evening in 1946 at the Bar du

Pont-Royal. She was wearing her tattered rabbit coat. They fought almost immediately.

You're late, Genet said reproachfully.

I'm not late! replied Violette.

Sartre wrote of Genet in his book *Saint Genet:* "He hates matter. Excluded he looks at the goods of this world through a pane of glass, like poor children looking at cakes through a shop window. . . . It is as a refugee that he settles in literature. He dislikes things but relishes the words that represent them; hates flowers but loves their names."

Genêt is a flower, broom—a large yellow flower that sits on angular branches. These branches are often made into brooms. Genet would rather be the tool broom than the flower broom—because he was coarse rather than soft. He wanted nothing pretty, a dingy hotel room was fine.

"The only time Violette saw Genet indulge in something delicate," Lili said, "was when he used an Elizabeth Arden face cream after shaving. She was amused. Otherwise, he lived in squalor and chaos in his room at the Hôtel de la Fleur-de-Lis."

Until he was an adult, Genet had no idea who his mother was—his father was never positively identified. He was born in 1910 and immediately abandoned to the Assistance Publique. By the age of ten he was sent to his first reform school, after being caught stealing. For the next thirty years he lived in some of that harshest prisons of France. He was arrested for begging, smuggling, stealing, and prostitution. *Genet was like my mother,* Violette said. *They will neither of them forgive others for their childhoods.* Genet's salvation was to write.

"At the Institut du Monde Arabe," I said, "I saw an exhibit about Genet. What I remember most was a tiny handmade notebook, no bigger than one and a half by two inches. He made the notebook from the paper he stole in prison—it was given to the prisoners for making sacks. On this paper he wrote *Our Lady of the Flowers.*"

"Yes," Lili said, "and eventually he was pardoned from serving a life sentence for robbery. This was due to the efforts of many of France's most famous writers. They recognized his genius and took a very strong position."

Violette was fascinated by Genet. He had the three major ingredients necessary for her adoration: he was a homosexual, he had had a ghastly childhood, and he was a brilliant writer. She said, *I see him so sad and fragile. I can open Genet everywhere. The griefs and agonies in Genet are my litanies.*

And here lies the biggest difference between the two. Violette employs her art, her writing, to seek understanding and forgiveness. Even though she was yearning to exact revenge for her wretched childhood, she was also attempting to integrate her life, to give herself a reason for living. But Genet's attempts at comprehending himself are crowded with fury—it is hard for us to find the redemption in his work.

Genet was occasionally kind to Violette," Lili said. "More often, he was like her mother—not wanting her around, tired of her neediness, bored with her repetitions, and yet attracted to her brilliance. Genet and Violette had a tumultuous relationship that continued for a number of years—on again, off again."

On again: Violette invited him to dinner. Off again: Genet was infuriated with her fawning during dinner and . . . *rose from the table, pulling the tablecloth toward him.*

"Come on," he said to his lover, Lucien, *"we're fucking off."*

They left the flat at a run, amid the muffled noise of bottles rolling on the floor, the cracking sound of breaking plates, and the frivolous shattering of glass.

Violette followed Genet to his hotel, and unashamedly fell to her knees and begged his forgiveness!

"Is it over now?" Violette asked him.

"Yes, it's all over," Genet said.

Genet invited Violette to the opening of his play *Les Bonnes, The Maids.* Later, he asked her if she liked it. She said nothing.

"I want to talk about Les Bonnes," he said.

". . . Very well. Since you wish it, we'll talk about Les Bonnes. *No, I don't like* Les Bonnes, *I don't like the production. . . ."*

"I don't want to hear about the production. Tell me what you think of Les Bonnes."

Violette threw herself back onto the divan.

She told him: *"I prefer your books."* She waited.

"Go on," Genet said.

Violette flung discretion into the river. *"Does one expect Racine to write poems by Rimbaud? Does one expect Rimbaud to write Racine plays?"*

She stood up. Genet shoved her back down on the divan and stormed out the door.

The next time Violette saw him on the street, he shouted *"Fuck off!"* at her without breaking his stride. Off again.

"Simone," Lili said, "once remarked that Violette 'turned her life into the raw material of her works, and that gave her life meaning.' This, she and Genet shared."

The telephone rang and Lili excused herself.

I heard her speaking to someone about an appointment at her publisher's. It was time for me to leave.

When she returned, I said, "I think we should stop here. You seem tired."

"Yes," she said, "and I have some work to do."

"Could I take you to dinner on Sunday?"

"I'm so sorry, but I have an engagement. Let me arrange my schedule and I will ring you."

We walked to the foyer, where I got my coat and said goodbye.

"Lili, I have so many more questions to ask. I'm afraid we won't have enough time."

"Don't worry," she replied, "we will figure something out."

· XVI ·

When I returned to my hotel there was a message from Lili, asking me to meet her at eight-thirty that same evening at the café on the corner of the Rue Racine and the Rue Corneille. I was relieved to get the call.

What a funny little café it was. There were three tiers of people. The first tier sat on the street, with the tiniest possible tables—barely large enough to hold two cups and the ever present ashtray. The next tier was two steps inside the café, and the third was like a balcony floating above the other two, as if suspended in the air. Lili was waiting up there. I could see her from across the street.

When I approached her my heart caught a beat. Something was wrong. "Lili, are you okay? You look pale."

"I'm not sure, I don't feel that well. Let's talk for a little while and see how I do."

I sat down and we ordered tea.

"Nineteen forty-seven was a momentous year for Violette," Lili said quietly, "so I thought we could start there. In that year, Violette was still living off her profits from the black market. After being estranged for years, Gabriel finally asked her for a divorce. And even though they agreed, she blamed herself. She called herself *a forty-year-old beaked and ancient monkey.* She suffered pangs of remorse and bouts of self-doubt. She trailed Gabriel to sneak a look at his fiancée."

Around the same time, Genet convinced his friend Jacques Guerlain to read *L'Asphyxie.* He told Guerlain, "She's crazy, ugly, mean, and poor, but she has a lot of talent." Then Genet introduced Violette to Guerlain, and another important devotee was added to her circle.

Violette would meet with Genet almost every Wednesday at the home of Guerlain. Genet would read his new work aloud to Violette. This was a serious time for speaking about writing and language. They were both skillful at their art and had passionate discussions.

Yet Genet could be deeply cruel. He used Violette as a finely tuned ear. For years she listened. Later, after both Violette and Genet were dead, Guerlain was interviewed about the two writers and their relationship. He said Genet had told him, "A woman who writes, to me, is an insufferable zero."

Guerlain, like Genet a homosexual, was the scion of the famous perfume-making family. In 1955, he privately published an elegant edition of Violette's third book, *Ravages.* Later, he helped her financially, going so far as to give her large amounts of cash and helping furnish her apartment. Violette loved Guerlain passionately—in her usual perverse fashion—and this desperate and impossible love lasted until the end of her life.

1947. Excerpts from *L'Affamée* were published in *Les Temps Modernes.*

"Every other week, usually on Thursdays, at two in the afternoon, like clockwork," Lili said, "Simone would ask Violette the eternal question: 'Are you working?' It had become their custom to meet at the Café de Flore or go somewhere special for dinner. During these meetings, Violette would experience terrible anxieties after hearing Simone's suggestions for changes in her writing. Yet two weeks later, Violette would be impatiently waiting for Simone to read, discuss, and edit her work.

"One time, Violette was no more than two or three minutes late for lunch and was greeted by a furious de Beauvoir. 'Violette, do you realize that it is past two!' Violette was too eager for approval—she begged Simone for forgiveness.

"Genet would ask Violette every time upon meeting her, 'How are things?' This would create a similar anxiety. At first she would reply, 'What do you mean?' and Genet would look at her with 'that look.' She finally understood that he meant, 'Are you working?'"

Around this time Violette was invited onto the editorial board of *Les Temps Modernes,* but she refused to go to the meetings.

I wouldn't open my mouth if I did, she said. *I don't know how to argue. I should be a gaping carp.* She was easily embarrassed in front of de Beauvoir.

"Simone was Violette's lifeline," Lili said. "She held Violette's hand in the way Berthe never did. This gesture gave Violette hope, which in her world was often missing.

"We were all beginning to feel hopeful again in those days. Grapefruit appeared for the first time since 1939, although it cost an ordinary working person four days' wages. 'Renaissance Française' was stamped inside the newly made underwear appearing on the shelves in our shops—though we were rationed to only one pair per person.

"In June, Alain and I took Violette to the Opéra-Comique's *Les Mamelles de Tirésias.* It was described as a 'superrealist drama by Apollinaire.' We were captivated and delighted. We thought it was a comedy! We were delighted to be given complimentary tickets—the prices were terribly expensive."

As Lili was speaking, I happened to look downstairs to the main floor of the café. "Lili, excuse me, who is that woman with the three men?" I asked. "Everyone is staring at them."

"It is Marguerite Duras, with her usual entourage. She is as famous in Paris as movie stars are in Hollywood.

"In 1948, daily life in France changed," Lili resumed. "This was the last year of German prisoner-of-war farm help. Finally there were more jobs for the French. Wine was no longer rationed, but we couldn't get it—the Germans had taken it all. What was newly made, or found on the black market, was called baptismal wine—water had been added to make it go further. Food was still scarce."

Sartre wrote, in an issue of *Le Gauche,* "Hunger is already a demand for liberty." The Eiffel Tower was lit for the first time since the beginning of the war, and tourism, especially of American visitors, increased.

L'Affamée was published, and even though it was critically acclaimed, it did not sell.

"Violette was on a psychological descent," Lili said. "I remember speaking to Alain about her health. She was slipping into a half-sane state of paranoia. She would roll into one mood and slowly, almost imperceptibly, curl into another. This went on for some time. There was a brief respite when she called us, very excited, to say that Gallimard was giving her a monthly stipend.

I shall receive, from now on, a monthly allowance of 20,000 francs; I shall be able to write in peace. . . . I imprinted a long kiss on Simone de Beauvoir's wide brow in the Cartier-Bresson photograph. I owe her my monthly payments, I owe her everything.

"I've read conflicting reports about this money," I said. "One biography says that the money came from de Beauvoir, another says it came from Sartre."

"The money was given anonymously by Sartre, although it was arranged by Simone," Lili answered. "They decided to tell Violette that it had come from her publisher. She learned the truth in 1950, when Genet spitefully revealed the source."

"Did Sartre like Violette?" I asked.

"Sartre did not really know her. I understood he liked her work, and we all know he respected de Beauvoir's opinions."

Maybe, I wondered, he felt a connection to Violette because of her homeliness. He once wrote, "The mirror had told me what I always had known: I was horribly ordinary."

Violette's relationship with de Beauvoir became more intense. De Beauvoir was romantically involved with Nelson Algren. She was spending more and more time away from Paris, from Sartre, and from Violette. When de Beauvoir told Violette about an up-coming six-month trip to America, Violette threw herself in front of a truck and barely escaped being hurt. Her intentions were probably more theatrical than suicidal.

She said about de Beauvoir, *Without her, I wouldn't be able to find my way. Without her, I would never find my stride. She has the sense of form that I lack.*

Lili didn't look better, even after her tonic of hot tea. "Maybe we should stop here," I said.

"No, no, another cup of tea will help."

I ordered.

"In 1949, France was well on its way to recovery," Lili continued. "But that summer was especially difficult because of a severe drought that continued into October—each day was so dry that it broke apart like old newspapers. And unbelievable as it may seem, France was at war again, this time in Indochina."

1949. The fourth year of Violette and de Beauvoir's meetings. Violette brought her flowers to celebrate. And they spoke enthusi-astically about another writer of autobiography, Colette, who had been appointed the first woman president of the Académie Goncourt.

Violette wrote in 1964: *I very much liked Colette, who was a good writer and very wise. But in reading her, I had the feeling that she had not dared, that she withheld things. . . . As for me, I am going to dare.* Violette was referring to the fact that Colette never wrote about her lover, Missy. Violette, however, wrote about her female lovers freely.

Violette felt secure in her history of loving women. When she was a young student there was the schoolgirl romance with Isa-belle, consuming in its intensity and drama. They were found mak-ing love in a dormitory bed by the boarding school matron, and Violette's mother was told. Berthe removed her from the school, and Violette never saw Isabelle again. Before she was thirty, she had already been in a long and passionate relationship with Her-mine, called Thérèse in her books.

Hermine was Violette's friend in Paris. They were together until Violette met Gabriel. She wrote about her women lovers with sensitivity, with love—they understood her. Most important, they understood her embarrassment about her looks—her looks didn't bother them.

Violette liked men, but between her looks and the fear that her mother had instilled, she was convinced that men were not interested in her. She was petrified of being rejected. So she often dressed in severely tailored men's suits with elegant ties, spit-polished shoes, and a fedora tilting to one side of her head. She carried a man's suave posture well on her long, slender body.

To Violette, sexuality was an embrace of her life. First she chose women, then she chose men, finally she chose to be alone. Her looks and her sexuality were a confused bag of words. Sometimes she pulled out a positive adjective, other times she came up with a negative noun. Her life was a spin of choices—one day this, another day that. By the time Lili met her, she had abandoned the romance of loving women and had been married and separated from her husband.

"But I think her confusion about her sexuality," Lili said, "was only one of the many reasons that Violette's world was disintegrating. She was seeing enemies around every corner. They were crowding into her days, pushing her to the periphery. Paranoia had become manifest."

I am broken on a wall, I am a zig-zagging chalk line of pain. Paris, you are too big. I have to escape your walls, I am a pink spider swinging on a pink thread.

"Violette wandered deeper into illness. Many times when she visited us on the Rue du Temple, she would dissolve in front of our eyes. She was a woman haunted by passion, possessive of her friends, intolerant of the mundane, begging for sympathy, self-deprecating about her looks, and perpetually in tears. Alain and I were always exhausted by the time she left. Sometimes she stayed overnight, when her feelings of persecution were too intense for us to let her go home alone. We tried to help by encouraging her to talk, by suggesting a psychiatrist, by telling her to rest."

She resisted. Her moments of lucidity were spent in preparing for her hours of mental illness. She would clean her house, visit her friends, write, and write some more. Then the tethers of her sanity would come untied, and she would start to drown. Nevertheless, when she returned to shore, her house would be clean, her friends would continue to check on her, and a few more pages would be written.

Things I cannot understand always fascinate me. She had a deeply wholesome sense of survival, and it astonished everyone she knew.

Sometimes when she felt herself sliding she would travel, embarking on each adventure with great determination. In 1950 she took a three-month journey to the Loire region, where she wrote about the local people. She enjoyed the traveling but she was lonely. She wrestled with despair. She often wrote to de Beauvoir, in care of Nelson Algren. She missed her meetings with Simone—they had helped keep her feet on the ground.

When she returned from the Loire, she began to shadow de Beauvoir, who had also just returned to Paris. De Beauvoir would find her standing across the street from her apartment building—gazing at her front door. Violette took to writing her almost daily, declaring her love, and her sexual attraction. This was too much for de Beauvoir to bear. She said no emphatically, without the slightest opening. Violette apologized.

"There was nothing Alain and I could do," Lili said. "Alain spent hours with her. She would agree to seek help and then do nothing. With Alain, she would wallow through a litany of her life, only to end with something disarmingly funny about an event or a person she had observed. Her saving grace was her humor, her self-mockery. She would terrify us with her pathology and confuse us with her clarity.

"In the spring, Violette told us that she had made a will, leaving de Beauvoir as her sole heir. She had decided to kill herself, she told de Beauvoir, again. But again, in her inimical way, she sidetracked herself into another misadventure.

"I don't know how this happened, but Genet talked her into making a movie, a movie in which Genet played her baby, in a baby carriage. When I saw it, I was deeply embarrassed. There was Violette, the mother, pushing Genet, the son, who was dressed like an infant, and he was whipping her. The unconscious behavior I was watching, and later to hear her talk about it—it was astounding.

"Alain was angry with her for putting herself in that position. She was ashamed. She told Alain that when she saw the film, *I see a madwoman obviously just escaped from an asylum, a nut, a hag with*

Saint Vitus's dance. . . . Why didn't they stop me from plunging head-long into such idiocy, such absurdity?"

De Beauvoir had written about herself, through a fictional character, that she was "trying to compensate for the absence of God by an intense interest in herself." But it was quite different for Violette—God *was* de Beauvoir. And this makes sense when you consider that she was the only person who Violette thought did not "openly" judge her or her work.

But Violette was wrong. De Beauvoir often recited a range of unpleasant descriptions about her—calling her the "ugly woman" and maligning her writing whenever she was in the mood, depending on whom she was trying to impress. After many years, de Beauvoir finally stopped.

"At least, when Simone didn't like Violette's work, she suffered for how she was going to tell Violette. No one in Violette's life had ever bothered to give her this kind of attention. So Violette worshipped Simone as God, and launched her into the heavens with her adoration. She even prayed to her. Violette once wrote about Simone, *I have just dropped God off on the corner.*"

When she needed to leave herself, to move away from her earthly and painful existence, to escape people, she would sit *in my skin, in my kingdom of white clouds, in my armchair of dove's downs. I gazed down and listened to them.*

Violette also worshipped André Gide. She read his works when she was a girl, and often signed her letters "With Sympathetic Interest," just as Gide did. To her, Gide was the god of literature. He introduced her to the concept of pilgrimage. He showed her promise in the world, his world. She had the intelligence to cross over the difficult terrain and carry on. She became an explorer in the unknown.

In 1951, Violette left on a pilgrimage, hiking around the south of France. She wrote a journal during this time, *Trésors à Prendre,* that de Beauvoir thought awful. Actually, it is a very fine book. It tells of her journey to numerous religious sites, including Albi.

It is because of Violette Leduc's beautiful description that Joe and I went to Albi. Driving from Toulouse in heavy rain, on strange new roads, we wandered in the footsteps of Violette Leduc, who, in turn, had wandered in the footsteps of Simone de Beauvoir. Up along the red-banked Tarn, we wound our way toward the birthplace of Toulouse-Lautrec. The roads reflected the yellow headlights of passing motorists onto our faces, and that was a problem. I don't see well at night, and my husband has only one eye that works.

We found the old part of the town, then dropped our bags at a small inn and had dinner. The next morning, after breakfast, we walked outdoors into the startling red of Albi. The cathedral was beautiful, standing tall against the sky. I had expected it to be cold and forbidding.

I was so used to the traditional French gray-stone principalities that the red of Albi felt like another world. We walked along the old streets until we reached the cathedral, the center of the Albigenses, stronghold of the heretics of the Albigensian Crusade.

The Albigenses were Manichaeans. They believed in the principles of good and evil, represented by God and the Evil One, by light and darkness, by the soul and the body, by this life and the next, by peace and war.

I could see why Violette Leduc was fascinated with Albi. When she walked into the cathedral, she wrote, *I did not seek God in these walls. I found a thousand bricklayers raising the earth that they built. . . . The color is that of a violent/fiery rose, it is the color of the faith that we hold in our hands, bricks. . . . I am crushed by the citadel of these efforts.*

She also found something we didn't. She found the woman who made clothing for Toulouse-Lautrec's mother. The woman told Violette that she remembered making an onion-peel-colored dress for Mme. Lautrec.

Ce n'est pas possible. You are too young. You cannot have known the mother of Toulouse-Lautrec, said Violette.

She was wrong.

Lili had become silent. She looked pale, as if she were going to faint. I was frightened.

"I'm taking you home, Lili. This is enough."

She nodded. I asked for the check. Something was wrong. I came around to help her, and as I took her arm, she slumped forward onto the table. All my first-aid knowledge abandoned me, and not knowing the language well enough hindered me, but at least my anxiety propelled me—I cried for help. The waiter ran to the telephone. I loosened the scarf from around Lili's neck, picked her up, and eased her to the floor. She was ashen and her pulse was quiet, but there.

The Service d'Aide Médicale arrived, and without my quite knowing how, I was sitting in the back of an ambulance holding Lili's purse. I asked that she be taken to the American Hospital in Neuilly-sur-Seine. When we arrived, she was swept into the emergency room and I was asked to wait in the lobby.

Suddenly my shoulder was being roughly shaken. I wasn't sure if I was still asleep—I wasn't sure where I was. The green-clad person with the long green arm blended into the green walls. The sun was glaring into my eyes; it was morning.

"Madame," the green person said in English.

Sitting up, I answered, "Yes, how is Madame Jacobs?"

"She was moved out of intensive care two hours ago. She had a difficult night but the danger has passed. At first we thought she had had heart attack. But now it is apparent she has a rampant *grippe*. Because of her age, a *grippe* such as this one can be very dangerous. If you like, you may see her now." Then the green-suited man turned and I followed him.

We walked a long way and finally reached her room. I didn't recognize her. Her face was without makeup, her hair was awry, her thin arms were stretched out at either side of her body. She looked her age and more. There is nothing that frightens me more than seeing a face hovering between sleep and death. Lili opened her eyes and smiled, and I smiled back in relief.

"The hospital has been trying to reach my niece and nephew, but neither can be found. There is a problem. I will need someone to look after me, at least until a member of my family can be contacted. I hate to ask you, but could you come and stay with me for a few days? At least it will give us time to finish this business. Could you manage this?"

"It will be no problem at all," I said. "I'm happy to help you."

Arrangements were made, and the next day I moved into the guest room—the room, Lili told me, where Violette Leduc stayed when she was ill. It was a simple room, a lovely room, with a dormer window facing east toward a Parisian cityscape of chimney pots, steeples, and garrets. It was pretty, like my room at Saint-Désiré—only looking out upon a small cobbled street instead of a seasonal garden. The following morning I bought fresh bread and blood oranges, then took a taxi to fetch Lili in Neuilly.

She was waiting for me in the hospital lobby in a wheelchair. She looked better, but I couldn't tell if she was wearing makeup—not without staring at her. When I helped her into the taxi, it was clear that she was still quite weak. I marveled at how quickly she had been released. We arrived at the apartment and Lili went to bed.

My first evening in her apartment I made a pot of fresh chicken soup. I was delighted to cure Lili in my own Jewish tradition. We ate together in her bedroom and then she slept until early the next afternoon. I worked at a small table in her study, gathering my notes into some semblance of order. When she woke up we ate, and this time had a glass of wine.

"Do you want to talk?" Lili asked.

"Absolutely not, you must sleep."

"But I'm not tired," she replied, and laughed. "Get out your tape recorder and we'll do just a little bit. I promise to tell you when I've had enough. Let's talk about death. What day is it?"

"It's the twentieth of February," I answered, setting up the recorder. "Why do you want to talk about death now! Let's not. . . ."

"But I missed Gide's death day! I remember, the nineteenth of February 1951, when Gide died, it was just a few days before Violette left on her journey for the south of France. He was eighty-one and aware of his approaching death, and he said, 'If anyone asks me a question, make sure I am conscious before you let me reply.'

"Gide died during a mercurial winter—downpours, tempests, winds, and then sun, all within an hour's time, and many times a day. He died several months before the celebration of the *bimillé-naire*, which he surely would have enjoyed. Paris was two thousand years old on the eighth of July.

"Violette had left before the celebration too, to begin her pilgrimage. Alain and I usually departed for Saint-Désiré on the first of July and didn't return to Paris until the end of August. That year we stayed some extra days to participate in the festivities. We were particularly interested in hearing a concert at the Louvre. We had been involved in helping to organize this event. It rained, it rained without relenting, and the concert was canceled. We were terribly disappointed.

"I was worried about Violette. She had set off on this journey with very little money and only one change of clothes. She had told me she was determined to make this pilgrimage as a mystic seeking the truth. She wanted to discover the fields of van Gogh with the same hardship that he had endured. She wanted to find the cafés where he had stopped, and travel the same dark passageways."

I had eaten and drunk God when I read that Vincent van Gogh once qualified the smell of turpentine as mystic. That adjective has stayed in my bloodstream. Violette was praying for deliverance from an affliction similar to van Gogh's. She was racing to keep one step ahead of her madness.

So she lay at night in farmer's huts or on the ground under trees. She ate with the peasants, sharing her food and washing her clothes in the rivers alongside the people. She experienced visions of heaven laced with the fluttering wings of angels, and she crawled along paths on her knees, praying for relief from her tormentors. She had the innate sense that all pilgrimages are roundtrips. She knew that her return home would be as important as her devotions on the road.

❧

I believe the very act of pilgrimage acknowledges a universal desire for direction in both our external and our internal worlds. Formerly it was a search for God. Now it is a search for self. Today, we are taught that we may find God only through the search for self. Until this century, God certainly came first.

Joe calls my pilgrimages "walkabouts." He says that I remind him of an aborigine who occasionally needs to wander the bush to visit new places and old dreams. The aborigines leave mementos of their lives in the places they visit. I leave photos of my family hidden in crevices. I place poems under rocks. I offer the hair from my hairbrush to the birds for their nests. I mark my place on the earth. From my journeys are born the materials for my work as an artist.

I was once invited to travel to the Sinai. I had no idea what I was getting myself into. I brought a backpack, dehydrated food, vitamins, two changes of clothes, and too many books.

My friend Danny was interviewing the Jebalayeh, a group of Bedouins who have lived in the area of the Saint Catherine Monastery since the sixth century. Before leaving Tel Aviv, we bought chocolate and brandy to give as gifts. I was surprised—I thought Muslims didn't drink alcohol. Danny and his girlfriend, who was going with us, looked at me and grinned slyly.

When we reached the border, the Egyptian guards were implacable. We had to pay them off. It was December, cold, as we stood by the roadside with our thumbs out.

Eventually, a large jeep stopped and the driver gave us a ride down the main highway to Nuweiba at the mouth of the Wadi Wattir. We decided to sleep on the beach. I was exhausted from jet lag and shy with my traveling companions. So I ate some fruit and drank a large amount of brandy, then took myself and my sleeping bag out onto the sand.

I lay down under a palm tree, beside the Gulf of Aqaba, and listened to the sounds of the sea from Sharm Dabba, Saudi Arabia, just across the way. That night I tried to sleep, torn between anxiety and excitement. I thought about the Rousseau painting of the sleeping man with the mandolin—the beautiful starry night sharing the space above his head, a lion by his side.

The next morning we left early for the monastery, cutting across the yellow-sanded desert punctuated by tamarisks. This was the Wadi Zaghra road, and again we were hitching our way. We arrived at the guesthouse outside the monastery wall. The structure was built out of rock, with two guest rooms and one bathroom, sort of. The rooms had rows of three-tiered bunk beds covered with questionable mattresses. I wandered outside to watch the sacred mountain. Here I was, in the valley of my ancestors, feeling very little relevance. This troubled me.

Danny left to find his Bedouin friends. He had been told that

VIOLETTE'S EMBRACE

the Egyptian police required all visitors to register with their office and did not allow hiking into the mountains. Because he was already known to the police as a mischief-maker, Danny hid while we registered—leaving our passports and two permits each at the police station. One was a visitor's permit to enter the monastery area, issued by the Joint Egypt–Israel Commission; the other was a foreigner's temporary permit, issued by the Passport and Immigration Department of the Arab Republic of Egypt. These documents were the police's ransom.

Danny stayed well hidden. He was in the Sinai to complete a project he had begun while he was living there—before the Israelis returned the region to the Egyptians. Now that the Egyptians were in residence again, they were very serious about controlling their territory. They didn't want "foreigners" writing about their people. They wanted Egyptians writing about Egyptians.

Danny's unfinished project was to record folklore and myths of the Jebalayah before they were invaded by the contemporary world. This oral tradition was the only avenue of historical education for these people until the middle of the twentieth century. Now it was in jeopardy. Danny wanted to see an old friend, a native folklorist named Mahmoud, who was intent on keeping this tradition alive. But he had alienated the authorities as well. Mahmoud was known as a troublemaker, and they tried to keep him in the corner of their vision.

We stayed quiet in our room until nightfall. When it was dark, Danny told us to follow him without making a sound. We slunk around buildings and boulders, using the moon as our flashlight, until we came upon Mahmoud waiting for us in the shadows. This darkness was comforting to me. I was ashamed that my face didn't reflect the awe of being at the foot of Mount Sinai.

Mahmoud was a handsome man. He was dressed in the traditional Bedouin djellaba, a tweed sportsjacket with elbow patches, and plastic sandals. He spoke both Arabic and Hebrew, since his school years had coincided with Israel's occupation of the Sinai. He told Danny that we had to stay clear of certain patrolled areas. Later I realized that one of the villages tucked into the mountains was the drug capital of the Sinai, dealing primarily in hashish. The tenets of Mohammed were softly bent in the desert. The men smoked hashish at night, around the fires, while drinking brandy.

In the morning, before light, we slipped out of the guesthouse. Along with a camel, the camel driver, and Mahmoud, we headed up the mountain alongside the Wadi Nasb to Nawamis, where we camped. Everyone breathed a sigh of relief—we were now past the most serious patrols.

This stretch of the Sinai can be warm during the day, yet very cold at night. For some reason I couldn't sleep. Each evening I took my fancy feathered sleeping bag and set off by myself. I enjoyed the solitude, I needed it. I read by flashlight. One night I was glancing through my notebook and came across a quote from Violette that I had copied down. *Why not invent God, since one invents prayers?* I had never understood what she meant until that evening. I realized that I had been assuming that once I was on this holy land I would feel the way I had read about other people's feelings! Not so. I was still just as confused as I had been before. But inventing God interested me.

Early the next day Mahmoud happened to walk by while I was sitting in the sun. He greeted me, then suddenly stopped, standing stock still. After a moment, during which I instinctively froze too, he turned toward me with an apprehensive look on his face. Then he smiled and pointed about twenty feet away. The high grass was matted down to the earth, and when I got up to see where he was pointing, I saw spoor. He said, *"Nimmr,"* in Arabic, and gestured for me to come closer. Up behind us came Danny, and the two of them spoke excitedly in Arabic. Finally Danny explained that I had just spent the night with a leopard, and maybe her cub.

I liked this fact, much to everyone's confusion.

We left the site and trekked farther into the mountains. We stopped whenever we came upon a man. We never saw a woman. Danny, who seemed to know everyone, would simply sit on the ground and begin an interview. His questions concerned all aspects of Jebalayah life. He jotted down notes in a little black notebook filled with his tiny handwriting. Danny's notebook reminded me of Bedouin weaving—the upswing of lines slanting toward the end of the page and then back again.

Every time we stopped, even if we had been walking for only fifteen minutes, a small fire was built and tea was made. Tea. No, tea-flavored sugar! One-half sugar, one-half tea, far too sweet for me. My companions teased me for drinking tea without sugar. At mealtimes I gave away my dehydrated food to anyone who wanted it. I preferred the rice and pita bread. The pita bread was baked on hot rocks and sprinkled with thick crystals of salt. It was the most delicious food I have eaten.

One day we came upon two men harvesting olives. They shook the olives from the trees and picked them off the ground. Then they transferred them to goat-skin sacks which were closed with leather cords. Ibrahim, Mahmoud's uncle, told me that the olives stayed in the goat-skin sacks for forty days, after which they were washed and poured into other skins, but this time with spices. He offered me some cured olives—they were unique, perhaps *tart* is the word.

Ibrahim and I became immediate friends. He proudly showed me his summer lodge, or *khuss'ishshe,* stocked with dried fish, fruits, and vegetables. The lodge was like a large basket of food, with muted colors hanging from the rafters, spread upon the floor, strung across the room. Ibrahim was fascinated by my vitamins. I showed him how a vitamin A tablet was meant to be like his dried apricots, a vitamin E like his fish.

We swapped. I gave him all my vitamins for a bag of his dried apricots. I got the better end of the bargain. Ibrahim showed me how to cut the taste of too much sugar or too many dates by eating sorrel and allowing it to float in my mouth.

When friends of mine went to the Sinai two years later, I sent more vitamins for Ibrahim.

The evening after I slept with a leopard, we came upon another summer *khuss'ishshe.* Mahmoud insisted that I take his spot inside the hut to sleep. I reluctantly refused, but he ignored me. I watched while he dug a hole in the floor of the hut about three inches deep and the length and width of my sleeping bag. He filled the pit with small pebbles and placed dried sage on top. Then he set fire to the sage. He continued to add sage until the pebbles were red-hot. Then he covered the area with dirt and spread my sleeping bag on top. I climbed in, he handed me a hashish pipe, and soon I fell asleep—for the entire night.

Late the next day I noticed Danny looking at me quizzically and realized that I was mumbling prayers. I sheepishly smiled and walked away from the camp, and sat down on a rock. His catching me edged me into an understanding. I realized that by placing myself in this new situation, I had made myself vulnerable. And from this vulnerability would emerge new questions and, I hoped, new answers.

I had heard about a very old *hakîm*, a healer and wise man, who lived nearby. His name was Salah Salim. It was arranged, after we paid the police twenty-five American dollars, for us to visit him. We drove in a pickup truck owned by Salim's nephew. The truck reminded me of the low-riders in Los Angeles and Espanola, New Mexico. The windshield was hung with fringes of colored cotton balls, interspersed with amulets and a small plastic doll. The dashboard was a platform for the nephew's collection of religious artifacts. I felt right at home.

We arrived at the *hakîm*'s isolated *bayt*, whose yard was overrun with junk. Salah Salim was a kindly man. He wore a djellaba and a cable-knit sweater closed with gigantic safety pins. His white turban was wrapped over a ski cap that framed his face. He was genuinely gracious.

After the ritual tea serving, he announced that it was time for his prayers. He allowed me to photograph the stages of preparation. First he poured water from a large can labeled "Butter Oil" into the palms of his hands. Then he proceeded to wash his face, especially his eyes, ears, and nose. Last he poured more water into a large metal coffeepot and washed his feet and hands, and wiped them with a white rag. At this point I turned away, not wanting to intrude upon his actual praying.

After fifteen minutes he was finished. He asked Danny if anyone in our group was having medical problems. Danny's girlfriend said that her knee, which had been injured in an automobile accident, was bothering her.

The *hakîm* pulled up his djellaba and then his long underwear to show us his leg. It was an astonishing white next to his dark and grimy hands. He demonstrated to us what he was going to do, by touching here and there on his leg. We thought he would manipulate certain pressure points and marveled at how much he knew about Chinese medicine.

With great trepidation, Danny's girlfriend placed her knee in front of *hakîm*. He proceeded to fish around in the surrounding junk and happily produced a needle. Then he performed Islamic acupuncture. We were convinced she would get deadly tetanus from the needle. Instead, she later wrote to me, her knee has never bothered her again.

The last evening was spent trying to sleep on straw mattresses that didn't keep away the cold. I awoke at three in the morning, ill with the flu. It was no use—I was lying there with the chills one minute and flames the next. So I got up and packed and went to wait for the bus. The bus arrived at four and took me across the Sinai Desert, through Wadi Firan to Cairo, away from my friends.

· XVII ·

Lili asked me to make tea.

"There was a serious flu epidemic in Paris in 1953," she said. "We named it *la grippe*. There was a constant blanket of fog wrapping around Paris. I remember thinking it would never lift, that I would never see the sun again."

Nineteen fifty-three was the year of Colette's eightieth birthday. France was in a frenzy of celebration. The week of her birthday, January 28, the newspapers, magazines, and literary weeklies were competing in seeing who could outdo whom in reverence. Old letters were published from Proust and Gide and other dead writers, as well as new letters from living ones, applauding France's most famous literary figure. Meanwhile, Colette sat in her apartment in the Palais Royal and worked—writing more, racing the running down of her earth-time.

In 1954, on Palm Sunday in Monaco, Colette, tired but still charming, said to André Maurois, "At my age pleasure consists in not working." She died in August, after taking a sip of champagne.

That same year, Violette's book *Ravages* was censored by the readers at Gallimard. They tore its heart out—they gutted it, cut it to shreds. The male establishment was frightened and shocked by its intimate portrait of a love affair between two women. Violette's fictional passages about Thérèse and Isabelle move like a dream. They are not cruel, or mean, nor is one person dominant.

It is interesting to note the resemblance between Flaubert and Leduc. They both took chances with beautiful, sexual language.

Flaubert stood trial for "outrage to public and religious morals and to morality" and was acquitted. Leduc wasn't even given a trial. Her words were never entered into evidence.

They have knocked down my house with the tip of their finger. . . . It's murder, Violette said.

De Beauvoir tried to help Violette. She begged, then threatened to move her own writings to another publisher, but nothing worked. "Certain scenes were considered unpublishable," de Beauvoir said, "although they were no more daring than many others that had been printed; it was just that the erotic object in this case was a woman and not a man, which to the Gallimard readers was an outrage."

The same publisher had published Jean Genet's *Funeral Rites* in 1953. His erotic material was just as vivid as Violette's, yet he was considered germane: "My hand squeezed the cock a second time; it seemed monstrously big. If he sticks the whole caboodle up my cornhole he'll wreck the works."

I could find nothing as vulgar in any of Violette's works. Her writing about sensuality was exactly the opposite: *The veil brushed at the sole of my foot, the finger turned in thick white sun, a velvet flame withered in my legs. . . . I had been brushed by the scarf of madness that has no end, I had been caressed, yet also milled to dust, by a cramp of pleasure.*

❧

"Violette could not understand why her book was censored and Genet's was not," Lili said. "When she heard about it she grew quite ill. Simone telephoned her and that same day took her to the Bois for a walk. Then they had lunch. She had great empathy for Violette. She knew the book had been amputated and would not be as good, as a result.

"The next day Violette was worse, so we brought her to stay with us. She had a dangerously high fever and we were concerned. We felt so bad for her. She was undemanding, which worried us. She just lay there, deeply weary."

Flaubert said, "I have come to the desert in order to avoid the troubles of existence."

Ravages was published to mixed reviews and sold five hundred copies. Because it had been edited, the work was deprived of its spirit. Violette wrote to de Beauvoir, *I'm a desert that talks to itself.*

"I am tired," Lili said suddenly. "Perhaps I should rest."

I helped her settle in for the night and went to my room.

During the night I checked on her a few times. Once she woke up and asked for water. Another time, I took her temperature. It was a little above normal. I gave her her medicine and she fell back to sleep, holding my hand.

In the morning I looked into Lili's room and found her still sleeping. I went to the kitchen to prepare breakfast. While waiting for the water to boil, I stared out the window at another dark and rainy day. I heard Lili behind me.

"A good day to stay in bed," she said.

She looked better, but still fragile. There was no word from her family, which was fine with me. I wanted her all to myself.

Lili ate breakfast at the table and then insisted on taking a shower. I braced for the sound of a fall on the tiled floor—but when I saw her next, she was back in bed, dressed in a pretty bed jacket with a pink ribbon holding her hair away from her face.

"Are you ready to begin, my dear? Where were we? Oh, yes, 1955?"

I brought my tape recorder and sat down.

"I remember January of that year because the Seine flooded its banks and the quais went underwater."

This was the most horrendous flooding since the great deluge of 1910. The water was climbing at the rate of an inch an hour and the statue of the Zouave on the Pont de l'Alma was treading water that came up to his thighs. In 1910 the water had come up to his neck. The low areas of Paris, and all of France, suffered terribly.

"Our apartment house had a flooded cellar, but all our books were upstairs," Lili said. The few things saved from Alain's family, though, were in the cellar, and were ruined. Losing them felt like the end of a long struggle.

"Around this time, I remember, I needed to be in Munich on business. During a break in my meetings I took a walk along a street lined with booths, like an ongoing flea market. I saw a number of objects that were obviously French and stopped to look at them. My skin crawled. I realized that they had been stolen from French Jewish families—Passover plates, menorahs, siddurs, all inscribed in French and Hebrew. I asked the woman at this booth where she had gotten these objects and she said that they were given to her. It made me ill—her lie was a continual thread basting our society together.

"When it got warmer, Violette managed to take a holiday on Ibiza," Lili said. "She seemed more relaxed when she came back. She made up long and elaborate stories about the people she saw on the beach, about their wives, their husbands, their jobs, their dreams. Her humor really emerged when she was telling droll stories, and Alain and I found ourselves laughing helplessly."

In October, Violette attended a public reception honoring women writers that was held at the Académie Royale de Belgique. She was pleased but a little befuddled about a remark that Cocteau made about her and the publication of *Ravages*:

"In 1955, these books by our women, these American ballpoint pens that spot our pockets, these flames that shoot out of the lighter of the devil, far from pushing Colette into the shadow, send her this light which Violette Leduc would tell us 'falls rawly in the bedroom.'"

What an odd statement. Every which way I translate it, it is still odd. Yet when Violette left the reception, people crowded around her to shake her hand. She was amazed because she wasn't sure if Cocteau's comment was a compliment or a criticism. But she decided to take it as a compliment.

"The year of 1956 felt like one long spring. It was really quite strange," Lili recalled. "November was the warmest since 1899. Usually the sun greatly influenced how Violette felt, but now, even the weather was not affecting her. The persecution had begun.

"Then I heard that Jacques Guerlain was very concerned about Violette. When a friend of mine and Guerlain met Genet on the street, Guerlain asked, 'Have you seen Violette lately?'

"'She is a bluestocking, she is rotten with literature,' Genet replied.

"Violette began to see things that were not there. She heard noises coming from her closet and from beneath the floorboards. She growled at people on the street who happened to look at her. Simone persuaded her to see a psychoanalyst. She did, but, Simone told me, he did not offer much hope. Personally, I think she was taken to see the wrong analyst. Nevertheless, because Simone had referred her, Violette was determined to continue working with him. I would not be surprised if she made herself as perverse as possible."

Yet she continued to write, completing and publishing two books during this time. Both *The Old Maid and the Dead Man* and *Trésors à Prendre* were published to good reviews but miserable sales. Genet loved these books.

"*I willed myself to be a figurehead for the complexes inside me,*" Violette told Alain one day. They were sitting in the park, feeding the pigeons and reading the newspaper. Her hand was constantly going to her right shoulder. As with many traumatized people, complexes can manifest themselves physically and Violette was bothered with a painful shoulder. This is where she was shaken, where she was pushed, where she was pinned to the ground, against a wall, too often on a bed. She tried massaging, kneading, moving her shoulder in circles, sleeping on a hot-water bottle— none of it helped.

"Then she had a head-banging episode, followed by imaginary monsters pursuing her." Lili shook her head. "The obsessions got noisier. They created a cacophony, raging against the thick bone of her skull. It was unbearable."

One day in November 1957, Violette's demons won their battle. She left her apartment in the morning, after imagining that Sartre was making fun of her looks in an article about Tintoretto in *Les Temps Modernes.* He mentioned something about ugliness, and Violette, in her state of paranoia, assumed that he was writing about her. She walked across Paris to Sartre's apartment on the Rue Bonaparte to stand guard. Her friend Madeleine Castaing was driving past on the way to her antique shop on the corner of the Rue Jacob and the Rue Bonaparte. Castaing saw Violette cowering against the building, her eyes in a fixed stare, looking deathly pale. She got out of the car and went to her. But when she touched her, Violette became hysterical and threw herself on the ground, screeching. Castaing managed to get her into the car and drove her to her shop. There, she phoned de Beauvoir and asked for help. De Beauvoir arrived and took charge. She cajoled Violette into agreeing to go for help—and after some consultation on the telephone, drove her to a psychiatric clinic in Versailles.

For some peculiar reason, Violette's period of clouded reason coincided with a bizarre time in France. UFOs were being sighted everywhere, in all shapes and colors. A hotelkeeper, a policeman, the mayor of a small town, all respected citizens, saw a cigar-shaped object that they called *le Churchill*. Half-moon shapes frolicked in the nighttime skies over Lille, and more than one hundred people watched.

France sent a dog into space and Violette was upset. *Yes, I am a dog*, she said. *Like Frisette. Poor Frisette, poor little bitch being used out there in space. . . . You're not the only one, my poor Frisette. They're using me too. We are two unfortunate, defenseless creatures.*

"She said she was possessed," Lili recalled. "Once when I arrived to visit her in the hospital, I opened the door, and standing before me was a face smeared with lipstick from ear to ear. I walked in, stunned. She was whimpering, circling, crying through tears that she was a clown, and . . . *Why should anyone take me seriously?*"

De Beauvoir took her seriously. So seriously that she didn't give permission for electroshock therapy. But it was administered anyway, over her objections. Violette suffered the traditional grand mal seizures with accompanying disorientation. After a series of ECT sessions, Violette awoke to barred windows and a feeling of hollowness. She was sanely alarmed. She didn't respond well to the treatment.

De Beauvoir moved her to La Vallée-aux-Loups, once the home of the writer Chateaubriand. Like Violette, Chateaubriand was known for the synthesis of imagination and realism in his books. Indeed, he is regarded as the true founder of the school of Romanticism. It was at La Vallée-aux-Loups that Chateaubriand wrote *Memoirs from Beyond the Tomb*. And so, the Valley of the Wolves became a temporary psychiatric retreat. Violette arrived at the clinic wearing her Tuscan lamb coat and was immediately taken to her room and locked in.

In 1957 the property was owned by a Dr. Le Savoureaux, who was well-known in Parisian circles for his successful use of the sleep-cure as a remedy for trauma. The drug he prescribed, Benadryl, was a French invention similar to Valium. For the cure, it was combined with chloral hydrate and phenobarbital to create a lytic cocktail, a potion that brought on a deep sleep. The sleep-cure was used by both the French and the Russians in the 1950s and 1960s to treat what we now identify as post–traumatic stress disorder. When chloral hydrate is combined with alcohol, it produces another form of lytic cocktail, a Mickey Finn.

The therapy was administered to Violette for thirty days. She did not literally sleep for thirty days, as de Beauvoir reported. Violette was roused at least once a day to eat, use the bathroom, and do minor exercises. She was fortunate to survive such a treatment. French doctors were cavalier with this procedure. There are two main reasons why it is not used any longer: the danger of convulsions when the medication is stopped, and the possibility of serious melancholia. Violette, in the end, suffered the latter. She accused the doctor of turning her into a zombie, and indeed she fought this feeling for the rest of her life.

"She did calm down," Lili said. "But it was more than the sleep-cure that helped her. It was her friendship with the doctor's wife."

The two women took walks in the clinic's park, returning to the beloved natural world of Violette's grandmother. When she sat in the clinic garden she saw this picture in front of her life: She walked into her room, crossed a few years, sat down in her blue childhood chair—got up again and went to her cabinet—took out her inkwell—set it down on her invisible table—took up her peacock-feather pen—dipped it into the glass—and wrote until the sunlight arrived and settled warmly on her painful shoulder. This fantasy seemed to contribute to her recovery.

And so it was no surprise that toward the end of her stay at the clinic she started to write again. She wrote *The Old Maid and the Dead Man*. She wrote in her locked room, *I taunted the missing doorhandle*. But she wrote. This was her van Gogh room, with the same bars on the windows, the same locked doors. She was acquainted with him through their shared torturous experiences—and imagined following him along the pathway of her illness. She felt fellowship for van Gogh. She entered his painting as an invited guest. *The trees go through their crisis of despair*. She knew the way.

Violette never completely recovered from her paranoia. She still heard threatening voices at times of stress. But she never again dissolved into clinical illness. She wrestled with her madness for the rest of her days—but never became so radically lost. When she returned to Paris from La Vallée-aux-Loups she was given devastating news. All the unsold copies of her three published books had been pulped—made into new paper—for other people's books. She was crushed.

De Beauvoir comforted her. "When one knows the effort that is required to confront a virgin page, the tension needed to set one sentence after another, and the weariness of spirit that saps one's courage at times, this steadfast, dogged energy leaves one amazed—all the more so since Violette Leduc was persevering against a background of failure."

"All her friends stood watch," Lili said. "We made sure she was eating. We left little gifts outside her door. We took her to dinner. We drove her to the countryside. Then one day in late December, I collected Violette from her apartment on the Rue Paul-Bert and took her out for a special treat.

"'Violette Leduc paints tortured landscapes which resemble those of van Gogh,' Simone had said. I felt Violette would appreciate an exhibition at the Musée de l'Orangerie called *Van Gogh et les Peintres d'Auvers-sur-Oise.* These paintings had come from Dr. Paul Gachet's collection. He had cared for van Gogh until van Gogh died. And van Gogh gave the doctor and his family many paintings as payment and in gratitude.

"Violette was still agitated and uneven, and I knew that this work might further upset her. But I decided to take the chance. She was captivated. Her response was visceral rather than intellectual. *Et quis non causas mille doloris habet?* And who has not a thousand causes of grief?" With a sigh, Lili leaned back into her pillows.

· XVIII ·

Some say I am second-generation Jewish-American, some say I am third. I say I have not even arrived. I don't have a hundred years of wide-open spaces breathing in my bones, nor do I have that marvelous sense of American freedom and comfort living in my soul. I experience the traditional alienation tales that began with my grandparents.

My grandmother Rosa was a beautiful, fiery woman with a

crown of thick and curly silver, not gray, hair. She was the arche-typical bohemian. She always wore dangling earrings and singing bracelets. She continuously gestured with her hands. Her eyes were hazel, with dark black eyebrows and eyelashes. When I was young, I dreamt of being like Rosa. I imagined myself in a fantasy of Russian nights, with other artists, sitting at her table covered with a deep-red Persian throw, drinking vodka or tea in silver-bottomed glasses, smoking exotic-smelling cigarettes, and arguing until dawn.

Rosa's family belonged to the intellectual circles of Kiev. Her mother, my great-grandmother, insisted on teaching reading to the peasants. But it was against the law. Jews were not allowed to mix with the Russian peasants. The czarist government could not abide this breakdown in their racial and class system—so they sent her to prison. In those days the children of female prisoners went with their mothers. Thus Rosa and her three sisters went to prison with my great-grandmother. The family historians say they were there about six months, but no one really knows. Rosa remembered that there was very little food and they never saw the sun. When family members remarked about how difficult it must have been, she dismissed the trauma with a wave of her hand and her famous scowl. But we knew there was something wrong with the sisters—they were slightly off-kilter, not quite right.

As the eldest, Rosa was shipped alone to America to live with relatives in Pittsburgh. She was only ten years old and went to work in a factory, but this was not unusual at the time. Because of the pogroms, Jews were seeking safety wherever they could find it. She was assigned the task of making enough money so the rest of her family could emigrate. For two years she worked. Then she was sent word that her father had fallen ill and she should go home. She returned to Russia with enough money to make her father well—and to bring her parents, three sisters, and herself to this country.

Rosa's generation of immigrant women marched out of the shtetls and cities of Eastern Europe to the music of fantasies. They came to America believing they were escaping confining and pa-ternalistic rules. They were wrong. Soon their rancor and disap-pointment rubbed off onto our mothers in smudges that could not be erased.

When Rosa was sixteen, a cousin from Grodow introduced her to a struggling photographer in New York. (Of course, ages in stories may not be precise. The Jews arriving in America were born under the Hebrew calendar. Translating dates became quite a muddle. Indeed, it also gave immigration authorities an opportunity for meanness. My other grandmother, Leah, and all the people in her group of arriving immigrants were given December 25 as their birthday. The next group was given the next year's Easter date, the following group Ash Wednesday. Real birthdays were lost in America. People were given the opportunity to be younger, or older, according to the whim of the official.)

Rosa and the photographer were married, and soon afterward she gave birth to a daughter. Two years later, in 1914, the photographer left them to go to Hollywood. He worked on three- and four-reel films—but sent no money. In 1916, Rosa was living in a boardinghouse owned and managed by Sophie Tucker, the entertainer. In 1919, Rosa's husband returned to New York with an ulcer, and no money. Rosa sent him away—she had learned to take care of herself.

Rosa worked in New York City, or at least she said she worked, but she would never tell us where, or what she did. Her daughter, my aunt, was farmed out to the country house of Scott Nearing and his wife, who ran the first health food commune in the United States. The Nearings did not believe in giving milk to children more than one year old because, they claimed, it produced diseases that would appear when they were adults. One day, when Rosa was visiting, she noticed that her daughter was falling often and bruising easily—she was suffering from a severe case of rickets. Rosa was very poor but decided to bring the girl back to New York. She raided garbage bins in search of eggshells. These she would carry home, sterilize, grind into a powder, and mix with water; drinking the concoction saved my aunt from a severe disability.

Rosa was twenty-four when she met my grandfather Eli. They didn't get married, because Rosa was still married to her first husband. They had one child, my mother, who was born in 1920. It wasn't until I was born, in 1941, that my mother became legitimate. Rosa came to Nevada to be at my birth. It was the law that if you set up residency in Nevada for six weeks, you could request a legal divorce. She stayed six weeks, divorced her first husband, and married Eli.

Rosa was fierce when it came to health. Eli had his first heart attack when he was thirty. She was a fanatical follower of Carlton Fredericks, who pioneered the use of vitamins and organic foods for better health. (She kept Eli alive for more than fifty years by controlling his diet. When he was seventy-five and had yet another heart attack, he begged his wife to let him go. He was tired of bland food, he was tired of sneaking cigarettes from his friends at Union Square.)

In New York City, before the Second World War, you were given one month free rent when you moved into a new apartment. So most poor people moved every year—and most poor people took in boarders. When my grandparents moved, they always took their boarder with them. I remember one boarder named Boris who lived with my grandparents in Harlem. I watched him and listened to him with sympathy. One day he took my sister and me for a walk over the George Washington Bridge. I was afraid, but he held our hands tight. I could hear the wind roaring, telling us to go home quickly.

I loved Rosa because she said I was as beautiful as she was. Later I was to learn, and understand, and be disappointed, that she loved only beautiful objects, not people. She scoffed and demeaned anything living outside her concept of beauty. Yet when she sang American cowboy songs of lost love and wide-open spaces in English with her thick Russian-Yiddish accent, I could overlook her failings.

Her apartments in New York were always as red as a Matisse painting—with red-lacquered Chinese furniture, Persian rugs, day beds with mounds of pillows and long-fringed paisley shawls. I think she even burned incense—and I know she and Eli occasionally smoked marijuana with their friends.

She refused to march in political parades, always disliked Stalin, and openly repudiated the Communist Party. She was an anarchist. Once, when Paderewski was conducting in New York, Rosa attended the concert. After the performance, a line of pretty young women formed on stage to offer him bouquets of flowers. Rosa was in the line. When it was her turn, she walked up to him, spat in his face, and threw the bouquet at his feet. She created chaos, as usual.

While Eli was organizing communist cells up and down the New England coast and in Canada, Rosa was making love. Some of her lovers were dignitaries in the party. There is a family fable that Eugene Debs was one of her lovers. I hope this story is true. We were always shushed when we brought up the subject.

Unlike Eli, her lovers were mainly musicians and painters. And also unlike my grandfather, most of her lovers had lots of hair. My mother remembers one man in particular because of his great mop of hair and beautiful guitar-playing. When Rosa rebuffed him, he took to following her on the street and threatening her with his guitar raised over his head.

My grandparents stayed together for the rest of their lives. Maybe it was their children, maybe they couldn't afford otherwise, maybe they really loved each other.

Every two or three years they rode the Atchison, Topeka & Santa Fe to visit us in southern California. In the 1940s it took two hours to drive from Compton to the train station in Pasadena, where the atmosphere was always one of great drama and celebration. But my mother was quiet. I could feel her anxiety, and I remember her frenzied preparations for these visits. My father, the eternal optimist, would soothe and placate her while she scowled, fretted, and waited for the train.

Off the Pullman would step my grandparents with their parcels and trunks. Everyone pretended that everything was fine. But by the time we had arrived at our house, Rosa would have succeeded in upsetting my mother and there would be an argument. My grandfather and my father refereed, and I would sit silently, waiting for the trouble to subside. It was obvious that Rosa and my mother disliked each other.

Then the trunks would be opened and a summer Hanukkah was celebrated. Small bags of Barton's chocolates—real chocolates from New York—were given to us. I loved this candy and would try to snatch the pieces with my favorite fillings before my sister could. With a metal nail file, I would bore a small hole in the bottom of each one to see what was inside. If the chocolate was filled with nuts or a cherry, I would carefully put it back in its little brown paper cup. If it was solid chocolate or marzipan, I would put it in my mouth and keep it there as long as possible.

As I grew older, I realized that Rosa was a sad woman who had hidden behind her beauty until it was too late—and then found herself old and alone. She communicated by using her infamous scowl, the scowl inherited from my ancestral grandmothers, all her life. It was the scowl that said, "Don't bother me, you are in the way of my life."

She died in the Bronx Hebrew Home for the Aged—silent, refusing to speak, out of spite, out of despair.

· XIX ·

Lili fell asleep after finishing her cup of tea. I wandered around the apartment looking at family photographs. While I was in the living room, the telephone rang and a woman asked for Mme. Jacobs. I asked if she spoke English. She said no. I asked her to speak slowly.

The call was from Italy; it was Lili's niece. She said she had received a message that her aunt was ill. I explained to her that, yes, Lili was ill, but she was much better now. When was she coming back to Paris? Not for another ten days, she said. Who was I, she wanted to know. I told her I was a friend of Lili's from America. When I mentioned a book about Violette Leduc, she said her aunt had written something to her about me in her last letter. She asked if she needed to return to Paris right away. No, she didn't, I said, nor did her brother. I'd be able to stay as long as Lili needed me. But could she leave me her number, just in case? Thank you. *Au revoir*, good-bye .

I went back to Lili's room. She was awake.

"Who was on the telephone?"

I explained that it was her niece, that she was in Italy and it didn't seem necessary for her to return immediately. She would be back in ten days anyway.

"Thank you," Lili said, and paused. "It has been wonderful having you here. I am enjoying myself." She smiled.

"So am I," I said softly.

I reached over and turned on the tape recorder. "It was Wednesday, the twenty-eighth of May, 1958," Lili started, "and thousands of protesters were marching down the Boulevard Voltaire to the Place de la République, protesting against de Gaulle and the French war in Algeria.

"Alain and I, as active members of the Comité d'Action et de Défense Républicaine, were part of this demonstration. We were amazed at the number of people there. The newspapers said five hundred thousand, and it certainly seemed like it. Everyone marched in his own particular section. We were in the Beaux-Arts group along with a number of communists, including Simone and Sartre. When we reached the Rue Chanzy, I saw Violette standing on the sidewalk, a basket over her arm filled with food, and her new friend René standing by her side. We beckoned to them both to join us, but only René did. He brought the message that we were invited to come for dinner at their apartment after the march.

"When we reached the Place de la République, it was obvious that no one had made any plans for speeches. There were no platforms erected, and although some people climbed a plinth and were waving banners, everyone else dispersed. We strolled back along the boulevard to Violette's place on the Rue Paul-Bert.

"Violette had truly fallen in love. René Gallet was a working-man, a mason, who resembled Genet physically. Unlike Genet, though, he was unpretentious and supportive—not an intellectual, and not ashamed of being a simple worker either. Violette thought he looked like an angel with his beautiful blue eyes. He appreciated her for who she was, and asked for nothing more. She worried that he might think her too intellectual, too worldly, too ugly, and turn away. He didn't, and she couldn't believe her good fortune. For one of the few times in her life she was comfortable with herself. She marveled at their intimacy, she was awed by his interest. And he thought she was beautiful.

"We arrived at her apartment—she had moved to the sixth floor, which she now shared with René. The apartment was shining. Her worktable was cleared of papers and the polished surface reflected the lights in the room. Her traditional Joseph Gilbert school exercise notebook was closed, with her old friend the Blanzy-Poure pen waiting on its cover. The room was scented with cooking smells and the perfume of a simple bunch of violets.

"Violette was a good cook. Alain shared her love of food, so he took himself into the kitchen to see if he could help. I sat and talked with René—we had a quiet conversation about work. He was doing a masonry job on a building across the street from the soon-to-be-constructed skyscraper called Antigone. We laughed at the ludicrous name. It was to be the highest skyscraper in Europe, he told me, and the ugliest—fifty-nine stories, replacing the old, dilapidated, but splendid Gare Montparnasse.

"I told him I was translating George Sand's *The Haunted Pool* and enjoying it immensely. She wrote about the customs of Berry, the landscape, the oral tradition. Since this was my home too, I was captivated with how she used words to paint the tone and character of this beautiful part of France."

"You know, Lili," I interrupted, "I had not known, until recently, that George Sand painted pictures. There's an exhibition of her paintings right here in Paris at La Galerie on the Rue Guénégaud. Would you like to go sometime?"

"*Bien sûr!*" Lili sounded well and fit again. "Maybe later this week."

"But tell me about Violette's dinner," I prodded. "Do you remember what she served?"

"Of course I remember! It was steak with a lovely salad and fresh bread, and red wine. Then came dessert—Violette's favorite, a rich layer cake filled with berries—and then coffee.

"During dinner Violette told us that Simone had suggested that she write her autobiography. Violette was fifty-one years old and still struggling, psychologically. But she always had the ability to stand aside and examine her behavior. As she grew older she became more aware than ever, though more detached—it was the ideal time to begin this book, which would be *La Bâtarde*.

"Over there on my dressing table is an envelope. I set it aside this morning. Could you get it for me? I remember Violette wrote a note to us around this time." Then I handed the envelope to Lili and she shuffled through its contents. "Here it is," she said, relieved. "It is dated Sunday morning, July 13, 1958. She writes, 'I am fragmented, but can still discuss Rimbaud while listening to Bach's Cantata number 170.' . . . She was stranded with very little money in Paris, with only one hot summer Sunday for a holiday. *To write means to give out warmth.*

"It took her from 1958 to 1962 to write *La Bâtarde*. By the time she finished, she had ended her relationship with René. She had tortured him with her jealousy. She had seduced his brother and flung this information in his face. He could not take it any longer. He left her. She lamented this loss until the end of her life. But *La Bâtarde* was not ravaged by sadness—it was enhanced at last by her need to be special, genuine."

Lili coughed. "Could you get me some cold water, please? Also, would it be disgusting of me to ask for a cigarette?"

"No, of course not," I lied.

After the smoke, she seemed tired again and agreed to rest. I decided to take this time to shop for food. After seeing her settled I went into the kitchen to fetch her string bags, then left the apartment. It was raining, as usual, but nice to be outdoors. I walked to the Rue Rambuteau.

· XX ·

During the forties and fifties in Los Angeles, the Chicano community seemed magical to me. I loved the *pachuco* gangs, the girls with their *estiletes*—daggers—stuck through their beehive hairdos, the boys' leather jackets and duck-bill haircuts. They swaggered into the Cinco de Mayo celebrations at my father's school and I tagged after them. They adopted me as their *chiquilla*. It was thrilling to be treated as special.

Maria Rivera was a real *pachuca* and lived in my house as a foster child. In her room she tacked to the wall hundreds of photographs of movie stars. She told me their names, whom they were married to, how many children they had—and the best part of all, who their lovers were. I adored her room and greatly admired this sixteen-year-old older woman.

I was told that her mother was a prostitute and had recently abandoned her. Maria was always into some trouble or other, and I know she suffered, because I heard her cry behind her closed door. To my world, she translated her suffering into a melodramatic Technicolor serial movie.

One day Maria invited her gang to our house and I went with them into the backyard. They spread blankets on the grass and then took surgical tape and stuck it to their thighs, marking their boyfriends' initials. They stretched out in the sun to tan their legs. After hours of talking about boys, they ripped off the tape, and there, on their skin, was the fleshy declaration of their love.

I experienced my first love for an older man when I was eight. His name was Eddie Martinez, he was sixteen, and he made me swoon. I remember being invited by Eddie and my older girl-friends to the Mexican side of town to celebrate Día de los Muertos, the Day of the Dead. We stayed up all night and visited the graves of my friends' loved ones. We licked sugar skulls, ate pumpkin with sugar cane, sweet rice, and *pan de los muertos*, bread of the dead—shaped like a human skeleton. During the night people picnicked in the cemetery, singing songs, chanting prayers for their dead. The graveyard was perfumed with the sweet smell of burning copal and decorated with bright-colored flowers and hundreds of flickering candles. People did not go from house to house to ask for candy; you didn't ask, you gave. Candy was offered as a gesture to someone's memory. I refused to eat a sugar skull with my name written on it in icing because it frightened me.

My friends believed life and death were two opposite forms of existence that could each not live without the other—life was a dream and death was the awakening.

A mask symbolizes one's ancestors and the return of the souls of the dead. It is a chrysalis, representing a transformation of the self that is hidden from the view of the world—a form of social disguise.

My husband is an artist and occasionally makes masks. Joe once made a life mask of me that I was afraid to touch. He covered my face with Vaseline and placed a straw in each nostril. Then he applied layer upon layer of cloth saturated with plaster of Paris. This was allowed to harden for a few minutes and then removed, creating a mold. He made the mask by pouring plaster into the mold. To my surprise, my face was much smaller than I thought.

Joe's masks line the hallway of our house. At night, when I walk past them, I see a rogues' gallery of nightmares. If only I could believe that my god lives in my mask. Then, by wearing it, I could finally unite with the holy spirit.

But I am afraid of masks. And yet I understand we live our lives as mask-wearers. It seems that we mask ourselves in the light, to disguise the reality of darkness. Which way do we travel, how far behind ourselves do we follow?

· XXI ·

We were tired of chicken soup and its lingering smells in the apartment. We craved fresh salad, bread, wine, and anything chocolate. I returned, damp through and through, to Lili's apartment with all our wishes.

Lili was still sleeping as I made our dinner. She slept on. It was already eight in the evening. Every half-hour I went to check on her. She kept sleeping. I ate my dinner at ten-thirty. I wanted to go to bed but felt that I had to keep watch. I made coffee, took it into the study, and settled on the sofa, with the gentle reading light above my head and an old Irish blanket wrapped about my legs. It was raining heavily outside—I didn't need music.

Simone de Beauvoir wrote Nelson Algren in 1951 that she had urged the ugly woman to spend the next summer taking a walking trip in France and writing in her journal. Then Violette wanted to publish it. The writing was terrible, Simone told Algren, because Violette was "insincere, morally."

Bizarre. De Beauvoir later wrote in the foreword to *La Bâtarde* that Violette had a "moral healthiness," that "her scrupulous honesty has the value of a moral challenge," that "she judges no one." And in public, she supported *Trésors à Prendre*, finally published in 1960, as being lyrical and well written. Indeed, Violette even dedicated it to her.

Did de Beauvoir feel envy toward Violette? It is widely agreed that Violette was the better writer. De Beauvoir's fiction is clumsy, and although her nonfiction is better, she lacked the music of Violette's words. De Beauvoir is known to have remarked that *La Bâtarde* and Sartre's *The Words* were two of the most "enchanting" books she had read in years.

Simone de Beauvoir could be mean and petty and narrow-minded. After a dinner with Genet, Leduc, and Cocteau, she defined Cocteau as "a famous poet and pansy" and in a gloating way called herself the "only heterosexual among them." The truth was that de Beauvoir was interested sexually in both men and women. She hid her feelings for people by calling them names. In her letters to Algren she never referred to her women friends by their given names. She called Bianca Lamblin her "Jewish friend," just as she called Violette "the ugly woman." De Beauvoir had a nasty streak—even though she vehemently denied it. She wrote her own script. Her books tell us how she wanted to be known; she extended the myth. She was so important to the history of literature and the emancipation of women that people continue to be fierce about protecting her. She wore a mask of words tied with a purple ribbon.

I checked again on Lili and found her sitting up in bed. "Lili, I was getting worried about you. It's almost midnight. How do you feel? Are you hungry?"

"I'm starving and I would love some coffee. I feel as if I had been plunged into a bottle of thick lotion. I need to wake up. I think I am over the worst part of this *grippe*."

"But since it is so late, maybe you ought to try to go back to sleep until morning?"

"No, I love working at night, it is my favorite time. Let's talk some more. Is this okay with you?"

There was no need to answer; she knew it was fine with me. I love this time also—the most private part of the day.

After she ate, we went to the study and made ourselves comfortable. She picked up the next stitch in Violette Leduc's life as if she were knitting a sweater.

"In the middle of Violette's writing *La Bâtarde,* the French detonated their first nuclear bomb in the Sahara. Violette didn't seem to be bothered by this, but Alain and I were terrified. France was behaving abominably in Algeria, and we were marching all over this country in protest."

In contrast, Violette was an apolitical creature. She seemed oblivious to day-to-day events. In the autumn of 1960, she left Paris for a holiday in Marseilles. Lili received a postcard from her saying that she wasn't happy there. The city was too big, and she realized the only way she could enjoy a holiday was by being outdoors in nature. She wrote that she had decided to leave and was meeting her friend Thérèse Plantier in Vaison-la-Romaine, in the Vaucluse. Thérèse was a poet, who wrote always in red ink—a tornado of exuberance and indignation. Her work was rough-hewn, manly, yet feminine too. She tried to turn poetic gender on its head. She said the more Violette wrote about her life, the less anyone believed her. They were an odd couple.

On this holiday Violette was very worried about money. She was poor in those days, yet committed to sending money to her mother every month. She made do on very little. Sometimes she hitchhiked when she was traveling outside Paris.

But this time, Violette took a bus and traveled up through the Midi to Avignon. Here, she changed for the local bus to Vaison-la-Romaine. The bus drove due east, through Petrarch's town of Fontaine-de-Vaucluse. Petrarch wrote about this "fountain" as the source of the Sorgue. He described how the river sprang, fully formed, out of the mouth of a cave during the rainy season. But the sun was shining for Violette that autumn day.

Tired from the ride but excited about this new adventure, Violette arrived in Vaison-la-Romaine to meet Thérèse. She worried that if she didn't behave properly, Thérèse would abandon her. Far from abandoning her, however, Thérèse was at her side, sampling pastis with her every café in town—the Bar de l'Orient, Le Central, Le Siècle, the Café du Commerce, the Casino, Les Vacances. To her delight, Violette discovered a new concoction, a *tomate*—pastis with a drop of grenadine.

They were happy as they drove away from Vaison-la-Romaine in Thérèse's car. Although Thérèse had to leave for Digne early the next morning, she wanted to show Violette her mother's village, Faucon.

Faucon was to be the purest love of Violette's adult life. She knew when she saw the village in the distance that Faucon would be her home. She squirmed with excitement on her seat. They approached beside what Violette called *the mountains of the angels*—the outlying ridge of the Provençal Alps, unfurled for the seeker by the wide green carpet of the Rhone valley.

When Violette wrote about discovering Faucon in *La Chasse à l'Amour*, in 1964, she asked the reader to hear a confession: she had changed the time of her arrival from autumn to spring. The violets were already hidden by the fallen leaves. The parading grapevines were already golden. The hills were already many shades of yellow. The bark of the trees had already turned blue with frost. Although it was really autumn, she yearned to write about the flowers and how they bloomed in Faucon in the spring.

Violette adored the ancient walls around the village, and autumn flowers living in the cracks between the stones, the butterflies and bees hovering in the flowers, and especially the famous falcons for which the village was named.

One of the adolescent Violette's mentors was the writer W. N. P. Barbellion, author of *The Journal of a Disappointed Man*. In the book is a passage Violette could never forget: "To have a Falcon's soul, a Falcon's heart—that splendid muscle in the cage of the thorax—and the Falcon's pride and sagacious eye!"

She never lost her passion for the village, which became her deliverance from exile. *Je l'avais toujours connu ce paysage.* Faucon knocked at the door of Violette's heart.

That first night in the village, Violette was surprised to hear that Émilie, Thérèse's mother, had read some of her work. She was told this as the three of them ate dinner, and it made her feel welcome.

That night she slept in the basement, which she detested. It was made of concrete and reminded her of a tomb. The only redeeming feature were the three tiny windows. If she stood on her toes she could see a lovely cherry tree.

She couldn't get warm. It was the time of the mistral. Stepping outside invited a furious buffeting. Violette felt sorry for the twisting trees—but she loved the drama of the wind. She had a hard time falling asleep. The next morning Violette missed the bus to Avignon.

Thérèse hated Faucon. More likely, I'd guess, she really hated her mother. She wrote in a poem that Faucon was a village "cracked congealed chewed bruised blue . . ." But Violette felt that being in Faucon was an answer to an unspoken prayer. Émilie asked her if she wanted to stay in her house for a while. She was taking a short holiday. Violette would have to feed the cats and the plants. Violette was thrilled.

The first day, after Thérèse and her mother had left, Violette started to write. She wrote with her head in the shade and her legs in the sun. After completing three pages, she decided to wander the village. She asked the egg lady and her brother if they knew of a place outdoors for her to write. They looked at her strangely.

They didn't realize that writing was work. To write, to write what? they asked. A book, she said. They stared at her as if they had never met anyone like this before, then pointed to a path leading to Jaux, a small woods belonging to the village. Violette found joy in the name and took the path . . . *to walk in the valley of my crowning.* On the path she found a grotto and was pleased not to see garbage. Instead, tucked into the crevices of the stones were wisps of sheep's wool and animal hair. She saw this as a good omen, an offering.

And then she noticed the statue of the Virgin. She was made of cast metal and seemed to have been there a very long time. Violette sat at the base and gazed at the purple-gray hills around Faucon. They consoled her. She walked on and found a chestnut tree motioning her to sit down. Her head filled with solitude.

The next day she wrote five pages, two more than usual. She was calming down. "Nowhere am I so free as in Vaucluse," Petrarch wrote. "Nowhere so full the air with amorous cries. No valley ever offered such sorrowing quest, such deep seclusion, leafy overgrown. . . ."

After three weeks at Émilie's, Violette was growing nervous about not having her own place to live in Faucon for the rest of the autumn. She was having what she called a *crisis of liberty.* And although it was difficult for her, she was trying to make friends.

One was Mme. Rialvait, who ran the Café Mama, which also sold tobacco, wine, and bread. Violette loved to sit inside and listen to the people congratulating each other on the beautiful weather. Much to her relief, they didn't discuss politics; it was not appropriate in this village. At the end of the day, everyone went home. She marveled at how quiet it was while she ate her dinner—canned tuna, potato salad, cheese, lemonade, and fruit.

"Speaking of eating, I am ready for the chocolate torte!" Lili said. "Could you bring more coffee too? My head is clearing and I am beginning to feel well again."

I went to the kitchen to prepare our midnight picnic.

"You know, it would be nice to have a fire," Lili said when I returned with the dessert on a tray. "The fireplace has not been used since Alain was alive, but it has been cleaned every year. There is some firewood stacked outside the kitchen, in the pantry. Do you know how to make a fire?"

"At my home in the mountains it's a winter evening and morning ritual," I said.

I found the wood neatly stacked—oak from Saint-Désiré, I supposed—and a basket of branches for kindling and a few pieces of coal. It made me sad to see how well supplied this urban apartment was with its country-grown reminders of Alain.

"Did you know," I laughingly asked Lili, "that the Latin word from which we get 'carbuncle'—*escarboucle* in French—means 'small ember'? And in Greek, it translates to mean a beautiful gem of a deep red color. These gems, or burning embers, were used to treat fevers because they embodied the spirit of fire. According to legend, you must carry an ember in your pocket. And when the ember becomes cold, or you feel ill again, you have to replace it with a new one."

I crumpled some newspaper, placed kindling on top of it, then arranged the wood like a tepee and lit the fire.

Lili smiled, gazing into the new flames. "That would be very dangerous—perhaps a gem instead, maybe a garnet."

Violette made friends with a villager named Édith Maurel, who was so kindhearted that she would pick grass to feed the rabbits at six in the morning, while it was wet with dew. She was sensitive to Violette's loneliness and brought her small gifts. On one of Violette's first evenings in Faucon, Édith presented her with a rose and told her not to be afraid. Violette put the rose in the same glass as her false teeth! But she still hadn't found a house to rent. She would have to return to Paris.

The night before she left, Violette drank most of a bottle of

Pastis 51. She called it her *ravigote*—her pick-me-up. Late the next afternoon she left Faucon with her suitcase. She got as far as the cemetery and decided to spend the night sleeping beside a gravestone. Édith went looking for her, found her, and pushed her back toward the village, insisting on carrying her suitcase and promising to help her find a place to live.

She succeeded, though it was less a house than a very old shed, with no glass in the windows and only bedsprings, no mattress. Another new friend, the postmistress, loaned Violette some sheets, a few old towels, a pillow, and a blanket. She borrowed a chair with a broken back and a rickety table for a desk from Émilie. She piled old grain sacks to soften the bedsprings. Within an hour of moving in, she had found a butane stove that she installed on a crate—and so, she created a home.

She scrubbed the floors until all the old hay and its residue were gone. She arranged the space as van Gogh had done in his painting of his hotel room. She stacked crates to make a closet and a bookshelf. And she borrowed two buckets—one for fresh water and the other for a toilet.

In the evening she put her candle on the broken chair and read. The bed—a *grabat*, a pallet, a litter of rags—was very uncomfortable. But even in this discomfort, at fifty-three years old, Violette wrote about hearing the birds and how her little cell lit up with their songs.

She would awake at six-thirty in the morning and fetch fresh water from the *lavoir*. She would wash herself in an old blue basin and comb her hair in front of a small mirror she had nailed to the wall. (The landlady allowed her only one nail.) For her work day in the woods, she took an amazing assortment of things. Into one side of her basket she put: a blue-handled knife, an empty Amora mustard jar full of water (with a lemon peel), a pair of earplugs in a box with a sphinx on its lid, a piece of bread wrapped in a napkin, radishes, fresh garlic, some fresh parsley, a muttonchop she grilled just before leaving, a small sausage, salad greens (sometimes a *salade Ventoux*, consisting of escarole, goat cheese, ham, and olive oil), Bonbel cheese, an apple, a pear, chocolate squares, and petits-beurres. In the other side of the basket she put her notebook, pen, ink, a rag to clean the pen, a book, her knitting, a sweater, a wool vest, a pair of shorts, a tube of suntan lotion, handkerchief, compact, lipstick, comb. Since it was still so warm, she also packed a two-piece bathing suit whose top was too small, so *my breasts often hop outside as I write.*

She would leave at eight-thirty and walk for thirty minutes until she reached her spot in the Jaux, greeted by the shrill sounds of the cicadas. Then would she change into her bathing suit and do yoga for a few minutes—the standing-tree position was her favorite.

Promptly at nine-thirty she would start to write. She wrote for three hours, until her fingers ached and her stomach began to mutter. She would read while eating her lunch and then knit. At two she would write again, and continue until four or four-thirty. Her discipline was admirable.

When she returned home in the evening she would bring two bunches of fresh dandelions she had cut in the yellow-lit fields. She would put one bouquet in an old pastis bottle on her scrubbed table, the other in a wine bottle on the windowsill. She kept a dried olive branch on her desk—she loved the smell.

One April day in 1956, when the weather was only imagining spring, a killing frost destroyed most of the two million olive trees in the Vaucluse. From then on, the linden tree became the natural resource of Faucon. In the spring, the buds were harvested for herbal tea; they had to be picked before they actually blossomed. They were gathered by the villagers and placed on large pieces of rugged canvas called *bourras.*

Some of the bundles of linden buds were stored above Violette's head in her little shed. When the wind blew through the attic, she heard the linden move ever so lightly. After several weeks, when it had dried, it sounded like *frou-frou, frou-frou,* the swishing of the waves in the sea.

Only a month after Violette had settled in the shed, the landlady told her that she had to leave. Her daughter was coming home. Violette was thrown into turmoil. She said she was being made *to abandon the hard sand, the adolescent olive trees, the dancing roots of thyme, the Roman tiles, the wall, the pigeons, the white butterflies on my hat, on my shoulder, on my pen. It's my beautiful life.*

Quoi faire? Violette asked. The mayor offered her an abandoned isolated farm on the plains. Violette had noticed this ramshackle structure during her walks. But she turned down the mayor's kind offer because she was too afraid to be that alone. She found it comforting to be in the village with neighbors.

She walked down the path to the Virgin and her chestnut tree and kneeled for fifteen minutes asking for help—but there was no relief. That evening she was hysterical. She banged her head against the wall and wept with abandon. She ran through the village barely dressed until she was rescued by the postmistress, who took her back to the shed and put her to bed with soothing words.

The next morning Violette left the shed to take her dirty clothes to the *lavoir*. She was preparing to return to Paris, defeated. In front of her on the path to the *lavoir* was a thin woman dressed in black. She was a laundress by profession, and also the proprietor of the Café du Progrès, adjacent to the church. Violette reached the *lavoir* and began washing her clothes. Her tears fell into the wash water, and the laundress noticed her misery. She asked Violette why she was crying. Violette answered: She was being chased away from Faucon, from her little room. "All is not lost, don't be upset," the laundress said. "I have an idea."

She said her neighbors were a family from Paris and they would not be coming to Faucon for their holiday this year. The laundress would write them on Violette's behalf. Meanwhile, she took the risk and gave Violette the key and allowed her to move in. A few days later the Parisians said yes. Violette paid two thousand francs a month, about eight American dollars, for a beautiful house without electricity—but satisfactory in every other respect. Her bedroom, formerly a chapel, had painted yellow beams that made Violette smile every time she looked up. She slept on a hard bed, her *little stone mattress*. She could see Mont Ventoux from her second-story window. Here she could embrace the moonlight. She had paid a thousand francs more per month for the shed. She stayed until the middle of winter, then returned to Paris.

"Now Violette, after searching through her dreams, found one come true," Lili said. "*Fluctuat nec mergitur* is the motto of the city of Paris. I think it comes near to describing Violette's position in life—she is tossed in the waves but she does not sink."

I got up to put another log on the fire. I was sleepy from listening to Lili's pleasant voice, from the warmth of the fire and the hour—it was two in the morning. Lili was wide awake. I needed more coffee.

"What were you and Alain doing at this time?" I asked. "Did you still see a lot of Violette when she came back to Paris?"

"Well, yes, of course we continued to see her. But by 1961, Alain and I were spending most of our free time with a group of writers working on a referendum that we hoped would lead to a negotiated peace in Algeria. It was a disheartening job.

"Alain was a great believer in natural justice. He did not hold God accountable after the Holocaust. He felt strongly that meanness, cruelty, brutality, barbarous behavior were man's responsibility, not God's. He used to say God's responsibility was to be a reminder to people: there are good and bad ways to live, and we should treat other human beings as we treat ourselves. I envied his belief—I was the cynic."

Lili directed me to a pack of letters in the third drawer on the left side of her desk. "Please get them for me, and more coffee too, please."

I walked to the kitchen and put on the water. Then I went back into the study. I found the letters and brought them to Lili. After a few minutes I heard the kettle whistle, and I answered.

I was hungry again, so I prepared a tray with coffee, biscuits, and fresh orange sections and carried it into the study.

"Violette wrote to us while she was in Faucon," Lili said, as she poured coffee into her cup. "Short notes in blue ink hurried across the page, just to keep our connection. Here, I will read them to you.

"'March 26, 1961. At seven in the evening I paid homage to Nerval. I saw in the Halle aux Vins ... *his poetry sputtering like sparks between these little brick pavilions.*'

"'March 27, 1961. One of my former employers, M. de Saint-Ange, who was very kind, was sent off to the war. I stole a pen and lighter from his desk when he left. I knew he would die. I paid for my ancient guilt with a beautiful tulip with the same name, Saint-Ange.

"'*He was one of the first to be killed.*

"'Now he has bloomed in all his glory and I feel he has been reborn. He was planted on the balcony in a flower box, waiting for spring. He began to open pink, like a corpse. I forgive myself.'

"'May 15, 1961. Nine-twenty in the morning. I relish my Faucon. I watch the day unfold. I hear the day awake.'

"'May 18, 1961. I continue to write. I wrote about an old woman whose husband has just died. An old woman who continues to hear her husband whispering in her ear.'

"'May 22, 1961. The mistral is blowing. Maybe it is the wind left from the tail of Lieutenant Gagarin's spaceship as it circles my earth. Maybe it is to mark the death day of Victor Hugo, again. But on this day, I marveled at the poppies, dark pink against the hills— the masses of purple-bearded wild irises bending, in concert, with the wind, the wild narcissus, and the mauve Judas trees, in harmony with the tamarisks.'

"'May 23, 1961. A lingering cold has settled upon the Vaucluse. Nevertheless, I set off to the writing site under my favorite chestnut tree, just beginning to produce its bristly burr-houses to protect their sweet nutmeats in the autumn.'

"'May 24, 1961. It is raining and I am sentimental, worrying about the water-soaked outdoor furniture. My flowers didn't warn me about a long rain.

"'June 15, 1961. Summer has thrown its warm blanket around me. *I am inside the calyx of a flower, the calyx of nature as it grows warm.* This June week brings the summer solstice and the first harvesting of wheat. The air is filled with the remainders, the morsels left for the birds. The singing blackbirds of Provence, the merles, are offering their hallelujahs.'

"And that August," Lili sighed, "the Berlin Wall was built. We didn't know what to do with our dismay. The world seemed hopeless to me. Would it ever get better, I asked myself. Violette just ignored the entire action."

She continued to read from the blue note paper.

"'August 27, 1961. It is hunting season here in the Vaucluse. It is said there are now more guns in Provence than birds that sing. When I hear shots, I hide behind a wall of broom bushes and lavender perfume. I am anxious for my safety.'

"'September 15, 1961. I copied a prayer and placed it in my purse. I will need a prayer to keep me safe on the streets of Paris.'

"'September 17, 1961. My friend Madame Maurel took me to visit Grignan. The Grignan in Provence is the later home of Madame de Sévigné. I am impressed by her fourposter bed with a canopy. *It would keep me safe from the noises and the eyes looking down from the ceiling.* The ever present mistral lifted our skirts over the cobblestoned terrace. We were embarrassed, and held down the fabric—only to see that a visiting priest saw us too.'"

Violette returned to Paris for the coldest winter in ninety-two years.

In July 1962, after a very late Paris spring, the independence of Algeria was proclaimed.

"Then the tulips finally bloomed in the Louvre gardens, and we knew peace had arrived," Lili said.

Alain beamed with optimism. His hopes were confirmed. He traveled with de Beauvoir and Sartre to the Movement of Peace Congress in the Soviet Union—where Sartre spoke about how culture should not be used as a weapon. Lili received an excited letter from Alain telling her that Khrushchev had allowed *Pravda* to publish "The Heirs of Stalin," a poem denouncing Stalinism by Yevgeny Yevtushenko. Alain was even more excited when he found out that Solzhenitsyn's *One Day in the Life of Ivan Denisovich* was being published, legally, by Novy Mir.

"Violette was again in Faucon. So while Alain was away, I traveled by train to Orange," Lili said. "Violette met me at the station with a taxi. She was wearing a simple white dress and white ballet slippers. Her hair was pulled back on the sides with puff bangs across her brow. She wore no makeup and seemed tired, but not harried. I knew she was working on a new book. I hoped she would allow me to read the manuscript."

The taxi took them across the Carpentras River to Vaison-la-Romaine and then along the small valley of Gournier to Faucon, tucked against the mountains of the Ventoux and perched above the Ouvéze River. Violette pointed out the houses where some of her acquaintances lived.

All the houses were designed for the individual needs of each family over the centuries. They were built in the traditional architecture of the Midi—stone with mortar. Each house was built on the foundations of other houses, some dating back to the twelfth century. Violette's rested on the foundations of a fourteenth-century structure.

"Can you imagine—this was the same century when Petrarch was living in the Vaucluse!" Lili shook her head in awe. "Then the taxi stopped at the Avenue de la République, which was actually a narrow stone path. We got out and walked up the path a short way until we came to Violette's house. This was the third season she rented it—and she continued to rent it until 1965. It was very much as I imagined. It had a roof of Provençal tiles, which are shaped by being molded over the potter's thighs. Her front door was small, but you could see one of the original arches that had framed a much larger opening.

"The bottom floor, until the war, was probably used to house livestock. During the winter, the heat from the livestock would rise through the cracks in the floor and keep the family living there warm. I even saw a small stone gutter hiding under the stones which must have been used for draining the animals' sewage.

"The house shone from top to bottom. Every day Violette honored the stone floors with her broom—she had even dusted the interior ceiling beams. Glass panes had been installed in the windows. The table was set for dinner with a vase of wild flowers in the center and a bottle of Côtes-du-Ventoux close by. We ate and talked about Paris.

"But I was more interested in her life in Faucon. She told me about the village and the people, and because she was such a keen observer, I could visualize her descriptions as if I were at the cinema.

"She decided not to write while I was visiting," Lili said. "Instead, on Saturday morning we packed a lunch and took a bus to Carpentras and then a taxi to the Abbey of Sénanque. Violette had discovered this abbey in a surprise canyon, the Sénancole, that appeared around the bend of a mountain. She always knew when she had come upon the monastery—lavender was planted everywhere, long rows of pale purple blossoms. At this time of the year the lavender was harvested and the air was filled with the sweet smell of burning stalks. As we came closer to the monastery, the fragrance grew stronger, from a smoky scent to the perfume of sachets.

"The monks greeted Violette quietly. She was obviously familiar to them. She asked if we could sit in the chapel. It was cool, and the pale limestone walls were soft. There was no decoration except for a simple wooden cross at the apse and a small gold-framed icon of the Virgin Mary on the wall. We sat still for about thirty minutes. Then she smiled at me and we rose. As we walked up the aisle, a monk came to meet us. He rather timidly handed us each a simple wooden cross, shook our hands, and went out another door. Violette carried this cross in her purse until her death. Mine is sitting on a bookshelf next to Violette's books and her photograph.

"We had our picnic on the far end of the lavender field. Violette said that when she walked to her writing place in the Jaux, villagers would hand her fresh food as a gesture of friendship. Of course, they also made fun of her short skirts, large hats, and bare legs. She refused to talk about her new book, except to say that Simone had agreed to write an introductory essay. Of course, this pleased her immensely and was all the encouragement she needed. I knew I would not be asked to read the manuscript.

"In the evening Violette and I had dinner with her friends Frédéric and Édith Maurel. Violette said she adored Édith because her clear blue eyes never lied. She was disarmingly truthful. She would not cut flowers, step on snails, or eat meat. Violette claimed that *hers was a face that Picasso could understand.*

"But sometimes Violette would become so angry with her that she would not talk to Édith for days and days. Édith would just ignore her and wait. Then, one morning, there would appear little candies and wry notes tied to the lower branches of the mulberry tree that reached across the path into Édith's garden—a mulberry tree with the arms of a devadasi, a Hindu temple dancer. She would sign these notes 'La Louloutte,' in childlike handwriting very different from her usual. Violette's embarrassment about her own behavior would always bring her to her knees. She would be overly kind and generous, like a shameful drunk."

In *The Personal Recollections of Joan of Arc,* Saint Joan told about a giant tree near her village of Domrémy. Some people called it the Lady's Tree, other people the Fairies' Tree. Villagers who were ill came to the fountain near the tree to drink its waters. They also walked under the tree's branches to receive its blessings. Saint Joan said girls hung gifts upon its branches as offerings to the fairies. Just like the mulberry tree, her tree produced blessings.

Lili got up and walked to the fireplace to warm her back. "This feels so good," she said. "I was getting cold."

She really does look better, I thought. I should start making plans to return to my hotel. The idea made me sad.

"As I was saying," Lili went on, "Frédéric, Édith, and Violette occasionally went on outings together in the summer. One Saturday they drove to Puymeras. They sat at a café, beneath a plane tree, eating and drinking. Violette was drinking her usual pastis. They were in a lively mood. Very discreetly, Violette reached behind her back and under her shirt, and undid her brassiere. She took off one sleeve of her shirt without exposing herself, slipped out of the first bra strap, and put the sleeve back on. Then she took off the second sleeve and slipped out of the second strap. She slipped the bra out from under her shirt, then placed it on her head, and *voilà*, it was an exact replica of a traditional hat from Brittany. They were all hysterical with laughter.

"Violette used to laugh about the Maurels' poodle, Mickey, saying the dog was spoiled in a way that only the French could spoil a dog. She disdainfully tossed her head and complained about how the French coddled their pets more than their children. Mickey always accompanied the three of them on their excursions.

"Although Violette never had a full-time pet, she did nearly adopt a wild black-and-white cat. She fed her outside the door, never inside. We loved hearing her stories about this cat. Violette grimaced when she told about its manginess—and purred when she talked about it curling on her lap. She named her half-pet Demi-lune."

Lili returned to the sofa and I put in a new tape.

"So that Sunday afternoon, when I was in Faucon, we walked three kilometers to the village of Mérindol-les-Oliviers for lunch. The cat followed us all the way—appearing suddenly by our side and then running ahead. Violette tried to shoo her home, but the cat was resolute. We strolled past rows of grapevines guarded by tall and slender cypress trees. Because the grapes were just becoming ripe, there was the song of birds everywhere.

"We ate lunch at a tiny café, La Gloriette, the only one in that village. There were five tables, each a different design—and all twenty chairs were twenty different styles too. Bouquets of wild flowers sat in vases in the middle of each table. After eating we took another stroll around the old part of the village, now in ruins.

"Violette told me that in June of 1944, when the village of Mérindol was deserted, two *gendarmes* were shot by the Germans along a pine-tree-lined path. Six of them had hidden in the woods and were engaged with the Germans in battle. When the two *gendarmes* were shot, the remaining four picked up their munitions and fled to the Maquis in the forest, behind the mountain.

"Violette and I had been friends for many years by now. This visit was the quietest we had ever had. Writing sapped her energy, left her weary and used up. Although we spoke and laughed together, she was not really there. She was in her childhood, with her remarkable memory, writing about what she knew best, herself. She said to write was to prostitute oneself."

It is to give the come-on, to sell oneself. Worse perhaps, because whores don't feel anything. Every word is a new customer. Want to come with me, adjective?

"At the end of my visit, Violette presented me with a strange gift. She was continuing to make art out of her dreams and nightmares—not only in her writing. I noticed a pile of gnarled chestnut wood in the corner of her kitchen. On her walks to and from the Jaux she had collected these roots and limbs, and used them to create small sculptures. She transformed dead pieces of wood into angels, into birds of prey, into boats sailing the River Styx. Once she told me that she would like to see a beloved friend *in a flowering chestnut tree, I hope in a ship with roots.* She gave these sculptures to friends in Faucon, who exhibited them in their living rooms. This pleased her very much. She gave one to Simone de Beauvoir, who admired it, although she thought it was strange. She put it on a table in her living room, where it remained until she died in 1986.

"The piece she gave me was of a bird ready to take flight. It is over there on the bookshelf."

Lili showed me the bird. It was no more than nine inches long, and gnarled like an olive tree. Violette had sanded it smooth and then oiled it—indeed a bird, abstract in shape, a metaphor in concept.

It was four-fifteen in the morning and I was exhausted. I wanted to keep going, but I was afraid I would miss nuances, sentences, crucial information.

"Lili, I think I have to admit defeat—I am really tired."

"You are valiant to put up with this late-night woman. Tomorrow—I mean, today—if I feel as good as I do now, we can go to the George Sand exhibition. Let me ask you something: Would you consider giving up your hotel altogether and staying here?

That way we can talk without sitting in cafés all the time. I think it would be more comfortable, don't you?"

The room was dark, except for the halo of light around us.

My whole mood brightened. "Yes, I do, but I really don't want to intrude."

"On the contrary," she said, "it would make me very happy to have you here."

"Then it would make me happy too." I smiled.

❧

We were ready to leave for La Galerie by noon. When we walked outside we were stunned by the sunlight. It was the first beautiful day in a very long time. We took a taxi to the gallery—there was no need to tempt Lili's health.

I wanted to own one of George Sand's paintings. Now was my chance. This was the first time her artwork had been collected and shown in one place. Two floors of the gallery were filled with paintings, watercolors, and drawings. The art wasn't great art, but it radiated a captivating atmosphere—a history that until now had only been words for me. One of the smallest works was a watercolor of three birds, maybe cranes. One was red, one green, the other a deep pink. Aha, I thought, I should be able to afford this. It took me a few minutes to figure out the exchange rate. I went over it again and again—I just couldn't believe it cost two thousand dollars! But it did, and I had to give up the dream.

After an hour, it was time to leave—Lili was becoming tired. We took a taxi to the corner of her street and the Rue Rambuteau and found a *bar-tabac*, where we ate lunch. I walked Lili home, then returned to the Hôtel Senlis to pack and move.

As before, when I had left my pink room for the hotel, I was loaded down with books, computer, clothing. Only this time, there were more books. Madame of the Front Desk was very nice—even though I had not given advance notice of my departure. She called a taxi for me, and after settling my bill, I left for the Rue du Temple. The vestibule of her apartment house was very dark and I had to grope around for the *minuterie,* the timed light switch, to see my way. It took three trips up and down the stairs to move my belongings into Lili's apartment.

Lili was still sleeping so I unpacked and read. An hour later she woke up, and we had coffee and ate the rest of the chocolate torte from the night before. She brought out the folder of papers and continued from where we had left off.

In the summer of 1963, Simone de Beauvoir drove to Provence for a holiday in Villeneuve-les-Avignon. While sitting in what she called a "mediocre garden" she worked on the preface to *La Bâtarde*. She had been reading and correcting Violette's drafts while Violette was writing. The preface came easily to her. *Les Temps Modernes* had already begun to run excerpts of the book. People seemed to be gearing up for it. Word had gotten out that Simone had written a long essay for it, rather than the usual short introduction.

"Violette returned to Paris in late September, chilled to the bone, almost finished with *La Bâtarde*," Lili said. "Soon after Violette's return, on Friday the eleventh of October, within six hours of each other, Édith Piaf and her friend Jean Cocteau died."

Cocteau was at his home in Milly-la-Forêt. Toward noon he recorded a final farewell to Piaf for the radio and then lay down for the last time. Feeling ill, he said, "The death of Édith Piaf is choking me again. The boat is sinking." And after suffering a closing heart attack, he died.

Violette was saddened by Cocteau's death. He was very important to her—providing literary support and a quiet place to work in Milly-la-Forêt. He was her link to Gide, to the literature she loved. She remarked that *Cocteau was sliding into old age like a simple peasant falling asleep in a farm cottage*.

She didn't attend the funeral in the churchyard of Saint-Blaise-des-Simples. But Serge Tamagnot attended, and later told her that it was a sad and lonely day.

In 1964, *La Bâtarde* was published. Violette's life flew with hope and soared toward the sun—sometimes too close. At least now she had enough pride to step back and take care of herself. She made new friends, and some old friends were assuming new positions. Around this time she met a man who would be a lasting and dear friend. The writer Daniel Depland and his family owned a house in Faucon. Daniel and Violette became friends in the countryside and then in Paris too. In fact, it was Violette who encouraged him to write his first book.

"One day Violette and Daniel were having lunch at the Pont-Royal, when they met Genet," Lili said. "Violette introduced Daniel to Genet as her good friend, and a good dancer too. Genet smirked and pointed toward Violette: *'And that one, do you make her dance sometimes?'*

"*'Oh, Genet,'* said Violette angrily, *'you are far too disagreeable!'* And she and Daniel left the restaurant."

People were beginning to appreciate Violette's distinctive character. Being an eccentric was becoming lucrative. It was now the trend to be friends with the writer Violette Leduc. She was photographed by famous photographers and written about too. The Italian painter Paolo Vallorz asked Violette to pose for him. His many paintings of her are exceptional in their content, and very beautiful. They capture her shyness about her physical self. One nude, in particular, is extraordinary. It is a long and narrow painting, as gangling as Violette. She stands with her legs in the delicate waterlike swirl of the painter's brushstroke, her hands clasped over her genitalia. Her breasts are small and shy. Violette's chin is tucked against her breastbone, her eyes avoiding the artist's gaze. She is thin and bony, with an eggshell pallor to her skin. When this painting was exhibited in Paris in the late 1960s, Violette was enraged. She was very modest. Another brooding canvas caught her in repose with her eyes down, her chin resting on the stripes of her sweater, and creases in her face pulling her chin even lower. She hung this one above her desk.

"Alain and I laughed with her about her fanciful hopes," Lili said. "France had discontinued its use of certain 'historic' telephone prefixes. The prefix named for Balzac, for instance, had been BAL, or 225, and that named for Goethe, GOE, or 468. When Simone insisted that Violette install a telephone, she finally agreed, then pretended to be distraught that she had not been assigned a historic exchange, especially now that she was becoming more well-known. Preposterous!

"In April, Alain realized a long-held dream. Truly, it was the end of a long-held nightmare. On a bitter cold spring day, more than five thousand people assembled at Père-Lachaise Cemetery to honor the fifty-six thousand French deportees who died at Buchenwald. For years, Alain had worked with a committee to raise funds to commission a sculptor, Louis Bancel, to create this monument.

Bancel was a Frenchman who had survived Buchenwald. His sculpture is of two standing men, starkly emaciated but dignified, comforting each other. The ceremony was conducted beneath a black, rain-soaked weeping willow tree. Alain finally got to say good-bye to his parents."

In 1965, Violette was famous, as if overnight. *La Bâtarde* was nominated for both the Prix Goncourt and the Prix Fémina for fiction. The literary critics of Paris had great debates about her book. Some writers claimed her work was so innovative as to warrant every available award; others said it didn't belong on any decent person's bookshelf.

All of this publicity catapulted the book to the top of the best-seller lists. More than 165,000 copies were sold. Violette was called scandalous and perverse, but she had the distinction of being recognized as persona grata of *Les Temps Modernes* by Simone de Beauvoir and most important French writers.

The uproar accelerated further when the Prix Goncourt and Fémina juries decided that the book was a work of nonfiction, not fiction, and therefore removed it from consideration. *L'État Sauvage*, by Georges Conchon, won the Prix Goncourt that year, although *La Bâtarde* far outsold it.

Violette's dream had come true. For several months she celebrated. She was invited everywhere—everyone wanted to be seen with her. She dressed elegantly in the designer clothes that were being thrown at her feet.

"She was an amazing sight," Lili said. "From behind, you would think she was a wealthy woman, expensively attired, with great taste. Then she would turn around and you were startled to behold a Breughel figure—a Flemish peasant, long in nose, small-lipped, with Lilliputian eyes whose folds almost entirely obscured them, and thick stiff blond hair."

For a while this charade stood center stage. But Violette was never one for falsehood—she knew the truth and soon tired of the dishonesty. She felt this success had come too late.

She made a great deal of money from *La Bâtarde*. Her earlier books were reissued and she was retained to write for many magazines, including American *Vogue*. In a way, the money made her nervous. Except for her black-market days, she had always been poor. She was terrified of being without any means of support, terrified of ending her life as a cleaning woman, terrified of being alone in her old age. This terror was a difficult habit to break.

"Alain and I spent time with her, going over her finances," Lili said. "We asked what she wanted more than anything else in the world. Her reply was no surprise. She wanted to own a house in her adopted village of Faucon. She bought the house, the one she had been renting, with the second-story window framing Mont Ventoux, Petrarch's mountain."

"Violette hired a contractor and began to renovate. She drove the contractor crazy. Alain was constantly going south for a few days at a time to ease the situation—or he was on the telephone calming everyone down. She was really impossible. A lovely bathroom was installed, but she used the bathtub only once. All the modern conveniences made her nervous—she continued to bathe in the kitchen from water heated on the stove."

Nineteen sixty-five was a busy writing year for Violette. In January, *Vogue* asked her to write about French couture. But rather than write in the traditional fashion mode, she chose to explore the skills of a shoemaker, two embroiderers, a glovemaker, a jewelry designer, a draper, and a perfume blender. With each artisan, she recounted personal stories, connecting herself to her subjects.

For the story, Violette visited Formentera, an island in the Balearics. She had a touch of sunstroke and was ill, sick to her stomach. She went to bed, in her room, on the ground floor of the Café Pépé. In her unique way, Violette wrote about vomiting *cocoons of white froth,* in the article itself—and this in a fashion magazine! She told how the proprietress, Señora Pépé, brought her armfuls of geranium leaves and told her to breathe in their aroma. Doing this settled her stomach. She used Señora Pépé as the example of a real perfume blender. The *Vogue* article was a success, and Violette was asked to write two more.

Her next article was about André Courrèges and his exposure of women's knees. Violette said he was a daring designer and that his fashions were a giant step into the twenty-first century. His clothes reminded her about how bad it had felt to wear dresses with starched petticoats when she was a little girl. Again, she brought her own history into a contemporary situation.

The last *Vogue* article Violette wrote in 1965 was about the making of the movie *Dr. Zhivago*. A 1920s Russian village had been constructed for the set ten minutes by car from Madrid. So Violette traveled to Spain to write about Russia. She watched Omar Sharif, Julie Christie, Geraldine Chaplin, David Lean. She observed them minutely—and responded with words of poetic precision.

She told a story about Alec Guinness. He had a pet parrot named Percy who whistled Scottish airs to entertain his master. One day Percy became angry with Alec for not paying enough attention to him, and he flew away. He was gone for many days, and poor Alec was beside himself with guilt and remorse. Then one evening a whistle sounded from a high tree branch. Alec looked up, and there was Percy. The two locked eyes. In dramatic grandeur, Percy flew down onto Alec's outstretched arm—and fainted.

Violette brought her childhood into this article too. She described meeting the Russians in 1914, as a seven-year-old war refugee in Valenciennes, and how frightened she had been. In the same breath she wrote about how odd it was to drink grapefruit juice instead of wine with her dinner at the movie set's canteen, and marveled at how this grapefruit juice came from a tap. She wrote about breaking her arm and being calmed by Sharif. Then she tossed onto the page a bizarre detail—she had forgotten to bring her false teeth to Spain!

Violette had great problems with her teeth. She had replaced one tooth here, one tooth there, but never the whole mouth. After *La Bâtarde* was published, she had the rest of her teeth removed—and treated herself to a new, expensive, full set of false teeth. De Beauvoir would talk about how Violette often went out without her teeth. Violette knew de Beauvoir was saying this behind her back, and she was very hurt. She took great pride in looking as good as possible. She was so mortified without her dentures in Spain that she hardly spoke the entire time she was there—and when she did, she kept her head down! Yet she had a droll sense of wit about herself that she used in her writing. The older and more well-known she became, the less fearful she was in expressing herself.

"I have some photographs in here." Lili pulled out a tattered accordion folder from under a stack of paper on her table.

She showed me a picture of Violette taken by Serge Tamagnot around this time. Violette is standing in a butcher shop wearing her new Tuscan lamb fur coat, with her hands in her pockets. Behind her hang two grisly carcasses, one with its backbone floating over her right shoulder. The animal's serrated spine mirrors the ribbed collar of her coat. You can see the butcher cutting a piece of raw meat, with a wall of diamond-shaped tiles in the background. To Violette's left is a rack of canned meat and BF dog food. She is looking directly into the camera lens, undaunted.

⚜

"It rained the entire summer," Lili said. "We had less than a week of sunshine. On the twenty-eighth of August, in the rain, Alain and I drove to visit Violette in Faucon. The house was in chaos. We took a room in the neighboring village of Mérindol-les-Oliviers, at La Gloriette, also a café, where we had eaten before.

"Her most disconcerting problem was the rats and mice in her ceiling. Violette was very upset by this invasion and further agitated by the use of poisoned corn to kill them. She was afraid that her birds, the ones who had been coming to her balcony, would eat the corn and die. Alain and I took over the discussion with the contractor while Violette wisely went for a walk."

In October, her house was finished. On the ground floor were a blue sitting room, the kitchen, and a very pink bedroom tucked beneath heavy beams. Upstairs were the bathroom and a small guest room with a tiny door that opened into a storage area. Everything was finally the way Violette wanted it.

In a letter to a friend, she wrote, *No I don't dream on a stone: I try to work. . . . The hills and the mountains are bathed in melancholy. I write you all gnarled up under a tree surrounded by juniper trees. . . . Gallimard would render me a service by buying me a Voltaire chair at the Prix Uniques store for 1200 francs and have it sent to me. . . .*

This year, 1965, was the most important in Violette's life. It was filled with work and travel and settling into her home. In letters to Serge Tamagnot she speaks about her anxiety with the house—but she writes mainly about writing. She was reading the life of Tolstoy and trying to understand Jouhandeau.

Lili took another photograph from the folder. "Here are Serge and Violette standing against a haystack. They had gone to the countryside outside Paris one weekend in December." The shadows say it is about three in the afternoon. Serge is on the left, his right arm by his side and his left hand holding a long-handled rake. He is grinning. Violette is standing next to him, almost as tall as he is. She is holding the rake too, with her black-gloved right hand. Her eyes are closed. They are mimicking Grant Wood's *American Gothic*. They don't succeed, because they are both smiling.

I have carried a similar photograph with me to Paris—one of Joe and me. I am standing on the left, dressed in paint-splattered overalls and a white T-shirt. Joe is in dungarees and a blue work shirt. We are holding a shovel between us. Grant Wood once commented that the idea for his painting came from his fascination with a low white farmhouse whose peaked gable had a solitary gothic window. He imagined "American Gothic people with their faces stretched out long to go with this American Gothic house."

Our house is made of mud. Not American gothic, but American adobe. My eyes caress its loveliness and embrace its simplicity. We built this house by hand, our hands and those of a few hired men, from the beginning of April until the end of November. Joe designed it and was the contractor and major builder. I helped by screening sand, mixing mud, and laying adobe. I pickled hundreds of board feet of ceiling planking with runny white paint and stained the vigas and the floor. I laid all the tile in the bathrooms, kitchen, and hallway—and if you look closely, you'll see it is a bit serpentine, and certainly handcrafted.

Our children were each asked to make a small bundle of talismans, and we did the same. We put these tied-up bags in an old clay crock and placed it in the footing at the doorway of our home. In Eastern Indian lore the feet are the seat of understanding. We were determined to set our footprints on this land, our very own.

We invested heavily in large trees, knowing saplings would not grow fast enough for us to appreciate since we were already in middle age. Fifteen-foot trees were planted eight years ago. Today they are more than thirty feet high and are firmly established. Their taproots have found the source of water and they are beginning to send out seedlings in their environs.

Now that our children are grown, the house is too large. Some days it feels as if something very important is missing. Those days I enter their bedrooms, fluff their pillows, and send them good tidings.

While I was in Paris, I missed my home. I remember last April: although great rolling snow clouds still called on us, the crocuses and the daffodils were blooming. Sadly, though, many of the daffodils' heads were bowing and scraping the ground, not strong enough to carry the burden of a recent spring snow. They were alive but tortured-looking. They made me want to stand up straight and pull back my shoulders.

Every summer I plant wonderful old roses. Inevitably, at least half of them die over the winter. I am undeterred and plant more. The wilder they are, with soft blooms that haven't been "designed," the more I like them. My favorites are the palest—those that smell like Giverny on a warm day.

When I sit on the porch of my studio, in the perfumed air of the roses, with a summer breeze ringing the Japanese temple bells, it is my daytime paradise. I survey my attempts at horticulture and find the rabbits have eaten the tops off many of the tulips and lilies. Part of this is my fault. I like the rabbits. They have made their own home under the porch, along with Ferdinand, our friendly bull snake. I leave old bread for them and they fight with the piñon jays for the crusts.

The house sits tucked in a small valley flecked with piñon and juniper trees. Facing west, I can see through a saddle in the hills across the Tesuque Valley, to the mountains. We have planted nothing but wild grasses in front of us. If there is a lot of rain, the grass can grow up to two feet; otherwise it barely shows above the earth and we spend the summer worrying and planning ways to save the field. Desert grass may look yellowed and dead, but it is only waiting for water. When it rains, the field comes to life like magic. We are learning patience.

One of the few nice things about a dry summer, when the grasses are low, is that we can watch Ferdinand as he slides out from under the porch. He keeps our house free of mice, mostly. He is long, almost five feet, with a crooked tail that looks as if it got caught in a door. His skin is dry and covered with diamonds. I often wish he would pause long enough for me to run my hands along his back.

· XXII ·

By 1966, Violette Leduc was considered a writer from the provinces, though she was living in Faucon only from May to November. Much to her amazement, when she was interviewed she was asked to give a naturalist's perspective. Violette laughed and asked, *What naturalism, the naturalism of neurosis!*

Although Violette never gave up her "working-class" Paris apartment, reporters decided that she had. They made a great fuss about how good writing just didn't exist outside Paris. The media's description of a serious French writer was someone who lived in Paris, wrote in Paris, rarely left Paris.

When Violette was in England on a book tour, reporters asked about her flower garden, rather than her relationship with Simone de Beauvoir and French literary life. She was disturbed when they asked about her private life. In France, she said, people were more respectful.

The year brought Violette more work and more acclaim and more money. Her *Thérèse and Isabelle* was published as a thin pink pamphlet by Gallimard, and she sent copies to her friends. Eleven years after the controversy of *Ravages*, a sexual relationship between women no longer shocked—times had changed. *Thérèse and Isabelle* was a great success.

Again American *Vogue* hired her, this time to write about the making of the film *How to Steal a Million*, with Audrey Hepburn and Peter O'Toole. In her usual fashion, Violette was more interested in the workers on the set than the celebrities. She was fascinated with the painter who was hired to copy works by Monet, van Gogh, and Picasso. She wrote about him, the makeup artist, and last the actors.

In March, the English magazine *Adam* hired Violette to write about Brigitte Bardot. Reportedly, Bardot had read *La Bâtarde* and said, "I adore this book of Violette Leduc's! Here at long last is a person I would like to meet. She is a woman who doesn't spare herself."

Violette, who considered herself one of the world's ugliest women, accepted an assignment to meet one of the most beautiful women in the world. With great apprehension, she interviewed Brigitte Bardot at her home in Bazoches.

Bardot spoke about her passion for animals, and Violette wrote, *I believe her. She's authentic.* Bardot told her how she would go to the market armed with cardboard boxes and money. She would purchase caged birds and squirrels and take them back to her gardens. There she would let them go, "one by one, it's their Christmas." When merchants needed more squirrels, she said, they would come in the night and trap hers.

Near the end of the Bardot article, Violette confessed her insecurity. *I fear again her suffering grimace for my history of haircuts and old clothes. I become silent.*

I cut in on Lili. "Not to change the subject, but that reminds me of the time I met Marilyn Monroe."

"Marilyn Monroe?" Lili was clearly curious.

"Believe it or not. I had dinner with her and Arthur Miller. I was nineteen years old and living in New York with my aunt, uncle, and cousin. Miller's daughter was a friend of my cousin's. The five of us ate together at Rocco's on Thompson Street in Greenwich Village. This is a wonderful New York restaurant, still there, thirty-five years later, with many of the same waiters. We sat in the second room on the left at a table in the middle. Marilyn sat facing the window and I was across from her. I was mute."

She was not wearing makeup. She was dressed in a black turtleneck sweater, black slim skirt, very high-heeled black shoes, and a startling mink coat the same blond color as her hair.

I was struck by her nearness, by my proximity to such a famous movie star, but I was taken most by her face. It was one of the loveliest I have ever seen. She listened to the conversation and her face glowed with interest and occasional humor. When she laughed, you heard lightly ringing bells, and when she was being funny, you were mesmerized by her expressiveness.

It was too long ago now to remember exactly what was said, but I do remember the restaurant smelling deliciously of garlic— and Marilyn drinking champagne—and a constant din in the background forcing us to lean forward to hear her, for she spoke so softly. She offered me a glass of champagne, and raised her own in a silent toast.

I felt christened.

She created an atmosphere of quiet excitement, gentle and generous, not at all brassy and self-serving. And there sat Arthur Miller, ignored. I barely remember him. I spent my time trying not to stare at Marilyn too much.

After dinner we walked with Marilyn and Arthur to Sixth Avenue to find a taxi. We said our good-byes and she brushed my cheek with a kiss. In the cold winter's air I caught a fleeting breath of her perfume. And then they were gone—up the avenue in a blur, lost in the maze of yellow taxis, just like everybody else.

But for both Violette Leduc and Marilyn Monroe it was impossible to wander through life unnoticed—Violette because she was so ugly, Marilyn because she was so beautiful. Both women's looks were so extreme that their lives were formed by their faces, instead of their beings. George Sand wrote, "I was neither ugly nor beautiful in my youth—a serious advantage, I think, since ugliness prejudices people one way and beauty another. They expect too much from a radiant face, and distrust a repellent one."

"Violette had said that *Giacometti was the only artist who could make an ugly woman look beautiful,*" Lili said, leaning back into the sofa. "She would project her own body onto his thin and mysterious figures, and those iron-gray pieces would console her. Violette wrote me when he died. In the letter she brought up her friend Clara Malraux, the ex-wife of André Malraux. He had denigrated and discarded her. Violette fiercely protected Clara—and Clara, in gentle kindness throughout the years, supported Violette both publicly and privately."

When the second volume of Clara's autobiography was published in the late sixties, it caused an uproar. She wrote the truth about her relationship with André, yet she wrote about him with tenderness and respect. Violette found her far more charitable toward him than she herself would have been.

For Violette, the worst event of 1966 was the publication of Simone de Beauvoir's *Les Belles Images.* The book was a disaster. It was widely panned, and deservedly so. Nevertheless, Violette felt very bad for her friend and suffered as if the negative reviews were meant for her.

"In January of the following year," Lili said, lighting a cigarette, "Violette was in Faucon for a brief stay. Then she came back to Paris to attend to business and have a physical examination. Simone had been encouraging her for years to go to the doctor. Now that Violette was more settled, she began to take better care of herself.

"One day we went to the Louvre to see a Cartier-Bresson exhibition. It was fascinating to walk along the path of these portraits—and then there was one of Violette Leduc. I will never forget how she gasped. She was shocked and pleased at the same time. It was not a flattering picture. In it her chin is resting on her right hand, which looks old and wrinkled. She is wearing a sweater she knitted the year before. Her eyebrows are pencil-thin and are like arrows pointing to her long nose. Her lower lip protrudes, as if she is speaking. Her eyes are smiling but vague, very unlike Violette."

I have seen the picture. Violette is sitting at a table—I assume it's in her apartment on the Rue Paul-Bert. Behind her is an ornate mirror reflecting a smokestack and continuing, smokestack after smokestack, into nothingness.

"Two weeks later," Lili went on, "Simone called to say that Violette's X rays showed a mass in her left breast. The doctor, an old acquaintance of Simone's, was convinced it was cancer. Knowing how difficult Violette could be, he called Simone for guidance about informing Violette. It was she who told Violette."

"But why did de Beauvoir take this task upon herself?" I asked. "It seems rather perverse with all the problems they had in their relationship."

Lili nodded. "Nevertheless," she said, "they were close, and Simone always kept an eye out for her."

De Beauvoir went with Violette to the American Hospital at Neuilly when she had the tumor removed. Violette was calm and optimistic, almost serene. The tumor was taken out, and the doctor told Violette it was benign. She was relieved. But de Beauvoir was given the truth—it was a malignant tumor. Simone and the doctor told Violette it was normal to have radiation therapy for a benign tumor. Again, Violette believed them.

While the therapy was being administered, Violette stayed in a hotel next door to the offices of Gallimard, her publisher, so she wouldn't have to climb the five flights of stairs on the Rue Paul-Bert. De Beauvoir and Lili were working in the area and called on Violette during the day.

The year ended with the death of Violette's forty-four-year-old half brother, Michel Dehous, in an automobile accident.

"Was she close to him?" I asked. "I haven't been able to find much information about him."

"No, they weren't close at all," Lili answered. "Violette always considered Michel an interesting but distant relative. You have to understand: In 1920, when Violette's mother married Ernest Dehous, she sent Violette away to a boarding school in Douai. Then she and her new husband moved to Paris. Violette was just thirteen years old and she was miserable, but her mother would not listen. Three years later, Michel was born—further driving a wedge between Violette and Berthe."

Within a few months, Violette was having her first affair with a classmate, Isabelle. And three years later she was caught in bed with a new friend, Hermine, and expelled. Violette was now free to move to Paris to be with her mother, stepfather, and Michel. But as usual, Violette didn't fit in. Her family was living a traditional French bourgeois life—and Violette was already on the fringe. She halfheartedly attended the Lycée Racine during the week and stayed outside Paris with Hermine on the weekends. Violette never graduated.

"When Violette's stepfather died in 1954, Berthe turned all her attention to her son. So when Michel died thirteen years later, Violette was sad, but it was not a complete tragedy for her—for now she was left alone with her mother."

Violette's relationship with her mother was still heartbreaking. After her success with La Bâtarde she had proudly gone to visit her, convinced that her mother would finally be able to accept her. Her excitement at the imaginary reconciliation, as Lili described it, was sad to hear and profound to see.

Berthe didn't respond to the book, or to the radio interviews and newspaper coverage, or to her radiant daughter. During their visit, all Berthe spoke about was Michel's daughter, Claude, and a minor school examination she had passed. She was very proud of her grandchild. Daniel Depland, Violette's friend from Faucon, said Violette's mother "didn't say a single word of kindness to her, she didn't even mention her books." And Violette's bitterness would never be washed away. Her mother never saw the house in Faucon. She was never invited.

In 1968, the doctor realized that removing Violette's tumor was not enough. The cancer was lurking around the edges of the wound. Her left breast had to be removed. Violently and massively, it was gone. She was told it was cancer—and to everyone's wonder, she took it calmly. She reported to de Beauvoir, *The surgeon says it was cancer, but a cancer of no sort of importance.* She had considerable pain while working to regain the full use of her left arm. But she complained very little. And she continued the radiation therapy.

That year Violette left for Faucon on May 1, considered the first day of summer in Provence. She left in time to avoid the students' revolt that set Paris on its well-coiffed head. Alain and Lili, of course, supported the students, found their demands for educational, social, and political reform just. The Sorbonne was under siege. The male establishment was under siege too. The Mouvement de Libération des Femmes had begun to organize women. Between this and the student movement, France would never be the same.

This week in May 1968 was catapulted into history by the audacity of the Sorbonne's rector, Jean Roche. On Friday afternoon, the third of the month, he called in the police, the Compagnies Républicaines de Sécurité, to clear a courtyard of small groups of students who were rallying to approach the administration with their complaints. He was afraid they would disrupt exams.

"Alain and I participated, the following Monday," Lili said, "in the largest march Paris had ever witnessed. One million students, intellectuals, and workers moved from the Place de la République to the Lion de Belfort statue at the Place Denfert-Rochereau. We waved red flags and sang the "Internationale." This dignified procession was three miles long. There was no violence. And finally the administration and the government backed down. The students' demands that the Sorbonne be reopened, that the students be released from prisons, and that the police be removed from the area were all granted.

"But now Paris was on strike. No mail, no newspapers, no food stores open, garbage everywhere, and television screens wavy with lines because electricity had been cut back. Even *l'horloge parlante*, the time given over the telephone, was on strike. People hid the shoes of their children, in a desperate effort to keep them off the streets.

"On the nineteenth of May, de Gaulle made his first statement about the situation. *'La réforme, oui: la chienlit, non.'* We all ran to our Larousses," Lili said. "*Chienlit* means 'carnival mask.' The news announcers read definitions out of every dictionary they could find. It wasn't funny at the time because we took it as the insult it was meant to be. Reform, yes: a carnival, no.

"And all the while, no sunshine. Just cold, gray drizzle, day after day. And then, every two or three days, a downpour.

"By the twenty-third of May more than nine million people were on strike. No cigarettes, no mail, no Métro, no school—even the Eiffel Tower's elevator operators were on strike. Some friends told me that the only provision that had not been disrupted was the American Diaper Service!" Lili laughed.

"Finally, on the thirty-first, the sun appeared. And just as miraculously, sugar materialized in the shops. Petrol gushed out of the tanks. The cinemas at the Place de l'Odéon were open, with lines of people waiting. Flowers were being sold on the street corners again, and the cafés were filled with people.

"On June second, Pentecost Sunday, Violette rang us, almost hysterical. She had been worried, she said, because all communication with Paris had been cut off for a week. We were surprised to hear from her by telephone—she rarely called. But recently she had become more alert to the people around her. And more generous to her friends."

❧

If 1968 was a turning point, then 1969 heralded new destinations. Samuel Beckett won the Nobel Prize for Literature—and a spaceship landed on the moon. Violette was amazed at the moon landing, but disappointed too. She couldn't understand the astronauts' language: "Oh boy, did we hit it good." There they were, turning the theology of heaven and hell upside down, and they couldn't see the poetry of it, let alone remember their grammar.

Violette stayed for longer and longer periods at her home in Faucon. But she kept her apartment in Paris and was usually there from November to February. While she was in Faucon she continued to correspond with the Jacobses—not long letters, but enough to inform them about her well-being. Medically, there was still trouble. Her breast was not healing well and she was discouraged. She wrote to Serge Tamagnot that she was suffering where the breast had been cut. She went to a hospital in Avignon and was given medication for an infection and exercises for her left arm— and more radiation therapy. After a week she was writing again. She was coming to the end of *Mad in Pursuit*, a volume of autobiography that narrated her life up to 1950, and sending chapters to de Beauvoir as they were completed.

All around Lili and me, on the sofa, on the table, on the floor, were Violette Leduc's letters, written on light-blue stationery— here was a sea of language, a roiling remembrance of a life.

Lili and I laughed about the mess.

"I am very much like Violette," I told her. "I like my work space to be in order. Once my mother told me that a messy purse was an indication of a deranged woman. Ever since then I have been very conscious of my surroundings. I have learned to hide my madness!"

❧

Later in the evening I placed a telephone call to Joe. We had arranged that he would meet me in two days in Avignon and then drive to Faucon. At first we thought we would have to change his reservation—but now that Lili was feeling so much better, I told him we could continue with our plans. He was delighted to hear the trip was on schedule. After our brief journey, he would go on to meet a cousin of his in Spain, and I would return to Paris for my last few days.

The next morning I told Lili about our plans.

"When you return," she told me, "please feel welcome to stay here. You will probably have questions after seeing the village and meeting some of Violette's friends. This afternoon I have to go to the doctor's, and tomorrow I will be with my publisher all day. Let's see how much we can do now."

We took our coffee into the study and Lili began where we had left off the night before.

By the time Violette was sixty-two, she had published about a thousand pages, though she had sent de Beauvoir many, many more—which de Beauvoir cut and cut and cut. Violette's involvement in her work was consummate. *Once my exercise book is closed again, I accuse myself of living.*

That summer, 1969, Violette met Simone de Beauvoir for the last time. De Beauvoir was driving to Italy and passed through Faucon to see her. They visited one afternoon and de Beauvoir returned her edited chapters of *Mad in Pursuit*. Violette refused to go for a drive.

"Although Violette admired Simone immensely, she was petrified to drive with her," Lili said. "Simone had been in numerous accidents, some quite serious. Yet she continued to think she was an excellent driver. She learned to drive in 1951, when her publisher loaned her money to buy a car. Genet went along with Simone to make the purchase. They decided on a new Simca Aronde. This poor car quickly became a battered wreck. Sartre thought Simone was a perfectly capable driver, but he didn't even drive! He would encourage her to pass cars at the worst times— and she would oblige with a heavy foot on the gas. Once when she was upset about a love affair, she drove her car into a wall. She got out and looked at the damage, shrugged, got back in, and drove off. A little later that day she plunged into a stone marker on the highway. She arrived at her destination with the front of her car all dented and the passenger door hanging by a thread. She spoke about her car as if it were a person and she a victim of its abuse."

Violette was reading more than ever. She read Trotsky's *Diary in Exile*, which she thought beautiful and simple, and reread *The Brothers Karamazov*. De Beauvoir marveled at Violette's intellectually rounded world. She also envied her courage in leaving Paris, wishing she had more time to write herself and fewer interruptions. De Beauvoir was constantly besieged with requests and had a daunting social schedule. Violette now had all the time she desired, or so she thought.

July 23, 1969. Violette wrote to Lili about living in Faucon: "The heat, the boredom, the solitude. As I anticipated, I am an agreeable prisoner of this house, confined in my village and cut off from the roads that climb over my heart."

September 6, 1969. "I write to you in nature, on the edge of a little path near the pigeons' roost. I hear the fine cry of the guinea hens, two young cocks fighting a little, it's not serious. Sun and rolling thunder."

October 19, 1969, eleven fifty-five at night. *Grave chiaroscuro, that of the end of the world. My battered doors and my struggle. My wild rose leaves are lost in the evening. This is a white evening. The giants box my doors. Who leaned the iron chair on the edge of the church stairs? The wind?*

Mad in Pursuit was published in 1970. It didn't receive the same attention as *La Bâtarde*—still, it was anticipated as a literary event. It was the sequel, the continuation of Violette's life after the Second World War, in all its perplexity. Violette gave many interviews to promote the book. But there was a melancholy surrounding her success. In one of her last radio interviews, for the series *Radioscopie* on April 25, 1970, her lovely voice responded to the interviewer as if she were reading numbly from her book:

I have been ugly. I'm still ugly. Old age means respite. I know that at my age I will never meet someone with whom I could share my life. It's too late. Being old is consoling. I have no regrets. If I had been beautiful, I would have had a lot, but right now I would be forced to give up so much of it. I shall depart as I arrived. Intact, loaded down with the defects that have tormented me. After a few minutes, her voice seemed to glide, her dialogue drifting in the air.

She celebrated the return of the nightingales to Faucon in April. In June there was a postal strike, and since Violette did most of her business by mail she was forced to go to Paris. She met Lili one Thursday evening at the Café de Flore. They sat in the back, against the upholstered wall, drinking their coffee.

"We were talking about Simone's *The Coming of Age*, which had just been released," Lili said. "We both found it exciting and courageous. But as we sat talking in the café, I got an uneasy feeling. There was a murmur in the night air, something different. Suddenly we heard this enormous roar and the café seemed to explode in slow motion. We put our arms around our heads and dove onto the floor. The windows shattered and I could see the demonstrators yelling their protests, surging onto the Place Saint-

Germain-des-Prés. Then there was terrible screaming, which re-minded me of sounds I had heard during the war.

"It was over in a moment. Violette was sobbing—the back of my head was covered with small pieces of glass. My body had shielded her face from the exploding glass. We held each other until the medics arrived. They wanted to take me to the hospital, but I couldn't think about anything except getting home. I asked Violette to find us a taxi.

"We sat in my apartment, with a bottle of wine between us, and Violette picked the glass out of my hair. She left the next morn-ing for Faucon. She was very shaken from our misadventure."

Her friend Daniel Depland met her at the train station in Avi-gnon. On the way to Faucon in his car, Violette was quiet. Finally she turned to him and told him what had happened at the Café de Flore, and said, *If I die, I don't want to be buried like a dog. I would very much like a little blessing.* He assumed that she was still upset about the incident at the café.

⚜

Near the arroyo a short distance from our house in New Mexico is a mulberry tree, similar to Violette's in Faucon. It has the same shiny leaves the silkworm loves—but without the silkworms. It is said there is no silkworm industry in the United States because there is no cheap labor to hand-harvest the leaves.

In the Vaucluse, if it gets too cold, the women keep the silk-worm eggs warm between their breasts. When it becomes warmer, they carefully place them in a special silkworm room. Then the silkworms begin to eat, so noisily that you can hear them.

Our mulberry tree looks like a stage prop. The nursery we bought the tree from unloaded it before we noticed that the branches grew from only one side of the trunk—it was really only half a tree. We knew that if we returned it, the mulberry would be destroyed. So here it grows, slowly, as if wearing a slouch hat to protect it from the sun.

In March and April, when the desert mistral blows through the trees and knocks against the walls of the house, we close the doors and windows tight. After a few days of continuous winds, it is wise to stay indoors to save ourselves the trouble of having to apologize to each other for being irritable. Unlike the wind of Provence, our mistral is not bitingly cold; it hurls fistfuls of warm, dry, dust-ridden wind. Finally, in May, the winds become still, our eyes caress the cleared skies, and we embrace the silence.

❧

"Violette seemed content, but I knew she was worried about her health." Lili took up the narrative at 1971. "On the fifth of February the bells rang in Maillane to celebrate Saint Agatha's and to warn away treacherous winter storms. Violette wrote that even though the bells were far away, she could hear their knelling in her imagination. Again, she was not receiving mail, for there was yet another postal strike. It was frustrating to all of us.

"When the mail started up, I received a letter from her asking if I was going to sign the manifesto supporting abortion that had been written by women of the Mouvement de Libération des Femmes.

"I had already signed it. But many of the women with whom I discussed the manifesto were concerned about their employment, and that their families might be harassed, that perhaps they would be arrested."

The author of the manifesto, the attorney Gisèle Halimi, created a publication titled *Choisir* to protect the signers, strengthen their solidarity, and provide information. Eventually, three hundred forty-three women from all areas of French life admitted, in print, that they'd had abortions. The Manifesto of the 343 was signed on April 5, 1971, and published in *Le Nouvel Observateur.* The manifesto demanded that women be given the right to legal birth control. De Beauvoir (although she had never had an abortion), Halimi, Colette Audry, Catherine Deneuve, Jeanne Moreau, Christiane Rochefort, Françoise Sagan, and Violette Leduc all signed it and took their chances.

❧

On the fifth of April, the day the manifesto was signed, I was five weeks pregnant with my second child. I felt fortunate to have had the first. Now I was living in the dominion of grace.

I could appreciate Violette's decision, but I had made a conscious decision to have this baby. Eight months minus a few days after the manifesto was signed, I lay in the bathtub surrounded by warm water, trying to float. In a few hours my child would be born.

I insisted on being alone, in the water, with the lights off and the sweet smell of violets filling the air. The water rocked me and soothed me while I listened to Bach. A great aged cello beckoned me with its deep, mournful tones. My body ranged over the crescendos. I was enchanted to see the mountain of my torso move through a lively andante di molto to a dancing gavotte en rondeau—and then settle deep into the water during the melancholic sound of an adagio. I floated, pleased with the idea of the two of us suspended together in the water, in the music.

Violently, without warning, a massive iron fist found my pelvic wall and left me senseless. The pain arched me out of the water like a bloated skin bag. As I breathed deeply between contractions, I felt as if my body had filled the tub so there was no longer room for the water.

I had landed on the shore and was beginning the ancient journey. Driving to the hospital was difficult. I didn't want to leave my son. I kept asking myself why I had to go through this ritual in an antiseptic environment, away from home. I wanted to lie in the fluids that my body was discharging—to inhale their earthiness—to see their colors—to respond to their measurable rhythms. I didn't want to be cleaned and sterilized for the doctors.

Upon arrival I refused a wheelchair and walked to my bed in a row of cubicles on the second floor. It was past midnight, and I wanted to be left alone. I was intense with concentration. I listened to every change. Sensations were roaring within me.

I wanted to be submerged, along with the child, in those safe waters at home. The winds rocked and buffeted me against my pain, and then for a few moments the sun would come out. I'd give a sigh of deliverance, grateful for the in-between spaces. The struggle was ferocious, both physically and metaphysically. I was maligning the male God for having no compassion. If He was so caring, why did women have to suffer this ravishment?

And then I was working so hard at staying with the timing of my body that I didn't realize I was being wheeled into the delivery room. The lights were too bright, there were too many people, the sounds were harsh, grating, and I had to behave. Could I bear to bear this child?

When the birthing began in earnest, white, cold people bustled around me. Hard, cold instruments thrust against me.

The male doctor said, "It looks like it's a boy," and my heart stopped singing.

"No, no," he said sadly, "it's a girl."

My dear heart. I am happy that you were born into the family of women.

❧

I handed Lili some letters, and as she sifted through them she would touch down on passages here and there, and give me the highlights.

"May 1971. 'Spring has arrived in the Vaucluse, along with terrifying electrical storms. The lightning comes in the evenings. I continue to write every day under my chestnut tree. Sometimes the temptation to wander these fields is great. . . . Yesterday I hurried through my lunch and didn't read the Proust I had taken along. I walked to Gauthier, wading across the Eyguemarse River and traipsing through fields of wild iris and narcissus. It takes me a long time to walk across a field, for I try to avoid stepping on the plants. The earth and the sky have filled with an abundance of activity. The swallows are feeding on the wing above my head. And I hear the lengendary male nightingale singing day and night, beckoning. . . .'

"Ah, *The Taxi* has recently been published. It is making a minor but noisy splash in the publishing world. She writes, 'The words emerged out of long-ago passions, strange for a sixty-four-year-old woman. I hope the incestuousness of the two young people will be read as a metaphor.' This is the first book that Simone didn't edit."

Lili turned over another blue page. "Okay, June 1971. 'Yesterday I went with my friends Frédéric and Édith to the fête at Tarascon. We left at four in the morning for the long drive'—they must have just completed the autoroute. 'Do you remember last year when we went to the flower festival? We were too late to find any of the rare plants I had in mind for my garden. This year I am determined. I found nineteenth-century tea roses that looked as if they were hand-painted on tissue paper, peonies sashaying from a very deep pink to almost white in their centers, the same mauve iris that Virginia Woolf describes in her garden. . . . We were finished by noon and home in time for me to plant everything but the irises—these I will keep in a cool and dark place in the back of the grotto until October. . . . This summer I have planted tarragon, thyme, rosemary, savory, jasmine, mimosa, and lavender along the east- and south-facing stone walls. The perfumes attract the constant attendance of cicadas. In the old stone grotto, I placed shade-loving potted plants. Along the north wall I planted a privet hedge interspersed with lilacs, my favorite flower. I love the privet's aroma, *if I have my wish, it will be the odor in my coffin.* Did you know it is possible to graft lilacs to privets? Now that would be a wondrous aroma to place in my box. I send you both my best regards. Violette.'"

Lili held the next page under the light. "'June 24, 1971. Dear Lili. Last night I sat on my balcony and watched the fires blazing on the hilltops around the village of Valréas. Tomorrow is Saint John's Day.'" Lili looks up and tells me, "In the Vaucluse they celebrate it as a time for gathering medicinal herbs. 'I am thinking of planting a Saint John's garden of catnip, thyme, sage, hyssop, and wild hypericum. . . .' She goes on to talk about where she wants to plant it, and then says, 'Did you know ladybugs are known as Saint John's hens? I didn't.'

"My dear, I have to stop here. Reading these letters—I feel anxious. I would like to take a short walk. I need to move around. Will you come along?"

"Of course, but is something wrong?" I asked.

For the first time since I met her, Lili hesitated in answering. "I can't explain clearly, but Violette's letters have made me terribly lonely. Some of my favorite people are gone and I am just filling my life with things to do, none of which is important. Come on, let's go to the air."

In this life, I have been dependent upon literature. As a little girl, I hid behind anyone willing to stake a safe spot for me. And because

I could trust only a few human beings, the safest place was behind a book. Reading has been my passion, my solace, my moral education. Without understanding, I found the perfect ruse in which to ignore my disquiet, to escape my reality. Books were, as de Beauvoir said, "the only reality within my reach."

When I was ten years old, I came across a two-volume edition of Victor Hugo's *Les Misérables*. I was drawn to the old red leather bindings engraved with gold letters, tarnished then with time—its letterpress-printed leaves feeling like gooseflesh—its knife-cut, deckle-edged pages.

I was Fantine's child, Cosette, saved from desolation by the brave Jean Valjean. I was no longer abandoned, denied, thwarted from my path. I experienced the revelation that I, by pure and graceless happenstance, was living in the wrong place at the wrong time. While the walls of the Bastille were being scaled by brave and hardy men, I was lying on my bunk bed, facing the wall, avoiding all contact with my family. Falling off to sleep I lamented the dreary town I lived in, and dreamed of Paris. In school I daydreamed, to such an extent that I was continually reprimanded for these so-called disorders.

Years later, when I was in London with my two children, I begrudgingly bought tickets from a scalper to see *Les Misérables*. I was convinced that it would be a trite puff of a musical, and we would want to leave at intermission. How could Hugo abide his art's being trivialized, made into a carnival? But quickly I found myself transported once again to the Paris of 1817, madly in love with Valjean—and tearfully trying to compose myself so as not to embarrass my teenage children any more than usual. At intermission I moved down to another seat and sat next to a woman who was crying just as pathetically as I was. To my delight, this introduction to another time still held the range of emotions I had experienced as a ten-year-old.

My children pretended they didn't know me.

⁂

Lili and I decided to walk to a Jewish delicatessen on the Rue des Rosiers. It was a cold day, clear and very windy. The wind was strong enough to move us along the sidewalk faster than we cared to walk. Lili held on to my arm. We passed storefront synagogues and a flashing neon Star of David installed against an old stone wall. Everything was in Hebrew—it felt like Jerusalem again. All those familiar signs led us down the street, chez Jo Goldenberg.

The window was lined with giant jars of bright red peppers alternating with jars of deep-green kosher pickles, interspersed here and there with jars of pickled sunny lemons. Hanging from the window frame were kosher salamis, their deep red casings encrusted with white rind. They dangled and tempted, and reminded me of home.

We entered and sat down. Lili ordered first. "A bowl of borscht, with a *tas*, if you please."

I asked for blueberry blintzes and farmer's cheese, with that extra dollop of sour cream, if you please too.

"Now I feel better," Lili said, after the first few spoonfuls of borscht. "This is where Alain and I used to come whenever we needed a *remède*, medicine for the soul. Alain said that the accents of the owners and the smells reminded him of his home when he was young. Ever since he died, I find myself coming here more and more often."

After our meal, Lili left for her doctor's appointment, and I walked to the Bibliothèque Nationale with copies of Violette Leduc's letters in a case under my arm. I was given a seat, way over on the left-hand, quiet side. I began to translate.

September 8, 1971, Wednesday, three forty-five in the afternoon. The day is dim. A dog barks. A hiding insect coos with ardor. Here is the magpie. . . . Sometimes the country coughs. Stop. My ecstasies are no longer kind. . . .

September 18, morning. Everything lives in nature. The dead branches balance the dead leaves. Everything dies under my contemplation. If I no longer need the human voice it is because I am underground. I rest my heart where I can rest it. I ask myself if literature still exists.

Break. I have been coming here for ten years. . . .

September 21. I weep on my exercise book. I found the Virgin. The Virgin is in the west—Mont Ventoux is in the east. I will be at home. . . .

September 23. A new wall . . .

September 23. Do I dream that she exists? Step to the sun. I went back and wrote five pages. I settled down. Old age rests its chin on its hands and its hands on the staff. I am confident in old age. Old age is watching me pass by. . . .

Sunday, September 26. Road from Faucon to Mérindol, ten-thirty in the morning. Two heavy baskets, content, alone in the world. The dry earth will follow me in my long coffin. The mauve butterfly . . .

⁂

I stood up, got my pink card, and left the library for a cup of coffee. It was four in the afternoon, but already dark, and raining again. From the *bar-tabac* I phoned Lili, who told me the doctor said she was fine, not to worry. She was going to bed early because of her full day tomorrow, and she would see me in the morning. I sat at the table drinking my coffee and impolitely eavesdropped on four touring Englishwomen.

One of them said to the others, "Don't you just feel the hot soup going down to your cold feet?"

"What are these bits of green things floating on top?" another woman asked.

"I think it's parsley, or one of those fancy, *hoot-cruising* herbs," said another. (It was basil.)

"Well, the soup is greasy, ducky, but it's still scrumptious," firmly answered another.

The four women shared a cheap carafe of wine, which poured out to four small glasses. "No, you take the last drop," they argued. "No, you, dearie."

In the unrelenting, miserable rain, I walked back to the library, warmed by the Englishwomen's soup. I sat down at a nearly empty table and realized I needed to fill in Violette's life—walk across our biographical gap. In the soft glow of a shaded light, I imagined I could find Violette in beautiful weather.

October 16, 1971. Dear Lili, Autumn is beautiful in the Vaucluse. The vines are aging to red. In a week or so they will be golden, and reflecting the sun across this valley. Even today there is snow veiling the peak of Mont Ventoux.

Yesterday I walked to the market, the Halle des Fêtes, in

Mérindol and saw that the season for killing wild boar has begun. Their meat was hanging from the racks, it was gruesome. The alchemy of seasons is most obvious at this time of year. It makes me sad. Everything left after the summer is being harvested—walnuts, chestnuts; all have a pungent, earthy quality. The land is falling asleep and hushing its living creatures with a lullaby. I am feeling a strange calm, it is unsettling. Fondly, Violette.

November 6, 1971. Dear Lili, Thank you for the catalogue from the Francis Bacon exhibition. He puts to canvas my grotesque imagination. It is startling.

Today I watched an amazing event right here from my window. Thousands of sheep were moving across the valley. Their baaing had a rhythm that was not unpleasant, though it was very noisy. When they arrived at the walls of Faucon they were forced to split into two herds and move to the right or the left. There was much confusion at this point, and the din became frantic. Lambs were searching confusedly for their mothers, mothers panicked looking for their babies—there was bedlam. And then, suddenly, it was still. Families were back together and, in relief, followed their shepherd. I poured myself a pastis.

Winter wheat is being planted, and the olives, now brown, are being harvested. To remove their bitterness, they are cured with olive or vine wood ashes. After a week the olives are cleansed of the ashes and soaked in clear water that has to be changed twice a day. Finally they are put in a sea-salt bath and cooked with spices and fruit peels.

It seems peculiar, but November is really the beginning of a new agricultural year. There is an old country saying here, *"L'iver a ges d'ouro"*—Winter has no hours—and that seems to be true. Even though the weather has turned cool, I still manage to write under my chestnut tree in the Jaux. I come every day it is at all possible. Instead of bringing my bathing suit and cold water, I bring hot coffee and the blue sweater I was knitting when I saw you last. Otherwise I work indoors at my desk by the window, or in bed, as in Paris.

And of course, it is truffle season again. The trained pigs are out hunting for *rabasso,* or what we call "black gold." Each year it amuses me to see grown men leading pigs around. I will send you my annual box of truffles next week. Let's hope there isn't another rail strike.

Thank you for your concern about my health. I don't know what is going on, I just seem to be malingering, with no apparent reason. Perhaps it is because winter is here. Maybe I need a holiday. Love, Violette.

December 30, 1971. My dear Lili, Thank you for sending the books, and I'm happy the truffles arrived safely. I knew you were worried about my being alone this holiday, but I really did have a pleasant time.

On Christmas Eve, my friends invited me to go with them to the torchlight vigil and midnight mass in Séguret. This village wraps around the rocky side of a very steep hill. We entered through a covered passage onto the main street. Great torches of fire were parading in front of us, moving toward the church. If I hadn't known better, I would have sworn they were creating a path just for us. I had my old Bible with me—remember the one with Maurice Sachs's jottings in the margins?—such wicked illuminations. Yet I am always comforted when my eyes caress his handwriting.

I am generally tired but trying to write. I am very restless. I cannot seem to eat more than an egg and a slice of bread, sometimes a vegetable. Pastis is too sweet but whiskey is all right. I send you and Alain my best for a Happy New Year. Violette.

❧

Nine-thirty, and the library was closing. I walked back to Lili's. It was quiet on the street and quiet inside the apartment. She was asleep in her room; no light shone beneath her door. More than anywhere I have been, rain in Paris dampens noise, hushes light. People seem to pass into a melancholy mood. I slept with my window slightly ajar so I could listen to the rain.

When I awoke very early the next morning, Lili was already gone. Perched on my favorite cup and saucer, the one with the pretty pink roses, was a note: "Please leave anything here that you do not need to take with you. And keep your key. I will be gone all day and then have to go Saint-Rémy to be with my friend who is ill.

Please give my regards to Mme. Maurel. Your room will wait for you. I will wait for you. Lili."

I took a taxi to the Gare de Lyon. There I boarded the seven-forty TGV to Avignon. Four hours later I arrived, in sunshine, to Joe—standing there waiting for me on the train platform. I couldn't believe our timing. He had arrived at the airport only three hours earlier—all the way from New York—and then got to the train station easily. We immediately found a café and sat over coffee catching up on news. Actually, I did most of the talking; there was so much to tell him.

It was wonderful to be with Joe—he was excited about my time in Paris and ready for an adventure. We picked up our rental car and left for our first stop, Gordes. There we spent the night in a hotel perched high over the rolling hills of the Vaucluse.

The next morning, taking the most obscure roads we could find, we left for Faucon. Our eyes roamed the bare vines of the famous Côtes du Ventoux. We continued along the D86 to the base of Faucon. We could see some of the stone wall that has surrounded and braced the village since the eleventh century. The thorny bramble that grows between the rocks was now leafless; firethorn, with its clusters of bright reddish-orange berries and its prickly branches, decorated the roadside. Birds eat these berries for their sugar; they are poisonous to humans.

We passed through a herd of sheep being brought down from the Ventoux. They had patches on their coats that were dyed blue, red, or orange to identify their owners—a moving quilt of color. The sheep numbered about four hundred and were herded by at least two dogs and two shepherds. The weakest—the babies, the nursing mothers, the grandmothers and grandfathers—went first. They crossed before us on the D86, the shepherds paying us no heed.

We parked our car at the bottom of the village and walked up the narrow stone-paved road to the main square. We must have looked lost and confused, for within minutes a mailman approached us and asked if we needed directions. We told him we were look-ing for the house of the writer Violette Leduc. He didn't know which had been hers, for he had moved to the village only ten years before.

"Come with me," he said. "I will take you to someone who knows everything." Like good sheep we followed him down a lane to a house on the left. He marched to the door and flung it open without knocking. "Madame, I have brought you some people looking for the Madame Leduc house. Can you help?" A tall, reedy woman was introduced to us by the mailman. She didn't know which house it was either. The woman invited us in and, speaking her native English, offered the use of her telephone. Because Joe spoke French, he called Mme. Maurel to set a time for an interview. It turned out that Violette's house was the one next door.

The English-speaking woman's house was beautiful. Until 1975, she told us, it had been the village café and grocery store, and was used primarily by the elderly, who spent their days sitting and drinking and conversing. An old statue of the Republic once stood outside between the two windows, guarding the stone walls from intruders. From Violette's books, I knew this was where she had come each day to purchase wine, butter, and milk.

I wanted to ask questions, but I knew from my previous nosing around that the Fauconnais are very private and unto themselves, so I resisted. "What you want to know, you won't know," I was told by those who knew. Our appointment with Mme. Maurel was at three o'clock, so we asked the English-speaking woman if she could suggest a place for us to eat. She recommended La Gloriette—the same café in Mérindol that Lili had told me about. We drove the three kilometers through a pathway of oak trees, and had one of the most memorable meals of our journey. A simple lunch with an outstanding bottle of wine, a 1988 Côtes-du-Rhône Domaine du Faucon Doré. At the end of the meal we were quite drunk and having a wonderful time. With still another hour before our meeting, we decided to leave our car where it was and walk back to Faucon.

This was the same road, the D530, that Lili had told me about. Rows upon rows of waiting grapevines, intersected by vast dark ocher fields and beautiful stone walls meandering toward Mont Ventoux, led us to Faucon. We passed a few farmers who were tilling the land with modern machinery. Others were using the same *araires* that have been used to plow the earth for two thousand years. Smaller patches were being cleared by hand with scythes. It was a dance, a performance of balance and rhythm. It was another time.

Mme. Maurel lived across the lane from Violette Leduc's house, in a house that was called Café Mama fifty years ago. Édith Maurel had been another substitute mother to Violette, although she was sixteen years younger. She was small in stature, with red hair and a face that made me think of someone who had experienced a great tragedy. Indeed, she had recently lost her son to a brain tumor. With eyes of limpid blue—a face worn with grief—and beautiful, long-nailed hands, Édith had stood by Violette Leduc through her highs and lows.

We spoke all afternoon, moving from French to English and back again. Mme. Maurel spoke very slowly so we could understand. Her face was calm, her eyes steady, and her hands sat demurely in her lap. She was very interested in helping me with information. Between Joe's linguistic ability and my insistent questioning, I was able to garner a vast amount of information. She told me many things I already knew, but she also gave me a more thorough view of Violette's kindness, and in particular her slapstick sense of humor. She told me how Violette would speak in a ragtime tempo through the curtains of her kitchen window when a neighbor walked by:

Good / morn / ing / to / you / Good / morn / ing / to / youuu.

At first the neighbors thought she might be a little *too* eccentric. But in time they began to appreciate her zaniness.

"Faucon is known for its eccentric population," Mme. Maurel said. "We once determined the altitude of the village by measuring the distance to the top of the church steeple."

"Another odd story, also a true one," Mme. Maurel continued. "Until a few years ago there were two families who had lived side by side for generations. One family had three brothers and two sisters, the other family had three brothers and two sisters too. Not one of these ten people ever married anyone, much less anyone from the other family. I find this amazing!"

Mme. Maurel told us that truffles were introduced as an industry to the region after an epidemic attacked olive trees in the nineteenth century. Small landowners replanted their land with *chênes truffiers*, special oak trees. Under these trees, into their roots, they introduced truffle spore. In eight to ten years truffles began to grow in great quantities. Then one man decided to speed up the process. He injected truffle spore into the trees, but it took him years to come to a conclusion about his research because he needed the right amount of humidity before he could inoculate the trees in the first place. If he thought the season was going to be damp, he rushed around and gave the trees their shots. But year after year, the weather turned upon him from the opposite direction and he had to begin again. "Violette laughed at his failures because she knew the truffle man didn't like her," Mme. Maurel said. "He was a buffoon."

She showed us Violette's house, and Joe and I took photographs of each other standing by her door, next to the stone wall, under the mulberry. We could not enter the house itself because the owners were in Paris. The doors and windows were closed tight against our curious eyes, and the imposing pale-blue metal shutters with large barn hinges were locked.

We asked Mme. Maurel about visiting the Jaux, the small woods outside the village. She insisted that we had only enough time to see the graveyard before it grew dark. She couldn't go with us, so we said good-bye and started for the graveyard by ourselves.

We walked down the hill from the village, and passed through the stone archway. Opening before us across the road was a wide expanse of land, a bottomland, with rolling hills punctuating the horizon. And there, straight ahead of us, was a small graveyard with a path lined by two rows of grape arbors and two grand cypress trees. The area was bordered by a stone wall. We walked to a stone portal with a stone cross standing on top; the gates, which were of heavy wood, were aged and slightly aslant. They were not easy to open, and the more we pushed, inch by inch, the more apprehensive we became. The gates were not locked, but nevertheless seemed to be protecting their hushed citizens.

Finally we were inside. A few graves were decorated with red plastic roses. It was a traditional French cemetery with an occasional crypt housing a family, one family member on top of another. Mainly the graves were simple, the graves of farmers, wives of farmers, children of the land.

Joe and I walked up and down the gravel paths looking for Violette. It was late, the sun was low on the horizon, and it was getting cold. But where was she? We couldn't find her grave. Up and down we walked, again and again. We each took a row, examining every headstone. No Violette.

We met back at the gates and decided to trade paths, when along came an elderly woman. She was dressed entirely in black, with a wrinkled, sun-dried face. We told her we were looking for the grave of Violette Leduc, but couldn't find it. She looked at us, as some French do, as if we were either crazy or stupid, and said to follow her.

And there was the grave. We had walked past it innumerable times without seeing it. Because Violette Leduc was so physically obvious in her lifetime, we were looking for a dramatic gravesite. There was no drama here, only a highly polished gray granite slab in a modern, sleek design. The headstone was blank, serving only to prevent Violette from seeing the sun setting in the west. The stone that rested over her remains was engraved with serifed letters in gold:

VIOLETTE LEDUC

ECRIVAIN

Centered beneath this was a three-foot-long cross, raised about an inch high, in the same cold gray granite. Under the cross was inscribed, also in gold:

1907–1972

In front of the grave was a potted geranium with two branches, six leaves, and one faded, dying red blossom.

Violette Leduc would have been furious if she had seen how she'd been buried. She said she hated buildings made of concrete, they were human coffins. And here she was, interred in concrete and cold, cruel-edged stone. I know she would have preferred her Vaucluse stone, the rough-hewn stone that marked the neighbors to her left and right. She would have wanted stone that could age with rain and sleet and the mistral—not highly polished gray granite made impenetrable with modern materials. Violette would have wanted a small, lacelike wrought-iron *croix potencée* sitting silently by her head. Whoever ordered the stone with the ugly cross did not know Thérèse Andrée Violette Leduc very well.

Berthe, the cold, distant mother, outlived her daughter. It didn't seem fair. Since the death of her stepfather in 1954, Violette had been supporting her mother. When Violette died, her mother was in a rest home in Biarritz and not well. The authorities had to find Claude Dehous, the daughter of Violette's half brother, to sign the necessary papers.

Violette Leduc desired *the dry earth to follow me in my long coffin.* Instead she had a petit bourgeois burial—very clean, no dust.

It was almost dark, and Joe and I still had to walk back to Mérindol to get our car. There is a country superstition that says that after a person is buried, the straw upon which the person has been laid while being prepared for burial must be burned. Those living look for a footprint in the ashes. If it fits one of them, he will be the next to die. There were no ashes now, but enough mud to make us nervous. We decided to follow Jewish tradition instead. We each placed a stone on Violette's grave, paying homage, saying good-bye.

A few days later, after wandering around Provence, I returned to Paris; Joe continued on to Spain to meet his cousin. It was nice to be back. When I let myself into Lili's apartment, I found her in the living room. She had been reading and was now dozing, shaded by the lowering light of the evening. The sight made me sad—I knew our time together was drawing to a close. She woke and reached to turn on the lamp, and smiled and warmly greeted me. I told her about Faucon, Mme. Maurel, our adventures.

Her week was not nearly as interesting. "My friend in Saint-Rémy is not well," Lili said. "Tonight is the first evening I have been home. Her family finally arrived and took her to their home in Lille. It is sad—I feel I will never see her again."

"To cheer you up, let me take you to dinner," I said. "I'm starving. All I had on the train was a candy bar and two cups of terrible coffee. Do you feel well enough to eat at La Coupole? I have a craving for shellfish and their wonderful bread."

She laughed and said, "Of course. I would love some good food. All I have been eating is soup and more soup and stewed vegetables and soft bananas—a diet for the sick."

Lili put some of Violette's letters into her satchel, and we took a taxi across the Seine to the Boulevard de Montparnasse.

La Coupole was a favorite café of the Parisian literary elite when it opened in 1927. Now it still attracts the literary elite, but only the wealthy. When we arrived, there were but a few people, reading newspapers attached to bamboo poles. They were the regulars. We ordered the gigantic *plateau de fruits de mer*.

I told Lili how my grandfather had taught me to eat raw oysters. Then I told her about a previous experience of mine in Paris. "I wanted to order an omelette that wasn't runny. I kept saying to the waiter, *'Une omelette fermée, s'il vous plaît,'* and he kept looking at me as if I were crazy. Finally he said, *'Oui, une omelette non baveuse'*—and he brought me the 'closed' omelette I'd asked for. A man sitting next to me leaned over and said, 'Madame, there you have your omelette without slobber!'"

The waiter brought us a bottle of the season's Muscadet along with thick-sliced brown-crusted bread. He wore a long white apron that brushed the floor, and was tall and thin, just like every other waiter in the restaurant. I told Lili that it appeared they had been bred for the job. She laughed, and I took out the tape recorder.

"My dear, it is so nice to have you here with me again," Lili said. "I am going to miss you."

I couldn't answer. My eyes started to fill with tears, and I looked down and tried to catch myself. Together, we were quiet for a few moments. Then Lili began to speak again.

"Violette came back to Paris in January 1972. It was obvious she wasn't feeling well. There were new, large creases in her face, accentuating her long nose. Her eyes seemed to be set farther back into her skull, threatening to depart. Her long body was stooped, her neck disappeared into her shoulders. My immediate reaction was to suggest a visit to the doctor. Violette protested that she felt fine, just a little tired. We had a drink together at the Bar du Pont-

Royal, her favorite on the Rue de Montalembert, around the corner from Gallimard.

"Violette usually liked to sit near the front, facing the door. She liked to watch people come in, and speculate upon their lives and their work. She would make up fanciful stories about them from observing their clothing and how they held a fork and knife. She could write a novella from a lunch. But that day she sat quietly, her back to the door. When she did speak, her thoughts were introspective, lingering at the feet of her life. She reminded me that it was Simone de Beauvoir's birthday, and she proposed a toast.

"Raising her glass, she said, *'At the end of my life, I will think of my mother, I will think of Simone de Beauvoir, and I will think of my long struggle.'*

"She spoke about her work and her alienation. I'll never forget her face, and the somber tone of her voice. She said she had finally found her home, she was no longer in exile. I thought she meant her house in Faucon. But she said no, she had found her home in words. Words provided the comfort never given by her mother. She blanketed herself in words, they kept out the coldness of her estrangement. She was ever so grateful. Words had given her a place in the world. She said she was separated from the rest of society by a hyphen—not a period.

"Her words frightened me. When I returned home, I was devastated. Violette's life seemed to be moving and dissolving at the same time. It was like watching an old film disintegrating through the projector, frame by frame. I told Alain she was an apparition of her former self. He was convinced that Violette was simply fatigued after the publication of her last two books. But I could smell disease. There was a mustiness about her that had never existed before. It could not be eliminated by any amount of fresh air. It made my skin crawl. It was a busy time for us but Alain and I both felt we had to help her. We offered to drive her back to Faucon, and she gratefully accepted.

"On the fifth of February, as the bells were ringing throughout Provence for Saint Agatha's Day, we returned Violette to her home in Faucon. The next morning, after making sure that she had food for the week, we prepared to leave. She was sitting by the window, looking across the valley to Mont Ventoux. I asked if she was in pain and she said no, she was just very tired. She promised me she was fine and thanked us again for bringing her home. I leaned over to kiss her on both cheeks, and then it was Alain's turn. She put her long arms around him, which was most unlike her, and clung for a few moments.

"Her habit was to walk with us to our car at the bottom of the hill. This morning we went alone. She was simply too tired to make the effort—but she said not to worry, there was not yet a graveyard in her heart. We stopped across the way at Madame Maurel's and she assured us that she would tend to Violette, not to worry. We left for Paris in tears."

Ten days later Violette wrote to Serge Tamagnot in Paris.

February 15. Dear Serge, I'll be arriving at eight p.m. precisely on the platform at the Gare de Lyon, Monday the 22nd. Don't tell anyone. Could you come and fetch me? Can you please answer me by return mail? You'll be my guest. We'll have dinner together.

Could you buy a small package of butter, a small package of coffee beans, a little package of bisquettes for my breakfast the next morning?

I'll reimburse you.

I kiss you, and best regards, Violette Leduc.

Violette was slowly beginning to say good-bye to her friends. She had the physical energy to visit only one at a time. And from now on they would have to go to Faucon: Violette would never see Paris again.

February 17. Dear Serge, I am ill and I cannot even come Monday as we had decided. So we'll do that another time.

Give me some news from you.

My best regards, Violette Leduc.

"I decided to go back to Faucon in March." Lili looked sad as she said this. "Alain stayed in Paris because of some deadlines and an important meeting. But we had an understanding that if I needed him, he would come. For two weeks I stayed with her and sat quietly while she stared out the window. *'Ce qu'on est bien,'* she would say, and smile.

"For dinner I would prepare a simple soup for the two of us and encourage her to take a little. She had difficulty keeping food down. It was obvious to me she was dying. It was not obvious to her. We talked and told stories to while away the long evenings. We were still living, but time was dying all around us. It was a bleak month.

"Then, at the beginning of April, she needed medical attention. She didn't want to leave her house—it was her haven, her refuge. But she understood she had to do something. We packed a few things, in case she had to stay overnight. I drove her to the Hospital of Saint Martha in Avignon. It was raining hard, the roads were paved with mirrors, reflecting my headlights. She hardly spoke the entire way—only a reminder to feed her cat, Demi-lune, every morning. I assured her I would."

When they arrived at the hospital, Violette held back. She did not want to walk into the building. She loved the color green in nature, but hated those putrid green hospital walls and the smells of illness. She was cringing in apprehension. Lili handed her a lilac-scented handkerchief, and Violette held it against her face as she entered. She took a deep breath and walked to the admitting desk.

The staff would not allow Lili to accompany Violette to the examining room, so she waited in the entry hall. For two hours she waited. Finally a doctor came out to see her. He told Lili he would be keeping Violette in the hospital for more tests. The cancer had spread—she was dying. He said he could make her more comfortable by trying a new combination of drugs. He wanted to keep her for two days to balance her medication; then he would send her home.

Lili went upstairs to see Violette. She entered a room lined with white beds. It made her think of a Samuel Beckett play. She walked down the aisle looking to her right, then her left. There, at the end, was Violette, asleep. Her face was in repose, her skin so pale that death appeared to have set its mask upon her face already. She woke and smiled at Lili.

"'Violette,' I said, 'I will stay as long as you like.'

"'No,' she said. 'Go home, I am tired.'

"She probably meant to Paris, but I returned to Faucon. I worked at her table and spoke each night to Alain in Paris. On April seventh, Alain came by train for Violette's birthday. I met him at the station in Avignon and we drove directly to the hospital. She was surprised to see Alain behind the huge bouquet of fresh-cut lilacs.

"'Why are you here, Alain?' she asked.

" 'To celebrate,' he answered.

" 'To celebrate what?' she asked.

" 'Your birthday!' we said together. She had forgotten.

"That day, we took her home. She was delighted, especially with all the attention being paid to her by her fans. The table was piled with greeting cards from all over France."

Our waiter arrived with the *plateau de fruits de mer*, a collection of exotic raw sea urchins, succulent Belon oysters, clams and mussels, all smelling of the briny sea. He set it down on a silver three-legged stand, right in the middle of our table. I ordered another bottle of wine.

"That evening, at Violette's," Lili said, "the Maurels came by and we had a little party. We drank a lot of whiskey, smoked many Chesterfields, and told stories about the old days. Violette was in good spirits. The next morning Alain and I reluctantly left for Paris. It was obvious that my hovering was making Violette nervous.

" 'Please, I will be fine,' she kept saying—and there was no way to respond without telling her the truth. This I could not do.

"It was the saddest of good-byes, for we knew we might never see her again.

"Every few days I would telephone her. She was always cheerful and optimistic. She sincerely didn't believe that she was deathly ill. She told me about the spinach she had just picked and made into a salad, with new potatoes and a little olive oil. Or about the spring in Faucon and how beautiful it was that year. She said that Demi-lune insisted on sleeping beside her for the first time. Even Alain and I started to think that maybe this last illness was only a scare.

"Then, on Saturday, May thirteenth, we received a note from Édith Maurel.

Dear Monsieur and Madame Jacobs,

My husband, Frédéric, is a part of Violette's elaborate rituals. Every morning except Sunday, he passes Violette's window at eight, and every morning she waits by the window and syncopates the words "Good morning my little Frédéric" from behind the curtain. This morning he didn't hear her, and he became concerned. Instead of continuing to work, he turned around and came back to our house.

"Because you climb like a goat, you need to get up on the balcony and look through the shutters," he told me.

I climbed up and saw through the opened louvers that she was very ill. We used a key that she had left with us, and entered the house. She was lying on her bed fully dressed, afraid to move. She was in too much pain. I called the doctor at Vaison-la-Romaine and made arrangements to go there immediately. Frédéric and I held her between us as she walked up the path, past the old café, past the *lavoir* where she used to fetch her water, to the church, where the car was parked, and then drove her to the doctor's in silence.

The doctor was waiting for us, and he helped Violette into his office. We stood aside as he examined her, looked her in the eyes, smiled, and said, "Madame Leduc, you are fine, just suffering from a bad stomach. Go home and eat whatever you like." We knew he was lying, but pretended he was telling the truth.

Do not come to Faucon yet. It will only make Violette more nervous. I will keep you informed.

Sincerely,
Édith Maurel

"From this time forward Édith tended Violette. She slept by her bed and nursed her. 'I don't give you details,' Édith wrote me, 'they are not pretty.'"

On Friday, May 19, Violette wrote a letter to Daniel Depland. The letter was breezy, full of interest. She didn't complain. She asked her friend to buy her a belt at a store in Paris and to bring it with him when he came to visit on the twenty-seventh.

The following Thursday, May 25, Édith phoned Lili to say that the end was approaching. Lili tried to contact Simone de Beauvoir, but could not reach her.

"I don't understand," I said to Lili. "Where was Simone de Beauvoir during this time? Did she know Violette was dying? Why didn't she visit her?"

"It turned out," Lili answered, "that Simone was indeed in Paris during this time—busy correcting the proofs for *All Said and Done*, and not answering her phone."

In this, the fourth volume of de Beauvoir's autobiography, she recounted: "When [Violette] left [the hospital] she wrote and told me how happy she was to be home again and to know that her illness had not been at all serious. A little later I was told on the telephone that she had just sunk into a coma. . . . She died without having recovered consciousness."

This was not true. Violette had two good weeks at home. She was lucid. She wrote letters to her friends. She visited often with Édith and they had tea in her garden. During the last few days she traveled through consciousness, sometimes quite alert, and other times lost somewhere in dreams. She never entered a coma.

It did not surprise me that Simone was so remote from Violette. Although she helped certain writers, she kept a well-defined distance from them. When Violette died, she immediately put her letters and manuscripts up for auction. I understood why Violette wrote about Simone de Beauvoir, *She is my reason for living, even though I am not part of her life.*

"After I tried to reach Simone," Lili said, "I rang Alain, who was in London on business. He was out, so I left a message with his hotel about what was happening. Violette's friend Madeleine Castaing and I drove south together, and arrived in Faucon later that evening. Madeleine was carrying a letter for Violette from her old friend Jacques Guerlain.

"We found Violette in bed wearing her favorite blue dressing gown. She was so much thinner than before. Her skin was diaphanous, and I imagined I could see the blood moving through her veins. Madeleine sat by the bed and read Jacques's letter—but I don't think Violette really heard much of it. This made me sad, for I believe they had not seen each other for a while because of a quarrel. The letter spoke of forgiveness and friendship—it would have pleased her."

"From what I have read," I interrupted, "Jacques was a creation of Violette's imagination. Because he had helped her occasionally and because he genuinely admired her work, she transformed him into representing both a good mother and a caring father. Yet he was very much like de Beauvoir, indeed like her parents. He kept his distance too."

"Listen," Lili said, "I don't want to finish Violette's life across a table of soiled dishes and damp bread crumbs. Let's go to the Café de Flore—it seems fitting. I know she would love the gesture."

I paid an enormous amount of money for a meal worth every last franc, and then we took a taxi to the Boulevard Saint-Germain. Lili obviously knew the headwaiter, and after a conversation of very fast French, we were seated at "our" table. Although spring was still far away, the front door of the café was propped open—people had draped their coats over the backs of chairs—a whisper of warm weather settled around us.

We ordered cognacs and smiled at each other. It was time for the finale—for Violette Leduc's farewell. Lili took a sip of cognac and began.

"Violette still did not expect to die. She awoke in the morning feeling no pain, just a little sleepiness. She laughingly told us that she must have taken too many sleeping tablets. Then she lay back on her pillow and slept for two days. Édith, Madeleine, and I took turns staying by her side.

"The morning of Saturday, May twenty-seventh, I went to the open market in the square to shop. As I was buying bread, I saw Daniel Depland trudging up the stone path. We walked to the house together while I explained the gravity of Violette's condition.

"When we arrived he went upstairs and stood by her bed, gazing down at her for a few moments. Violette opened her eyes, saw him, and smiled. He was very dear to her. Daniel asked her how she was feeling. *Je voyage* . . . she said.

"On Sunday, May 28, 1972, the church bells rang for the ten-o'clock mass and we sat by Violette's bed, knowing this would be her last day.

"At lunchtime we ate in the kitchen while a friend, Jean-Sully Dumas, a dressmaker from Avignon, kept watch over Violette.

"When the church bells rang for the four-o'clock mass, Édith, Frédéric, Madeleine, Daniel, and I were sitting in chairs around Violette's bed. We were all quiet, listening to her breathe, but hearing only ourselves.

"At five minutes past five, while Madeleine held her, Violette lifted her arms toward the ceiling of her beloved house. She separated her fingers like the petals of a flower and brought them back to the bed in a flutter, then said, *How many strange things have happened in my life.*

"At a quarter past five, as the sun finally slipped over the edges of Mont Ventoux, Violette Leduc died.

"Frédéric walked down the road, the one in front of the church, to the office of the mayor, Germain Hommage, to report the death."

Violette became number AZ70413 on the register of the Commune of Faucon in the Vaucluse.

"Alain had flown into Paris that afternoon. But before I called him, I had an errand to do. Violette had told me about Sabinien, her shepherd friend in a nearby village, Aguillan. She occasionally met him on her way to write in the woods. They would stop to chat and he would tell her about his sheep—about shearing and spinning and his seasons in the mountains. Besides being a shepherd, he was also the village bell-ringer. Violette had asked that he ring the bells in Faucon when she died.

"I drove to Aguillan and found Sabinien, who honored his promise. We drove back to Faucon. He opened the church door, climbed the platform, and rang the bells. He rang the bells seven times, once for each decade of Violette's life. And then I drove him home.

"On Sunday, in the early evening, Paul, the headwaiter and general giver-of-news at Les Deux Magots in Paris, found Alain sitting outside and informed him of Violette's death. I have absolutely no idea how Paul learned about it. By the time I called Alain that evening, he had already made reservations for the early train to Avignon.

"Madeleine and I drove to La Gloriette in Mérindol to sleep. Daniel stayed with Violette and drank whiskey. His grief was painful to see—they had become very good friends in the past few years, he was going to miss her terribly. He put one of Violette's favorite pieces of Bach, a passacaglia, on the record player and turned on every light in the house. Then he doused himself with Violette's favorite perfume, Habit Rouge—produced by the firm of her friend Jacques Guerlain, and poured himself another whiskey.

"After sitting for a while, he got up, took a pair of scissors from Violette's desk, and cut a lock of his hair. He carefully placed it in the pocket of her dressing gown—now her shroud—then poured himself another whiskey.

"Another hour went by and Daniel stood up and went to Violette again. This time he leaned over her body and with the scissors cut a lock of her thick hair. This he put in his own pocket. He sat down, faced his friend, and had another whiskey. He finally fell asleep, just as the sun was rising.

"Violette's mother, in the rest home in Biarritz, was too ill to come to Faucon and sign the death certificate. On Monday, no one could find her stepniece. So, according to French law, the authorities were forced to seal her house. We had to do something with Violette.

"Frédéric Maurel lifted Violette from her bed, carried her outside, and put her on a table in the grotto beside her house. This made everyone very nervous, especially Édith Maurel's mother, whose bedroom opened onto the grotto. Violette lay "in state" on the table all day, in her grotto, clothed in her dressing gown. Édith covered her with a blanket for the night and slept beside her in a chair.

"Late the next afternoon, May thirtieth, the office staff of Berthe's rest home located Claude Dehous. When she arrived in Faucon, it was apparent why Violette had never taken to her stepniece. She was about twenty years old, plain, a perfectly ordinary young woman—soon to be married. She signed the papers. Claude Dehous and Berthe Leduc Dehous inherited most of Violette's estate.

"Violette was placed in her coffin, and Madeleine put Jacques Guerlain's letter in her pocket. I put a sprig of privet and a branch of lilacs beside her head—and the coffin was closed. She was carried by friends and neighbors down the hill to the cemetery.

"The entire village of Faucon came to her funeral. And from Paris there was Odette Laigle, representing Gallimard, and the writer Monica Lange, an old friend, and of course, Madeleine, Daniel, Alain, and me. Serge Tamagnot, who heard about Violette's death on the radio, did not have the money for train fare, so he spent the day in the Jardin des Tuileries in Violette's memory.

"Daniel was so shocked that Simone de Beauvoir didn't attend that a week after the funeral he wrote her an angry letter. She replied to him that she 'considered death so final that any funeral was meaningless.'

"The funeral was simple."

Lili paused and closed her eyes. She opened them with a sigh and smiled at me. "It was so long ago, but I still feel such sadness," she said.

We sat quietly for a few moments, before Lili caught the waiter's eye. *"L'addition, s'il vous plaît.*

"So my dear, this is the end of the story. It brings to a close all those years of my friendship with Violette. She once said, *'Along the tracks of all the tears once shed, I trotted on my way.'* I am convinced that her soul has finally been relieved of its sadness."

Lili stood and put on her coat. "Let's go home. I'm tired."

The next morning I packed to return to America. Lili and I spent the rest of the day talking and eating and walking and talking some more.

Now here, sitting on the desk in my studio, is a lily, my favorite flower. I know the metaphor. I know a lily blooms just once a year. But my lily continues to bloom. Lili is my mother, my friend— Violette Leduc is my sister, my shadow. I wear many masks, over, under, and around my soul. They all fit, and whether I like it or not, they are all indivisible in the singular me.

Leaving Lili was terrible. She offered to go with me to the airport, but I couldn't bear to prolong our parting. So we said good-bye at her front door. She kissed me on the right cheek, she kissed me on the left cheek. She kissed me on the right cheek once more. Then she took me in her arms.

ACKNOWLEDGMENTS

To my first readers and advisors, I extend my appreciation: Lynne Bundesen, Dr. Isabelle de Courtivron, Joseph Dispenza, Constanze Frank, Greg Glazner, Len Goodman, Roberta Goodman, Dee Ito, Phyllis La-Farge Johnson, Dr. Marsha Landau, Leila Matthews, Paul Matthews, John Menken, Reina Menken, Phyllis Meris, Kate Millett, Tony Pearson, Mary Powell, Meridel Rubenstein, and Dr. Vera John Steiner.

Violette Leduc's friends in France were always available to answer my questions and set me straight about French customs. Serge Tamagnot spent hours upon days telling me stories about Leduc. He kindly offered original letters and photographs, for which I am thankful. Daniel Depland answered pages of persistent questions with even more pages of his observations and memories. His being with Leduc at the end of her life helped me visualize her death. Françoise d'Eaubonne, the first person I ever interviewed, sat patiently through an afternoon, responding to my halting questions. Despite a busy academic schedule, Professor Michèle Gibault translated for me in Paris. Without her serenity, my intentions would have abandoned me forever. Carlo Jansiti and René de Ceccatty are both biographers and friends of Mme. Leduc's. They provided important nuances in understanding her. The Mottiers, from the village of Anceins in Normandy, graciously allowed two bumbling women to barge in at the end of their lunch one afternoon. They got over their surprise quickly and invited us in for coffee and many stories. Catherine

Collomp generously introduced me to Édith Maurel. It was Mme. Maurel's openness and descriptive information that made it possible for me to "visit" Violette Leduc in Faucon. And it was Cathie Bizard and Armelle Tozzi's hospitality that made it possible for me to research Violette Leduc comfortably in Paris.

Upon my return to America the following people helped me enormously: Dominique Mazeaud, who translated, both verbally and sociologically, everything that came my way *en français*; Suzan Campbell and Gary DeWalt, who edited with kindness, long before I understood what they were saying; Henry Chalfant, who led me gently through the French language; Victoria Zackheim, who was a good Anna; Elizabeth Zackheim, who told me stories about first-generation Jews in America in her unique, visual way; Lewis Z. Koch, who showed me Nelson Algren's Chicago; Professor Elaine Marks, who encouraged me when all hope was fading into the distance; Dr. Eva Sartori, who introduced me to Lili Jacobs; Dr. Gerald Rodriguez, who researched many questions concerning Mme. Leduc's medical history; Dr. David Metcalf, who helped me understand her psychiatric-hospital stay at La Vallée-aux-Loups; Dr. Reina Attias, who helped me understand Mme. Leduc's psychological structure, and some of mine too; Marion Fourestier, of the French Government Tourist Office in New York, who answered every question, no matter how difficult or mundane; Jeanette Woodward and Sherry Evans at the Fogelson Library, the College of Santa Fe, who ordered every book and article that I requested from Inter-Library Loan; Sybille Pearson, who insisted that I was a writer, and Kathleen Chalfant, who was my constant reminder; Anna Jardine, who sees through a typed page with kindly infrared vision; Christine Brooks, who believed in me enough to introduce my work to Betsy Lerner, who generously introduced me to my agent, Kathleen Anderson; and Kathleen Anderson, the Golden Archangel, the champion of my middle years, whose every notation was a lesson in writing. And at the end of this paragraph, only because she is the newest person in my writing life, I thank Julie Grau, my editor, fierce corrector, dear person, and constant supporter.

It is burdensome for me to live a "normal life" when I am wandering in an imaginary world, day and night. My husband, Charles Ramsburg, an artist, is often lost in his imagination too. Between the two of us we manage to get meals cooked and dishes done, and love each other. I am grateful to him.

And last, I thank our children, Ben and Maggie, who are always alongside me, even when they are far away.

The author gratefully acknowledges permission to reprint excerpts from the following:

Deirdre Bair, *Simone de Beauvoir: A Biography.* New York: Summit, 1990. Copyright © 1990 Deirdre Bair. Reprinted with permission of Simon & Schuster.
Simone de Beauvoir, *All Said and Done,* trans. Patrick O'Brian. New York: Warner, 1975. Reprinted by permission of Marlowe & Company.
Simone de Beauvoir, *Force of Circumstance,* trans. Richard Howard. New York: Penguin, 1968. Reprinted by permission of Richard Howard. Original copyright © 1963 Éditions Gallimard.
Simone de Beauvoir, *Letters to Sartre: Simone de Beauvoir,* trans. and ed. Quintin Hoare. New York: Little, Brown, 1991.
Simone de Beauvoir, *The Prime of Life,* trans. Peter Green. New York: Penguin, 1965.
Isabelle de Courtivron, *Violette Leduc.* New York: Twayne, 1985. Copyright © 1985 G. K. Hall & Co. Reprinted with permission of Twayne Publishers, an imprint of Simon & Schuster Macmillan.
Daniel Depland, written interview with the author.
Janet Flanner, *Paris Journal: 1945–1965.* New York: Atheneum, 1965. Reprinted by permission of William Murray.
Jean Genet, *Funeral Rites,* trans. Bernard Frechtman. New York: Grove/Atlantic, 1969.
André Gide, *Journals: 1889–1948.* New York: Penguin, 1956.

Jeremy Josephs, *Swastika over Paris*. New York: Arcade / Little, Brown, 1989.

Violette Leduc, *La Bâtarde*, trans. Derek Coltman. New York: Farrar, Straus & Giroux, 1965. Copyright © 1965 Farrar, Straus & Giroux, Inc. Reprinted by permission of Farrar, Straus & Giroux, Inc.

Violette Leduc, *La Chasse à l'Amour*. Paris: Gallimard, 1973. Copyright © Éditions Gallimard. Excerpts trans. Dominique Mazeaud and Michele Zackheim.

Violette Leduc, *L'Affamée*. Paris: Gallimard, 1948. Copyright © Éditions Gallimard. Excerpts trans. Dominique Mazeaud.

Violette Leduc, *In the Prison of Her Skin*, trans. Derek Coltman. London: Rupert Hart-Davis, 1970. Original copyright © 1946 Éditions Gallimard.

Violette Leduc, *Lettres à Simone de Beauvoir. Les Temps Modernes*, no. 495 (October 1987). Trans. Dominique Mazeaud.

Violette Leduc, *Mad in Pursuit*, trans. Derek Coltman. New York: Farrar, Straus & Giroux, 1971.Copyright © 1971 Rupert Hart-Davis Ltd and Farrar, Straus & Giroux, Inc. Reprinted by permission of Farrar, Straus & Giroux, Inc.

Violette Leduc, *Ravages*, trans. Derek Coltman. London: Arthur Barker, 1968. Original copyright © 1955 Éditions Gallimard.

Violette Leduc, *Thérèse and Isabelle*, trans. Derek Coltman. New York: Farrar, Straus & Giroux, 1967. Copyright © 1967 Farrar, Straus & Giroux, Inc. Reprinted by permission of Farrar, Straus & Giroux, Inc.

Violette Leduc, *Trésors à Prendre*. Paris: Gallimard, 1960. Copyright © Éditions Gallimard. Excerpts trans. Dominique Mazeaud and Michele Zackheim.

Violette Leduc, letters to Serge Tamagnot. Reprinted by permission of the Estate of Violette Leduc.

Herbert R. Lottman, *Flaubert: A Biography*. New York: Fromm International, by arrangement with Little, Brown, 1990. Reprinted by permission of Herbert R. Lottman.

Herbert R. Lottman, *The Left Bank*. New York: Houghton Mifflin, 1982. Copyright © Herbert R. Lottman.

André Maurois, *From My Journal*, trans. Joan Charles [pseud.]. New York: Harper & Brothers, 1948. Copyright © Héritiers André Maurois.

André Maurois, *Memoirs: 1885–1967*. New York: Harper & Row, 1970. Copyright 1942 by André Maurois, renewed © 1970 the Estate of André Maurois. English trans. copyright © 1970 The Bodley Head and Harper & Row Publishers, Inc. Reprinted by permission of HarperCollins Publishers, Inc.

Thérèse Plantier, *C'est Moi Diego*. Paris: Saint-Germain-des-Prés, 1971. Reprinted by permission of Jean Breton. Trans. Michele Zackheim.

Rainer Maria Rilke, *Letters on Cézanne*, ed. Clara Rilke. New York: Fromm International, 1985. Copyright © 1952 Insel Verlag. Trans. by Joel Agee, copyright © 1985 Fromm International Publishing Corporation. Reprinted by permission of Fromm International Publishing Corporation.

Maurice Sachs, *The Hunt*, trans. Richard Howard. New York: Stein & Day, 1965. Reprinted by permission of Richard Howard.

Maurice Sachs, *Tableau des Moeurs de Ce Temps*. Paris: Gallimard, 1954. Copyright © Éditions Gallimard. Excerpts trans. Dominique Mazeaud.

George Sand, *My Life*, trans. Dan Hofstadter. New York: Harper & Row, 1979.

Jean-Paul Sartre, *Saint Genet.* New York: George Braziller, 1963. Trans. © 1963 George Braziller, Inc. Reprinted by permission of George Braziller, Inc.

Stephen A. Shapiro, *The Dark Continent of Literature: Autobiography.* Comparative Literature Studies, vol. 5. University Park: The Pennsylvania State University Press, 1968. Reprinted by permission of The Pennsylvania State University Press.

Elizabeth Sprigge and Jean-Jacques Kihm, *Jean Cocteau: The Man and the Mirror.* New York: Coward-McCann, 1968. Copyright © 1968 Elizabeth Sprigge and Jean-Jacques Kihm.

Serge Tamagnot, interview with the author.

Hélène Vivienne Wenzel, ed., *Simone de Beauvoir: Witness to a Century.* Yale French Studies, no. 72.

Virginia Woolf, *Moments of Being.* New York: Harcourt Brace Jovanovich, 1985.

In addition, the author gratefully acknowledges the following sources:

Madeleine Chapsal, "La Folle Solitude de Violette Leduc." *L'Express,* November 25–31, 1965.

Mavis Gallant, *Paris Notebooks.* New York: Random House, 1986.

André Gide, *Neuchâtel: Ides et Calendes.* Paris: Poétique, 1947.

Violette Leduc, "Brigitte Bardot." *Adam,* June 1966.

Violette Leduc, "The Great Craftsmen of Paris," trans. Antonia White. *Vogue,* March 1965.

Ian Littlewood, *Paris: A Literary Companion.* New York: Harper & Row, 1989.

Valérie Marin La Meslé, "Genet, Violette Leduc: Admiration et Jalousie." *Magazine Littéraire,* September 1993. Excerpts trans. Dominique Mazeaud.

Adelaide Iula Perili, *Contresquisses: Trois Études sur Violette Leduc.* Rome: Bulzoni, 1991. Excerpts trans. Dominique Mazeaud.

Petrarch, *The Ascent of Mont Ventoux,* ed. Harold Bloom. New York: Chelsea House, 1989.

Lauren Helen Pringle, *An Annotated and Indexed Calendar and Abstract of the Ohio State University Collection of Simone de Beauvoir's Letters to Nelson Algren.* Ph.D. dissertation, The Ohio State University, 1985.

Maurice Sachs, *Maurice Sachs: Lettres.* Paris: Le Bélier, 1968. Excerpts trans. Dominique Mazeaud.

ABOUT THE AUTHOR

MICHELE ZACKHEIM has had a thirty-six-year career in the visual arts. She is now at work on *Einstein's Daughter*, a book on the life of Lieserl Einstein-Marić. She divides her time between northern New Mexico and New York City.